Dixie Moon

Redemption Mountain

Historical Western Romance Series

SHIRLEEN DAVIES

Book Four in the Redemption Mountain

Historical Western Romance Series

Avalanche Ranch Press, LLC
PO Box 12618
Prescott, AZ 86304

Book design and conversions by Joseph Murray at 3rdplanetpublishing.com

Cover design by Kim Killion, The Killion Group

ISBN: 978-1-941786-24-6

Books by Shirleen Davies
Historical Western Romance Series
MacLarens of Fire Mountain

Tougher than the Rest, Book One
Faster than the Rest, Book Two
Harder than the Rest, Book Three
Stronger than the Rest, Book Four
Deadlier than the Rest, Book Five
Wilder than the Rest, Book Six

Redemption Mountain

Redemption's Edge, Book One
Wildfire Creek, Book Two
Sunrise Ridge, Book Three
Dixie Moon, Book Four
Survivor Pass, Book Five, Releasing 2016

MacLarens of Boundary Mountain

Colin's Quest, Book One, Releasing 2015

Contemporary Romance Series

MacLarens of Fire Mountain

Second Summer, Book One

Hard Landing, Book Two
One More Day, Book Three
All Your Nights, Book Four
Always Love You, Book Five
Hearts Don't Lie, Book Six
No Getting Over You, Book Seven, Releasing 2015

Peregrine Bay

Reclaiming Love, Book One, A Novella
Our Kind of Love, Book Two, Releasing 2016

Sign up to learn about my New Releases:
www.shirleendavies.com/contact-me.html

I care about quality, so if you find something in error, please contact me via email at shirleen@shirleendavies.com.

Description

Dixie Moon, Book Four, Redemption Mountain Historical Western Romance Series

"The author has a talent for bringing the historical west to life, realistically and vividly, and doesn't shy away from some of the harder aspects of frontier life, even though it's fiction. Recommended to readers who like sweeping western historical romances that are grounded with memorable, likeable characters and a strong sense of place."

Gabe Evans is a man of his word with strong convictions and steadfast loyalty. As the sheriff of Splendor, Montana, the ex-Union Colonel and oldest of four boys from an affluent family, Gabe understands the meaning of responsibility. The last thing he wants is another commitment—especially of the female variety.

Until he meets Lena Campanel...

Lena's past is one she intends to keep buried. Overcoming a childhood of setbacks and obstacles, she and her friend, Nick, have succeeded in creating a life of financial success and devout loyalty to one another.

When an unexpected death leaves Gabe the sole heir of a considerable estate, partnering with Nick and Lena is a lucrative decision...forcing Gabe and Lena to work together. As their desire grows, Lena refuses to let down her guard, vowing to keep her past hidden—even from a perfect man like Gabe.

But secrets never stay buried...

When revealed, Gabe realizes Lena's secrets are deeper than he ever imagined. For a man of his character, deception and lies of omission aren't negotiable. Will he be able to forgive the deceit? Or is the damage too great to ever repair?

Visit my website for a list of characters for each series.
http://www.shirleendavies.com/character-list.html

Dedication

This book is dedicated to all of my wonderful readers. Your support means a great deal to me.

Thanks so much!

Acknowledgements

Thanks also to my editor, Kim Young, proofreader, Alicia Carmical, and all of my beta readers. Your insights and suggestions are greatly appreciated.

As always, many thanks to my wonderful resources, including Diane Lebow, who has been a whiz at guiding my social media endeavors, my cover designer, Kim Killion, and Joseph Murray who is a whiz at formatting my books for both print and electronic versions.

Dixie Moon

Prologue

New Orleans, 1860

Stretching in her rumpled bed, Magdalena Campanel opened her eyes, reaching a hand across the mattress. At the feel of the cold sheets, she sat upright and glanced around, seeing no one. A wary smile curved her lips as she stood, noting the slight soreness from the night before. Grabbing her wrapper, she peered out the bedroom door. All was quiet. Then again, it *would* be at this hour of the morning.

Closing the door behind her, Lena walked the short distance to the end of the hall of private rooms, stepped onto the second floor landing of the Orleans Saloon, and looked over the railing. Empty. Dashing down the stairs in her bare feet, she hurried to the back room, expecting to see him as soon as she pushed the door open. Again, nothing.

A small surge of dread sliced through her as she rushed back upstairs and into her room. Taking a quick look around for a note, anything which would explain his absence, a chill claimed her when she realized he'd left nothing behind—no message, no clothes, nothing. Dread turned into panic as she glanced at her dressing table. The jewelry he'd helped her remove the night before no longer lay on the handmade doily her friend, Isabella, made for her.

"Oh, God…" Her voice trailed off on the pray as she placed a hand over her mouth. A search of dresser drawers and her wardrobe proved futile. Everything of value had been taken by the man she loved, the one she'd given herself to only hours before.

A sick feeling crept through her at the realization she, and her business partner, Nicholas Barnett, had been deceived. She needed to find Nick, a man who'd been like a brother to her since they were kids, and do a complete search.

Changing into a day dress and grabbing a key, Lena ran down the hall, pounding on Nick's bedroom door. Getting no answer, she slipped the key in the lock, knocking once more before pushing the door open. The bed hadn't been slept in. Racking her brain, she tried to remember the name of his current mistress—an actress new to town, but the name escaped her.

Using a key to open the office, her heart sank at the sight of the open and empty wall safe. The picture which had concealed it lay on the thick carpet a few feet away.

A scream gurgled up within her throat, begging for release. Holding both hands to her mouth, she allowed a small cry to escape before tears clouded her sight. Using one hand for balance, Lena lowered herself into a nearby leather chair, the pain in her chest intense.

"What have I done?" she mumbled, uncontrollable sobs shaking her body. Her mind reeled at the betrayal and her own part in it. Nick had warned her to be careful, but she'd let her emotions, and the man's declarations of love, take over. She'd given him her heart, and he'd taken everything—their savings, jewelry, and her *virginity*, then fled. After the trust he'd placed in her, facing Nick would be unbearable.

She had to tell him the truth and hope he didn't cut all ties, sending her out to build a life without him. Her chest tightened at the thought, but she had no other alternative. She had to pray he didn't turn her away.

Chapter One

Splendor, Montana Territory 1867

"What the hell?" Gabe Evans muttered as Magdelena Campanel's eyes widened and skin paled before she slouched into his arms. Nick Barnett, her business partner and longtime friend, cursed at Gil Murton's announcement.

"What happened? Is she ill, Nick?" Noah asked, glancing between him and Gabe, his eyes narrowing.

"No, not ill. The news of the gold strike is what happened." Nick moved closer to Gabe, holding out his arms. "I'll take her."

Gabe ignored him, kneeling to the ground and setting Lena on a bedroll Gil had retrieved from his horse. He gently swiped strands of hair from her face, feeling the clamminess of her skin.

"What do we have here?" Doc Worthington knelt beside Gabe.

"She fainted dead away, Doc. She's only been out about thirty seconds." Gil stood to the side, his hands resting on his hips. "All I did was announce the name of the man who discovered the vein of gold west of our ranch. Don't know why that would bother her."

Nick shook his head, glancing around at the circle of friends who'd gathered to celebrate Abigail

Tolbert's recent marriage to Noah Brandt. The whole town had been invited to make the short trek up the hill behind town where Abby and Noah planned to build their home.

No one in Splendor would know the significance of the name William Randolph Carlyle, or the impact it would have on Lena. Nick did, and the knowledge such a scoundrel might cross paths with them again burned a hole in his gut.

Doc pulled a pouch from his pocket, retrieving a small bottle. He removed the stopper and passed the smelling salts under Lena's nose once, then twice, before she tried to bat his hand away.

"That's it, Miss Campanel. Open your eyes for me," Doc coaxed, using a damp cloth to wipe her face. "Gabe, why don't you put her in one of the wagons and bring her to the clinic? I'll keep watch until I'm sure she's all right."

"No..." Lena's raspy voice accompanied a hand lifting to rest on the doctor's arm. "I'll be fine if you'll help me up."

"Lena, you should listen to him," Nick warned, worry edged on his face.

Doc Worthington looked between the two. "Let's get you to one of the benches. If you feel all right in another ten minutes, I'll allow you to stay for the party."

"Thank you, Doctor." Lena gripped his hand, feeling a strong arm at her back. She looked over to see Gabe on her other side, Nick standing behind him.

Although Lena tried to brush off their help, she relented when Gabe's grip tightened.

"I've got her." Gabe glanced at Worthington, who nodded.

They walked the few feet to where benches and tables had been set up, several people asking if they could help as they passed.

"I'm fine, Gabe. Truly." Lena's color appeared to be returning to its natural olive tone.

When Gil Murton announced the gold strike by English miner William Randolph Carlyle, she'd gone almost white. The name held no significance to Gabe, but judging by her reaction, it certainly did to Lena.

"Sit down like the doctor said and have some punch." Gabe leaned toward her, keeping his voice low. "Then tell me who the hell this Carlyle fellow is." He looked up as a shadow covered them to see Nick close by, his gaze locked on Lena.

She returned Nick's stare, gripping her hands in her lap as she straightened her spine. "I don't know who he is."

Gabe couldn't miss the looks passing between her and Nick. "That so? Then why did you faint at the mention of his name?"

"I'm certain it was a reaction to being out in the sun too long, nothing more. Running the saloon leaves me little time for outside pleasures, as I'm sure you're aware, Sheriff."

Gabe studied her, noting she refused to look him in the eye. "All right. I won't push, but if there's anything you want to tell me or need my help with, let me know." He looked up at Nick. "That goes for both of you." He stood, not missing the fact Lena noticeably relaxed at his comment.

"Thanks, Gabe. I'll take care of her from here."

Gabe nodded, walking toward Noah and a group of other men as Nick sat down. "It may be wise to tell him about Willie, Lena."

"No, absolutely not." The thought horrified her. "Besides, it's been too long."

"He stole *thousands* from us. I, for one, would like to get the money back." He pulled a flask from his pocket, offering it to Lena, who took a small swallow before handing it back.

"It's been years. Besides, this may not even be the same man."

A hint of annoyance crossed his face. "Is that what you believe?"

She took a deep breath, looking around at the crowd before glancing up at Nick. "No."

Leaning forward, he rested his arms on his legs. "We must be prepared to see Willie in the Dixie. He's stayed away so far, but a strike like this will draw him into town, and eventually, our saloon."

"I know." Although anger knotted her insides, her body began to tremble at the prospect of seeing him again.

"I don't want you to confront him, Lena. If he comes in, I want you to get me." At her lack of response, he grabbed her hand and squeezed. "Do you understand me?"

She exhaled slowly, glancing at their joined hands, understanding Nick's need to protect her. "Yes, I understand."

"Have you mentioned Willie to anyone in Splendor?"

A look of surprise crossed her face. "Outside of a few people before leaving New Orleans, I've never mentioned him to anyone. All I want to do is keep him where he belongs—in my past."

"That may be, but I'm not optimistic you'll succeed. He can't be trusted, caring nothing of the damage his remarks may cause another. Don't mistake him for a gentleman, thinking he'll be quiet about what the two of you shared in the past."

She gasped, her eyes going wide. "No...he wouldn't. What possible good would it do him to bring that up?"

"Lena, the man is a snake. If he needs to use the information to gain favor with someone else or achieve his goals, he won't hesitate to throw it in our faces."

"Can I get either of you some food?"

Lena startled at Cash Coulter's voice before pulling her hand from Nick's and glancing up. "If you don't mind, perhaps you could accompany me to the food table, Mr. Coulter. I do believe I'm hungry."

"My pleasure, Miss Campanel." Cash held out his arm, noticing Nick position himself on her other side. "I hope you're feeling better."

"Much. Thank you. I don't know why I didn't think to bring my parasol."

"It might be best to fill a plate and take it over to where the other women are sitting." Cash nodded toward a large poplar tree with expansive limbs, where several women Lena knew sat on blankets, eating their meal.

"Thank you, Mr. Coulter. I believe that's just what I'll do."

Gabe sipped his punch, now flavored with liquid from Bull's flask, and watched Cash escort Lena to a spot next to Rachel and Ginny Pelletier. Shifting his weight to one hip and slipping a hand into a pocket, he tried to figure out why she'd lied to him about recognizing the name of the miner.

He couldn't have mistaken the look of panic on her face when Gil mentioned Carlyle. Until then, she'd shown little interest in the announcement of a gold strike not far from Splendor. The name of the minor triggered her eyes to go wide, as if she were a cornered animal. In an instant, her face paled as she collapsed into his arms.

"What do you think, Gabe?"

Bull's voice tore through his musings. Tilting his glass toward him, Gabe waited while Bull added a slight amount of whiskey.

"About what?"

"The gold strike. If it's deep and rich enough, it could change Splendor's future, attracting hundreds, maybe thousands of men looking to get rich." Bull's words sounded optimistic, yet his face didn't display any enthusiasm.

"As well as those who aren't so honest in their pursuits."

"True," Bull agreed. "But if the miners are lucky and find gold, they'll settle down, spend their money here."

"They may erect a tent city like those in other mining towns. The number of saloons, gamblers, and camp followers will swell. It will be more than a fulltime job to keep the peace."

"That's why you have Cash and Beau as your deputies." Bull glanced over at Cash and his friend, Beauregard Davis. They'd both fought for the South, then turned to bounty hunting after the War Between the States ended. For now, they'd made the decision to stay in Splendor, taking a break from chasing thieves and murderers.

"If the strike is big and word gets out, even those two might not be enough."

"It may turn out Carlyle's talk is bigger than the gold he's found. This may be a bunch of hoopla about nothing."

Bull might be right, but Gabe's instincts told him otherwise. "I'm going to grab some food before it's all gone. You?"

"I think I'll head over toward where Lydia is helping with the children. See if she needs any help." Bull cast Gabe a woeful glance, hoping he hadn't given too much away. For months, he'd been trying to hide his feelings for the oldest of the orphans who'd escaped a Crow camp and hidden in one of the caves scattered throughout Redemption Mountain.

"You ought to say something, Bull. Let her know how you feel." Gabe clasped Bull on the shoulder.

Bull shoved his hands in his pockets. "Someday maybe. I've got a lot to do before I make any firm decisions." He flashed a grim smile before heading toward Lydia.

Gabe continued watching the people, trying to cast subtle glances at Lena, now deep in conversation with Rachel and Ginny. He'd wanted her from the first moment she got off the stage and their eyes met. Tall and slender, with auburn hair and bright blue eyes, she'd sparked feelings he'd never experienced before. She'd come to Splendor to join Nick, who'd already built the Dixie into a thriving saloon with games of chance not found at the Wild Rose.

Rumors were that Nick and Lena were like brother and sister, not a couple as some imagined. Gabe hadn't made up his mind on the subject, preferring to use the possibility they were involved as a barrier to his feelings. Believing she and Nick were together made Lena less of a temptation.

Gabe's attention shifted as the sounds of shouting from the town below wafted up the hillside. He could make out a crowd of men standing outside the Dixie, arms flailing as if in an argument.

"What's going on down there, Gabe?" Cash nodded down the hillside.

"Don't know, but guess I'd better find out." Setting his empty glass on a table, he swung up on his horse, Blackheart, taking the short trail to town. He reined to a stop at the sight before him, Cash, Beau, and Nick pulling up alongside.

"What the hell?" Nick slid off his horse and pounded up the steps to the doors of his saloon, then turned toward a group of perhaps fifteen men, all talking at the same time. "What's going on here?"

A short, wiry man of indeterminable age stepped forward, shaking a fist at Nick. "We been waitin' hours for this place to open. Whoever heard of a saloon closing in the middle of a Saturday?"

"We got money to spend," another yelled, "and we aim to do it here."

"Gentlemen, the saloon has been closed to celebrate the marriage of two good friends. But seeing as how you're aching to spend your money, why don't you come on in and we'll accommodate you." Nick nodded to Gabe, then disappeared inside, followed by the men who'd congregated out front.

"Beau, I think it would be best to head inside ourselves to find out where these men got all the money they're so eager to get rid of." Cash slid from his horse. "Gabe, you may want to go check on Lena. You know she won't stay at the party for long without Nick." He didn't wait for a response before stepping into the saloon, followed by Beau.

Gabe watched them disappear inside, knowing Cash and Beau could handle any overzealous drinkers or hotheaded gamblers, then reined Blackheart around. He agreed that Lena wouldn't stay long once she discovered Nick had left. Halfway up the hill, he spotted her half-running, half-stumbling down the path.

"What do you think you're doing?" Gabe jumped from the saddle, grabbing her by the arm as her feet slipped out from under her on the rocky slope. Hauling her up to stand a few inches away, he glared at the confusion on her face.

"I'm going to the saloon, of course. Dax mentioned you'd heard shouting and rode down with Nick. I need to find out what's happening."

"Did you forget you fainted dead away not too long ago? As I recall, Doc told you to take it easy." He didn't loosen his grip as he spoke. If anything, he drew her closer to him.

"I feel fine. Did you forget it's my saloon, too? Now, let me go." She pulled free as he released his grip.

"In that case, I'll take you the rest of the way." Before she could protest, he grasped her waist in both hands and lifted her onto his horse, then boosted himself into the saddle in front of her. "Put your arms around me and hold on."

He could feel her hands tentatively slip around his waist, as if she wasn't sure about touching him. Impatient, he grabbed her hands, pulled them tight, and nudged Blackheart down the hill.

"I understand your concern, but Nick handled it fine without you," he commented over his shoulder. "Cash and Beau stayed with him, so there's nothing to worry about."

He could feel her scoot closer, leaning toward his ear. "I do appreciate your reassurances, Sheriff, but you'll have to excuse me if I feel the need to make certain for myself."

He smiled to himself, knowing her sugary voice mocked him. It didn't matter. His efforts were more focused on controlling his body's reaction to having her nestled behind him...the whiffs of her rosewater-scented hair, the softness of her body as she brushed against his back. It was a relief when they reached the Dixie and he slid from the saddle, then helped her to the ground.

"Thank you, Sheriff."

It didn't surprise him when she dashed into the saloon without waiting for his response. He considered following her inside, then thought better of it. From the quiet, it appeared Nick, Cash, and Beau had everything under control. Besides, he didn't need to be looking after a woman already tethered to another man—whether she accepted it or not.

He climbed back on his horse, looking forward to rejoining his closest friend and his new wife as they continued their celebration when the doors of the saloon slammed open and a man came flying outside, landing with a groan on the hard ground. Gabe watched the man flail a moment before righting himself, standing, and marching back up the steps with a determined look, coming to a stop at the sight of Cash in the doorway.

"It may be best for you to call it a day and head back to your camp."

"I ain't going nowhere, Deputy. Not until I win back what I lost."

Gabe had to hand it to the man. He stood a good eight inches shorter than Cash and was about half his girth. It took guts to stand up to anyone who held that much weight on you.

"I don't believe that's going to happen today. From what I saw, you already lost all you brought. Seems you're going to have to find more gold if you want to continue to gamble." Cash started to turn, then stopped at the man's laughter.

"Hell, I didn't strike no gold. I just work for the man who did. He handed out money and told us all to go celebrate."

"That so? And who is this man?" Cash asked, believing he already knew the answer.

"William Randolph Carlyle. He's some duke or something from England. From the way he talks, it sounds like he's got money to burn. Says the gold strike is nothing compared to what he already has."

Gabe cast a look at Cash, his curiosity about Carlyle elevating even more than when Lena had such a strong reaction to his name.

"And where's this Carlyle fellow?" Cash glanced inside, as if he expected to find him at a table.

"Oh, he didn't come into town with the rest of us." The man scratched his stubbled chin. "He's a strange one, that's for sure."

Chapter Two

"Do you think we should ride out and meet this Carlyle fellow?" Beau asked the following Friday when news of the strike had died down. He'd returned from checking on some missing cattle at a small ranch southwest of town, finding the strays a mile away in a dead-end canyon. Gabe wouldn't normally have sent him out, but the spread belonged to an elderly couple who worked the place by themselves.

"No need. He'll come to town soon enough. Noah's got the only miner supply store for miles, the same holding true for the general store and anything else he's going to need. I'm surprised no one in town has met him yet." Gabe whittled on a small piece of wood as he sat in a chair outside the jail, watching the comings and goings on the main street as the sun began to touch the western ridge. He never knew what to expect on Friday and Saturday nights. Most of the cowhands came to town on Saturdays after six long days in the saddle. Others celebrated on Fridays.

"I think someone has." Cash leaned his chair back on two legs, his arms crossed.

"Who?" The knife stalled in Gabe's hands.

"Lena. I don't believe her reaction had anything to do with the heat. I'd bet a month's pay she knows Carlyle."

Gabe continued to whittle, showing no reaction. He agreed, believing she knew and feared the man. In his mind, that made Carlyle a threat.

"Well...what do we have here?" Cash stared toward the south end of town, watching a man bob up and down in the saddle, holding his black bowler hat with one hand, gripping the reins in the other.

Gabe glanced up, then stood as the man stopped in front of them.

"Hello, gentlemen. I wonder if you can tell me where I might find Mr. Horace Clausen."

"I'm Sheriff Evans. And you are?" Gabe looked the man over, guessing him to be no more than thirty.

"Delbert Utley. I've come at the behest of Mr. Clausen, as well as Mr. Ernest Payson of Big Pine."

"Well, then, why don't you follow me to the bank and I'll introduce you to Mr. Clausen."

"I'd greatly appreciate it, Sheriff."

Gabe could've just pointed out the bank and gone back to watching the main street. Instead, he journeyed past the gunsmith, barber shop, general store, and the new restaurant that opened several months before, presenting a small amount of competition to Suzanne Briar's boardinghouse restaurant. Passing an empty storefront just before the bank, Gabe stopped, waiting for Utley to dismount and join him.

"You'll find Horace in here." He followed the man inside, nodding a greeting to Mrs. Sally Phelps, the bank secretary, and Abby Brandt, Noah's wife, who'd been working at the bank for several months.

"Good day, Sheriff. What can I do for you today?" Sally asked, smiling at Gabe.

Gabe didn't have a chance to explain before Horace walked out of his office.

"Hello, Sheriff."

"Horace. This is Delbert Utley. He says you're expecting him."

"Indeed I am," he answered, extending his hand. "It's a pleasure to meet you, Mr. Utley. I'm Horace Clausen, president of the bank." He glanced at Gabe. "Mr. Utley is planning to open a law practice in Splendor."

Gabe looked him over once more, not sure he'd put his trust in someone who looked this fresh out of law school. "That so?"

"Oh, yes. I'm delighted with the prospect of putting what I've learned from Mr. Payson to use in my own practice."

With no attorney in Splendor, Ernest Payson had ridden in from Big Pine to help Abby Brandt settle her father's affairs when he died. The town had long been looking forward to someone opening a local practice.

"Then I guess we'll be seeing quite a bit more of each other, Mr. Utley." Gabe turned away, strolling to Abby's window as the other men made their way to Clausen's office.

"Who is that man, Gabe?"

"A lawyer sent by your friend, Ernest Payson. Delbert Utley. He's going to open a law office in town."

"Mr. Clausen did mention that to me. I think it's wonderful news. It will be so much easier to work with someone from here, rather than having to travel to Big Pine to see Mr. Payson."

Upon the unexpected death of her father, Abby had inherited a vast fortune. Although wealthy, she continued to work at the bank, preferring to be a part of the daily activities of the town and meeting the new residents, who usually stopped at the bank when they first arrived.

She leaned forward, lowering her voice. "You know, Mr. Clausen is also expecting another gentleman to arrive any day now. He ran a newspaper in Missouri and plans to start one here."

"A newspaper, huh? Guess I never thought of Splendor as having enough going on to justify one."

"The town is growing at a rapid rate, and the gold strike could entice many more people to the area. For some time, my father had believed we were ready for one. Although, I think he wanted someone he could control regarding territorial politics and his ideas of how the area should expand." She'd come to terms with her father's gruesome death, as well as their differences. "Mr. Clausen says the man and his family should arrive any day."

"I'll watch for them. I'd better be heading back to the jail. I've got a couple of the Pelletier men in there. Men who worked your father's ranch before he died. I doubt it will be long before Luke and Dax clean out the riffraff and hire a few new ranch hands."

Abby nodded. For several reasons, she'd sold the ranch to the Pelletiers, creating the biggest spread in the western Montana territory. Dax and Luke had added hundreds of acres to their already expansive ranch, as well as some men she didn't expect would last long under the new owners.

"Time to close up, Abby," Sally called from her desk, grabbing the keys and locking the front door.

"I'll walk you to the livery." Gabe leaned against the counter and waited for Abby to lock the money in the safe.

"I'm ready." Abby closed her shawl around her shoulders as they stepped out the back door. The path led behind the stores toward Noah's blacksmith shop and livery at the other end of town. They'd gotten no more than ten feet when the sound of shouting followed by gunfire had Gabe dashing between two buildings toward the main street, Abby following behind.

"Stay here," he warned her as he stepped onto the boardwalk, waiting as Cash and Beau joined him.

Drawing their guns, they stopped cold at the sight of two wagons overflowing with men shouting and firing their weapons into the air. One wagon pulled to a stop in front of the Wild Rose saloon, the other outside the Dixie saloon. Laughing and slapping one another on the back, the men disappeared behind the swinging doors, leaving Gabe, Cash, and Beau staring after them.

"What the hell was that?" Beau holstered his gun. The three men looked around to see if other wagons followed.

"We'd better find out. Beau, you and Cash head into the Rose, and I'll go check the Dixie." He watched as they followed the miners inside, then turned to Abby, who held up her hand.

"Don't worry about me, Gabe. I can get myself to the livery."

Nodding, he crossed the street. Hearing piano music at the Dixie, Gabe slid his revolver into the holster and pushed through the doors. All the tables were full. The girls who worked there scurried around, taking drink orders and offering other types of private entertainment.

"Gabe, over here."

Nick motioned from his spot at the end of the bar and signaled his bartender, Paul, for another beer. Always watchful, he never let his eyes wander from the crowd of celebrating miners as he waited for Gabe to join him.

"Do you know what's going on?" Gabe asked, accepting the beer and turning toward the raucous crowd.

"From what I've heard, all the men who came in on the wagons work for Carlyle. The man with the long red beard at the table closest to the piano told Paul the more they dig, the wider the vein spreads."

"Have you met the man?"

"Carlyle?"

Gabe nodded, sipping his whiskey.

"I'm not certain. A man named Carlyle frequented our saloon in New Orleans, but I won't know if it's the same man until I see him."

"Cornelius, at the assay office, said he came in on Monday, had the gold tested and filed his claim. He got the impression Carlyle planned to ride back to town soon. Seems we'll all be able to get a good look at him then."

Nick took in the information without any noticeable reaction. Gabe wondered if Lena's response would be the same.

"Is Lena going to be around tonight?"

"She's here every night, Gabe. You know that. As long as the girls work, she feels the need to be here and watch out for them."

"Even with you around?"

"I keep an eye on the gambling and take care of the drunks and sore losers. She handles whatever comes up with the girls. We both deal with the men who get too rough with them. I can't tolerate a man who's violent with women. They have no place in the Dixie."

The sound of a chair scraping against the wooden floor, then falling to the ground drew Gabe's and Nick's attention. At the same time, one of the miners at another table reached out, pulling a girl onto his lap, planting a sloppy kiss on her mouth. The girl pushed away, smiling as she stood and straightened her dress.

"You want any more of that, mister, you'll have to buy a spot upstairs." Winking at him, she turned away, looking over her shoulder to see the man toss his cards on the table and follow.

The other table didn't fare so well, escalating as two men squared off, one pulling his gun.

No one paid attention to Gabe shouting for them to back away—until he accompanied it with the sound of his gun discharging into the ceiling.

"You want to set your gun on the table and back away?" he asked, Nick coming up alongside him with his gun pointing at the half-crazed man.

"Hell no. That man there cheated, Sheriff, and I aim to get my money back from him." The man took a step backward, still holding his gun.

Gabe glanced at the other gambler standing on the opposite side of the table, showing no fear. In fact, he looked almost bored as he stared at the man hell-bent on shooting him. Short and slender with a thin mustache and black felt derby sitting squarely on his head, he stood his ground, not going for the weapon which hung low on his left side.

"That may be. Anyone else see the man cheat?" Gabe looked around, noting several men at the table shake their heads. He glanced at the other two. "Guess you'll both have to come with me so we can sort this out."

"I ain't going nowhere until I get my money back." The man took one more step backwards, not noticing the piano player who'd come up behind him, a walking cane in his hand. Before the man could turn, the cane crashed down, knocking him unconscious.

The silence, which followed, ended when the man in the derby hat pulled out his chair and sat down. "Gentlemen, shall we resume our game?" Picking up his cards, he didn't once glance toward Gabe or Nick.

"When I heard all the noise, I thought you might be in here."

Gabe turned to see Lena standing next to him, her gaze focused on him.

"What do you mean?"

"There always seems to be some excitement when you're here, as if it follows you through the door." She moved to the bar, accepting a glass of whiskey from Paul before turning, surprised to see Gabe standing next to her, crowding her space.

Although not entirely uncomfortable, his closeness, the way he brushed against her when others pushed for space, reminded her of how she felt years before when another man's touch sparked the same sensations. After he'd disappeared, she vowed never to allow herself to be vulnerable again. Even though Gabe tempted her more than any man she'd ever known, she couldn't let herself travel that dark path once more.

Gabe tipped his glass toward her. "Do you ever wonder if it's you and your girls who create the excitement, and lawmen like me who have to squelch the fire you start?"

"What do you mean?"

Gabe tilted his head toward the action a few feet away. "Your business is providing men liquor, gambling, and other entertainment. Most of these men haven't been with a woman in a long time. The combination of alcohol and availability creates a powerful need waiting to combust. It doesn't take much for the fire to ignite."

"Surely you don't mean it's the *girls'* fault the men act as they do, pulling guns on each other and tossing out threats." Lena turned toward him, her brows knitting together.

Gabe reached behind him to grab the bottle of whiskey, topping off her glass and then his, missing the spark in her eyes. If he'd seen it, he might have decided to keep his next comments to himself.

"You don't believe offering what you do plays some part in the way men act?"

"And what is it we offer, Sheriff?" Unlike her girls, Lena wore dresses covering her legs, the scooped necklines revealing little. In fact, her clothes were often more suitable for the theatre, rather than a saloon in an untamed frontier town.

Gabe leaned away, letting his gaze wander up her body to the slim waist, ample curves, and smooth column of her neck before settling on full, red lips...lips he'd wanted to claim since the first time he'd seen her. He lifted his gaze, the heat he saw in her eyes a reflection of his own, choking rational thought from his mind.

He took a sip of whiskey, then cleared his throat, his voice husky. "Escape, Lena. You offer men what they can't find somewhere else—a way to forget their harsh lives, at least for a time."

His words knocked all the irritation from her. The look in his eyes, the undisguised desire and hunger, chipped away at the defenses she'd erected over many years. She took a step back, needing to create a shield from the onslaught of emotions his presence created.

Gabe tossed back the rest of his drink, setting the glass on the bar.

"It appears Nick has the saloon under control. I'd best get back to what the people pay me for." Gabe took one more glance at Lena. His lips parted, as if he wanted to say more, then clamped them shut. He stalked toward the doors, letting them swing shut on creaky hinges.

Lena watched his retreat, feeling an odd sense of emptiness when she glanced at the open space beside her. A shaky hand brought the glass to her lips. She took one sip, another, then swallowed what remained, letting the alcohol burn a path down her throat, numbing the hollow feeling in her chest.

Chapter Three

"Is the sheriff in?" Bernie Griggs, operator of the Western Union station and post office, held a message in his hand as he approached Cash.

"Nope. He's at the livery with Noah. Do you want me to take that for him?" Cash nodded at the paper Bernie held.

Glancing at the telegram, Bernie shook his head. "I'd better deliver this one myself." He dashed back into the morning sunshine, walking at a brisk pace toward the livery.

Cash waited a moment before grabbing his hat and walking outside. Bernie had a way of making all messages seem important, and perhaps they were when people lived this far away from family and friends. This time, however, Cash noticed a sense of urgency, maybe even excitement, in Bernie's face.

"Sheriff!"

Gabe glanced over his shoulder and stepped away from the forge where he'd been watching Noah prepare metal for a new tool Dax Pelletier ordered. He wiped a sleeve across his forehead and walked toward the door, letting the cool autumn breeze wash over him.

"What can I do for you, Bernie?"

"I got this message for you. Seems pretty urgent. Guess someone's been trying to reach you for quite a spell." He held out the missive, his gaze shifting to Noah as he raised his hammer to hit the metal resting on the anvil, then looked back at Gabe.

Gabe read it through twice, taking a deep breath before folding it and sliding it into a pocket.

"Do you want to send a response, Sheriff?" Bernie knew the contents of all telegrams coming into and going out of Splendor. Unlike some in other towns, he prided himself on keeping quiet about what he knew.

"I'd better. Noah, I'll be back later to discuss the changes at the jail."

Noah nodded, not liking the look on Gabe's face when he read the message. It had been months since Gabe had received mail from his parents or siblings in New York. His parents had never understood why he'd given up a lucrative position in his father's business or his uncle's hotel, preferring to brave what they considered to be the wilderness. Noah guessed perhaps this was another of the messages urging him to return home.

Gabe stepped up to the counter in the post office, scratching out a response and handing it to Bernie. He pulled out a coin. "That should cover it."

"I'll let you know when there's a response."

Stepping onto the boardwalk, Gabe dragged a hand through his hair, then settled his hat on his head. The last days of summer were giving way to the cooler breezes of autumn. In a few weeks, they'd experience their first snow of the approaching winter. Shoving his hands into his pockets, he let his mind drift as he crossed the dirt street toward the boardinghouse. Too late for breakfast and too early for lunch, he needed something to occupy himself as he thought through the urgent message from his father. Choices needed to be made, and soon.

"Good morning, Gabe. What can I get you?" Suzanne wiped damp hands down her apron, then settled them on her hips, noticing his thoughtful expression. "Is everything all right?"

"Coffee, if you have it ready." He made his way to a table, ignoring her last question. Before she returned from the kitchen, the front door opened, Noah walking in and pulling out a chair at Gabe's table.

"What's happened?" He leaned forward, his eyes locking with his friend's.

"Uncle James passed away."

Noah let out a slow breath, already knowing the implications of the news. It had been no secret Gabe's uncle wanted him to return to New York after the war and take over the thriving hotel business he'd started over forty years before. The last Noah heard, he owned three swank establishments catering to wealthy Americans and travelers from Europe.

The restaurants in each, which was where twelve-year-old Gabe first started working for his uncle, were considered first class. Bussing tables, hauling garbage, fetching carriages...whatever needed to be done, Gabe did it. He'd progressed until, at eighteen, he'd become the summer season manager of the newest hotel. Everyone expected him to take over one day, but that was before the war and his volunteering to serve the Union. It had caused a rift in the family that never quite healed, especially after Gabe and Noah decided to move west after the war.

"What will you do?" Noah nodded at Suzanne as she placed cups of hot coffee before them.

Gabe picked up his cup and took a sip, gazing over the rim. "Honest to God...I don't know."

Noah sat back, crossing his arms and wondering what he'd do if a relative left him all his property and money. Gabe had always known the estate and businesses would pass to him when Uncle James died. A lifelong bachelor, James had been celebrated for his generosity in bestowing scholarships to deserving young men, founding orphanages, and donating to medical clinics on the eastern seaboard. That money was a mere pittance compared to the land and buildings he had owned outright, which were now the property of Gabe Evans, sheriff of Splendor, Montana.

"How long do you have to decide?"

"Not long enough. January first." Gabe sat back, resting his hands on this thighs. He knew this day would come, he just hadn't expected it to be so soon. At fifty-five, Uncle James had looked and acted like a man of thirty. His uncle should've lived many more years.

"Four months," Noah murmured. "Did he include any provisions where you wouldn't have to move to New York?"

"I don't know. My father believes not. I've sent a telegram to my uncle's attorney. All I can do now is wait."

"More coffee?" Suzanne asked, setting bowls of stew before them. "I know you said you aren't hungry, but since this appears to be a long conversation, I thought you might need it. No charge, of course." She smiled and left them alone.

Noah watched her leave, thinking how much she reminded him of his oldest sister. Always taking care of everyone, never complaining, content to make life better for her family and friends.

"Maybe you'll be able to sell the hotels and invest the money out here." Even though they came out west together, if Gabe had to leave, Noah had no desire to return to New York. He'd built a life in Splendor with Abby. Both expected to start a family soon.

"That's my hope. There's a lot of opportunity out here. It's too bad Uncle James never found time to travel this way. I believe he would've been surprised."

"Good day, gentleman." Nick walked up, Lena a few steps behind.

The men stood, Gabe letting his gaze settle for a moment on Lena before pulling a chair out for her.

"It's a little early for the two of you to be taking lunch, isn't it?" Lena set her reticule aside, straightening her skirt as she tried to avoid Gabe's knee touching hers. Turning her head, she expected to see a smug expression. Instead, he seemed lost in his own thoughts, paying little attention to either her or Nick.

"A little," Noah replied. If Gabe wanted to share the news, he'd let him do it.

"I received a telegram about a relative passing. The news may require me to travel to New York." Gabe stirred the remaining stew in his bowl.

"And you'd prefer not to." Like the others at the table, Lena knew how long and tedious the journey east could be.

"I'll go, if needed." Gabe finished his stew, pushing the bowl aside and standing. "I'd better get going." He left without another word, leaving the others to stare at his retreating back.

"Is he all right?" Nick asked Noah.

"He will be. Gabe needs to sort out a few details and make some decisions, then—"

Noah stopped at the sound of gunfire. Pushing back his chair, he ran outside, crouching on the walkway, cursing while drawing his gun at the sight before him.

"What is it?" Lena pushed past Nick to kneel behind Noah, her face ashen. She leaned around him, a cry escaping her lips at what she saw.

"Go back inside," Noah growled, holding a hand up to warn her off.

Nick grabbed her arm, pulling her behind him at the same time he saw Gabe sprawled on the ground, blood pooling beneath him. "Stay in the boardinghouse until I come back to get you," he told her, slipping his revolver from its holster. He followed Noah, crouching low, making their way toward the Dixie, where gunshots still rang out.

"Did you see anyone?" Nick asked as they got closer.

"No." Noah kept his gaze focused on Gabe, pointing his gun up the street to where Cash and Beau made their way toward the Dixie.

"The saloon just opened. Who the hell would be shooting at this hour?" Nick ground out.

"I don't know, but I need to get to Gabe. Can you cover me?"

"Yes, but be quick." Nick shifted toward the saloon, pulling out a second gun and setting it beside him. "Ready?"

"Ready."

"Go!" Nick began to shoot as Noah ran into the street to Gabe's side. Not taking time to check the injuries, he grabbed his collar, dragging him back to the cover of the boardwalk, leaving a trail of blood behind them. Looking up, Noah saw the sign on the clinic window.

"Doc!" Noah pounded on the door, then turned his attention back to Gabe.

Turning him over, he spotted the wound low on Gabe's right side and pushed the palms of his hands on it to stop the flow of blood, not hearing the clinic door open.

"Move over. Let me take a look." Doc Worthington nudged Noah aside, tearing Gabe's shirt, putting pressure on the wound.

"What can I do?" Suzanne knelt beside them, clean towels in her hand.

"Apply pressure here." He looked at Noah and Nick, who still had his gun trained on the saloon. "We need to get him into the clinic. I want to get the bullet out before he regains consciousness."

As they began to lift him, Noah heard Cash's voice rise above the chaos in the saloon.

"Drop your guns." His booming voice rang down the street before he fired into the air. "*Now.*" The shooting had stopped the moment Cash and Beau entered the Dixie, each holding a pair of revolvers, angry expressions on their faces.

Figuring the two deputies had the situation under control, Noah concentrated on getting Gabe inside the clinic without causing further injury.

"Lay him on the table. Suzanne, I'll need you to stay." He looked at Noah and Nick. "You two need to leave." Nick took one last look at Gabe, then walked out the door.

Noah hesitated before Suzanne placed a hand on his arm. "Go, Noah. Doc will take good care of him."

"I'll wait up front." He closed the door between the room where Gabe lay unconscious and the front area with several wooden chairs aligned along two walls. Shoving both hands through his hair, he paced back and forth, trying to control the dread he felt at possibly losing his closest friend. His brother in all ways that mattered.

"Noah, where is he?" Lena dashed through the door, heading straight toward the patient room.

"Doc won't let you in. Might as well wait here."

"But..." she whispered, her voice trailing off as her shoulders sagged.

"He was unconscious, but breathing. The bullet didn't go through, so Doc is trying to get it out before Gabe wakes up. I have to believe he'll pull through." Noah scrubbed a hand down his face, then looked over at her. "You need to do the same."

Lena lowered herself into a chair, taking hold of Noah's hand as he sat next to her. Giving it an encouraging squeeze, she let go, lacing her fingers in her lap, wondering why she cared whether or not a man she'd known for a few months pulled through.

The answer unnerved Lena, knowing she felt much more than friendship for this man.

The instant she'd followed Noah outside to see Gabe's prone body, she felt a piercing pain stab through her, sharper than anything she'd felt since...well, since the man she thought she loved betrayed her. If he pulled through—*when* he pulled through—she'd be thankful for his recovery, grateful he'd never know she harbored such deep feelings for him.

"Noah?" Abby walked through the door, taking tentative steps, kneeling before him. "How is Gabe?" She wrapped her hands around his, the corners of her eyes lined with worry.

"I don't know. Doc and Suzanne are with him."

Abby closed her eyes and sent up a silent prayer, asking for Gabe's recovery, knowing Doc would do all he could to save him. For the first time, her gaze met Lena's.

"Are you doing all right, Lena?"

She nodded. "I decided to wait with Noah, but now that you're here..." Her voice trailed off when the door opened and Doc walked out. All three stood as he came closer.

"The bullet's out. If he can get through the next few days without infection, he should make it."

"Can I see him?" Noah asked, tightening his grip on Abby's hand.

"He's still out and should stay asleep for a while. You're welcome to take a quick look if it will ease your mind."

"You go ahead, Noah. I'll wait for you here." Abby squeezed his hand, then let go, wrapping her arms around her waist as she sat back down, watching Noah slip through the open doorway.

"I should be going. I'm so glad the surgery went well." Lena picked up her reticule without waiting for Abby's response, needing to get outside. Closing the door behind her, she took a deep breath and closed her eyes.

She felt conflicted. Until today, her feelings for Gabe hovered at the edge of awareness, waiting for her to acknowledge them. After the shooting, the possibility she'd never see him again forced Lena to accept how much she cared. The realization frightened her beyond reason. She'd allowed no room in her heart to love a man, trust him, and consider building a life together. She had responsibilities to Nick and to her close friend, Isabella Boucher, in Philadelphia. The two had supported her through all the depression and bad times when she thought she couldn't go on. They believed in her, and the trust they showed created a new, stronger woman who could face most obstacles—except loving a man like Gabe Evans.

Spotting the Western Union office across the street, she stepped onto the dirt road, knowing she had to get a message to Isabella. No matter the level of despair Lena felt, Isabella could always find a way to lift her spirits.

"How is he?" Cash found Abby still sitting in the clinic waiting area, twisting a hanky between her hands.

"Doc removed the bullet. Now all we can do is wait. He's still sleeping, but Doc said Noah could go in for a few minutes. Were you able to find the man who did this?"

Cash removed his hat as he took a seat near Abby. "It wasn't hard. He and a friend were in the saloon playing cards at a table by the window. Turns out, he was the same man who caused problems the other night. Seems he blamed Gabe for not letting him get his money back from the man he thought had cheated. He spotted Gabe coming out of the boardinghouse, went a little berserk, and shot him. One night in jail turned in to him almost killing a man. There's no doubt he'll be headed to the territorial prison as soon as the circuit judge arrives."

"But there were so many shots fired."

"There was one other gunman. After Gabe went down, I guess they just kept shooting. No one in the saloon tried to stop them. Paul, the bartender, hid behind the bar until he had a chance to grab his shotgun. By then, Beau and I were already inside. It all lasted less than two minutes." He fingered the brim of his hat, glancing over at the patient room door at the sound of voices.

"Thanks, Doc. I'll be back later today."

"Well?" Abby stood as Noah walked toward her.

"He woke for a moment and recognized me, which is a good sign. Doc's going to stay with him until I come back in a couple hours." He shifted his focus to Cash. "Did you find the man who shot him?"

Cash explained what he'd told Abby, adding they expected the judge within the next two weeks. "Beau's at the jail with the men who did the shooting. We let the others go. Seems all of them are from the same mining camp and work for Carlyle. I'm thinking of riding out there to meet the man."

"If you decide to go, I'll ride along."

"I might take you up on that, Noah. Beau will need to stay at the jail. It'll take time for Gabe to heal, although I doubt he'll stay down as long as Doc will recommend."

"The doc says he'll need to either stay at the boardinghouse where Suzanne can watch him, or have someone stay at his place behind the jail." Noah thought staying with Suzanne presented the best solution.

"What about Lena?" Abby asked.

"What do you mean?" Noah's brows drew together as his mouth spread into a thin line.

"Well, she stayed here until Doc gave us word Gabe would be all right. She obviously cares about him, and Nick can run the saloon until Gabe is recovered. I just thought..."

Noah exchanged a look with Cash, knowing Gabe would fight either option. A small smile tugged at the corners of Noah's mouth.

"We could ask her. We'd also need to find out if Suzanne has a spare room. The last I heard, all her rooms were taken."

"She'd make room for Gabe," Abby said, looking at Noah.

"Of course she would, but we can't have her giving up her own bed. Why don't you ask her, Abby?" The gleam in his eyes sent a clear message to his wife.

"I'd be glad to. In fact, I'll do it right now before I return to the bank. Good day to you, Cash."

"Abby." After she left, he glanced at Noah. "What was that about?"

Noah smiled, his brows lifting. "Gabe's been meddling in my life for as long as I can remember. It's about time I did a little meddling back."

Chapter Four

"No. I will not have Lena coming into my home to take care of me." Gabe groaned as Noah supported his back so he could sit up on the bed in the exam room. After three days in the clinic, Gabe decided it was time to leave. "I'll stay at Suzanne's."

"Can't."

"And why not?" Gabe's glare would have stopped most people, but all Noah wanted to do was smile.

"She's full up. All the beds are taken—except her own. I assured her you wouldn't want to displace her."

Gabe shifted his legs off the bed, resting his hands on his knees and cursed. "What about the room behind the stairs?"

"Taken."

"Maybe Nick would have a place for me."

"Good idea. That way, Lena wouldn't have to go to your place. Of course, she'd have to sleep at the saloon, too." Noah kept his expression neutral as he helped him into a clean shirt and trousers before sliding his arm around Gabe so he could stand.

"Damn, that hurts." He watched in disgust as Noah pulled the trousers over his hips. "I feel like an invalid."

"You *are* an invalid, at least until Doc says you're good to be on your own."

Grabbing Noah's arm to steady himself, Gabe cast a pleading look at his friend. "I can't have Lena at my place day and night. It won't work. Besides, I can't believe she agreed to it."

"She didn't at first. Then we discussed the alternatives. You can stay at either Dax's or Luke's. Both said they'd be glad to have you."

"They're too far from town. I need to be close in case there's any trouble. I'll stay at my place and make do on my own."

"That will *not* happen, young man." Doc walked in the back door. "You need help so you don't strain the stitches. If they break, there's a good chance the wound will get infected."

"I'll be careful. I just don't want to be fussed over by a woman."

"You mean you don't want to be fussed over by Lena." Noah grinned at having the chance to get back at his friend for his harping about Abby before Noah came to his senses and married her.

"Same thing. I'm staying at my place alone, and that's final."

"I'm afraid I can't allow that." Doc crossed his arms, glaring at Gabe. "You young men are all alike. It doesn't matter if you fought for the North or the South. All you ex-soldiers are stubborn as mules. Now, here is the way it is going to be. You can stay here and I'll tend to you. Or you can go to your own home, have Lena watch after you for two weeks—"

"But—"

"No arguments, Gabe. It's either Lena or me. What's your decision?" Doc Worthington didn't budge. He'd had it with stubborn men who made his life harder by refusing to do as he asked. This time, he wouldn't back down. Gabe's life could still tilt the wrong way if he didn't take care of himself.

He glared at the doctor, realizing the fight had already been lost. Mumbling a curse, he took a step forward, grabbing Noah's arm for balance. "Fine. I'll go to my place and Lena can come by when she has time."

"And she'll stay all day. That's the only way it will work."

Noah saw something flicker in Gabe's eyes. "What about the nights? Surely she can't stay with me then. The church women would have a fit."

"I'll be there after supper and stay nights until you're healed," Noah said.

"What about Abby?"

"We discussed it and she thinks it's the perfect solution. Cash and Beau will take my place a few nights."

Doc clasped Gabe on the shoulder. "You know, most men would be humbled by the number of people willing to help out. You ought to be grateful instead of grumbling like some old man."

Noah's bark of laughter filled the small room. "He's got a point."

"Are Cash and Beau out front?" Doc asked Noah.

"They have the wagon ready. Come on, Gabe. Let's get you home." Noah supported him on one side, Doc on the other. The one step off the boardwalk to the street presented no problem, but getting into the wagon did.

"Noah, you take his shoulders and Beau and I will take his legs." Cash positioned himself on Gabe's right, the side with the injury, and they all lifted on the count of three.

Gabe grit his teeth and crossed his arms, his face a mask. Several people stood around, watching or waiting to help, including Nick and Lena. Their faces barely registered as Noah, Cash, and Beau settled him on a pallet of blankets. Even that little amount of effort left him exhausted and wanting nothing more than his bed.

He let out a mumbled oath as the wagon took off with a jerk. Noah knelt next to him in the wagon, checking to be sure the bandages stayed tight without signs of leaking.

"You doing okay?"

"Fine," Gabe ground out. He'd been shot in the leg during the war, bandaged it, climbed back on his horse, and continued to fight until they'd won the battle, never noticing the pain. Afterwards, he gave himself two days to recuperate, then climbed back on Blackheart, resuming his command.

The wound to his side surprised him in its intensity. He couldn't stand without help, and it hurt to sit. His body continued to crave sleep, even though that's all he'd done since the shooting. The wagon jerked to a stop and he turned his head to see the roof of his house behind the jail.

"You ready to go inside?" Noah asked as he moved behind him to support his shoulders while Cash and Beau lifted him off the wagon.

"I can walk."

"Probably, but you're not going to." Cash tightened his grip as they carried him inside, positioning him on the bed and pulling up the covers. "Beau's riding out to the Murton ranch to speak with Ty. Someone's been stealing supplies."

"Probably miners who haven't made a strike," Gabe replied, trying to sit.

"Agreed," Cash responded as he grabbed a pillow while Beau set a glass and pitcher of water on a nearby bow-fronted chest of drawers. "I believe Noah's going to stay with you tonight."

"I don't need anyone to watch over me."

"From what Doc said, that discussion is over. I'll stop by later to see if you need anything." Cash followed Beau out the door, closing it behind him.

The silence which followed felt strange compared to the constant flow of his friends in and out of the clinic the last few days. Staring at the ceiling, he closed his eyes, trying to recall his last thoughts before the bullet hit him. He knew it had to do with his uncle's death and the inheritance—an idea which had taken hold in his mind while he and Noah were eating at the boardinghouse. The entire time he was at the clinic, it had eluded him. He hoped the quiet of his home would help him remember.

A rustling sound in the other room drew his attention. "Noah, are you out there?" His voice sounded raspy from lack of use. Trying to pick up the glass of water and not quite able to reach it, he tipped it over. Shifting again, he grimaced at the pain in his side, then fell back. "Noah, you still here?" Closing his eyes again, he waited, hearing the sound of the door opening. "You don't have to stay. I'll be fine on my own."

"That's not how it appears."

Gabe's eyes widened at the sound of Lena's voice and he reached for the covers, pulling them up to his chest.

"No need for modesty, Sheriff. I've been taking care of Nick's injuries for years."

"I'm not Nick."

"Clearly," she smirked, stepping up to the bed.

He watched as she righted the glass and refilled it, handing it to him before mopping up the spilled water.

"I'm making the soup Doc recommended."

"You cook?" Gabe never considered she might be capable of doing more than just handling the activities of the working women at the Dixie.

"Don't sound so surprised. I may not be the best cook in town, but I do pretty well when given the chance." She watched as he tried to reposition himself. "Here. Let me help."

"I can take care of it." Gabe scoffed at the idea she'd be strong enough to help him sit up, then thought better of it when she positioned an arm behind him and helped leverage him onto the pillows resting against the headboard.

"How's that?"

"Uh...good. Thanks."

"If you'll be all right for a bit, I'm going to check the soup and make biscuits. I found jam in the cupboard. It is okay to open it?"

"Why?"

"Because it would be good on the biscuits." She cocked her head, beginning to wonder if he might need sleep more than food.

"No. Why did you offer to help me?"

She clasped her hands in front of her. "The truth is, I didn't. When I learned Suzanne didn't have a room available and everyone else worked during the day, it seemed I was the only choice."

He didn't know why her response bothered him so much, but it did. A part of him hoped she wanted to be near him, help with his recovery, perhaps just spend time with him. Instead, she'd offered assistance out of a sense of obligation. The disappointment was acute.

"Well, I don't need any help, especially from someone who doesn't want to be here. Why don't you dish me up a bowl of soup, then get back to the saloon. It's where you belong." Although he believed it, he regretted the terse response the moment it left his lips.

His words slapped her across the face, heating her skin and burning her eyes. Instead of lashing out, she caught her lower lip between her teeth and considered what he'd said. She didn't want to be here, taking care of a man whose mere presence created conflicting emotions and a need to flee. And he was right. She belonged in a saloon. She'd grown up in one, built businesses around them. They were the one place she felt in complete control, and as ironic as it sounded, safe. Here, in his bedroom, she felt powerless and vulnerable, both of which she hated with a passion. She took a breath and stepped closer to the bed, noting his haggard expression.

"You're right, of course. I *do* belong in a saloon. However, I made a promise to be here, and no matter how rude or churlish you choose to be, I'll keep my promise. You'll just need to learn to live with it." Turning on her heel, she stormed out, muttering all the way to the kitchen.

His kitchen wasn't much larger than one of his jail cells, yet he heard her open and slam every cupboard in the room. With each crack, he felt himself flinch, and rightly so. He'd been an idiot, or as his mother used to say about a wayward cousin, a natural born fool. There wasn't a chance he could make it to the outhouse by himself, and he sure as hell wasn't using a chamber pot with Lena in the house.

Leaning his head against the pillows, he pinched the bridge of his nose, then ran a hand down his face, feeling the stubble. He must look a mess to Lena, who never appeared as anything except stunning. If he had the chance, he could stare at her all day, every day, without tiring of the sight.

"Here you are, and don't even think about setting it aside. You'll eat every drop if I have to sit here and watch." She set the tray with his bowl of soup and biscuit on the bedside table before helping him adjust. Once settled, she handed him the bowl and biscuit. "Call me when you're finished."

He should have invited her to dish up a bowl and join him, but he didn't want to get too used to her being around. It was best if she helped him as little as possible, keeping her distance the rest of the time. The sooner he healed, the faster she'd be out of his house and his life.

"Lena, are you still here?" Gabe couldn't find a comfortable position. He'd levered himself up as much as he could, then let his body sink back down as the pain in his right side increased. Lying on his back or left side worked best, but after several days, his body objected to either of those positions. Getting up and walking around was what he really wanted.

"You know I won't leave until Noah or Gabe come by. What do you need?" It surprised her how she looked forward to being with Gabe. His cantankerous nature had settled into a tolerable grumpiness as she'd found ways to relieve his boredom. She'd brought over a chess board after he'd mentioned playing it with his uncle while growing up. They'd also played cards, and spoke of life in Splendor, the Dixie, and people they knew. They talked of what they hoped for in the future, avoiding saying much about their pasts, which worked fine for Lena. Their friendship had come a long way in a few days, a fact not lost on either of them.

"I need to get up, walk around, maybe even sit outside for a while."

She set her hands on her hips, looking over his disheveled appearance. He needed a bath, something he'd ardently refused to do with her in the house.

"I'll help you into a chair outside, on one condition. You take a bath."

"You know damn well I can't get in and out of that washtub alone, and I'm *not* having you help me." He crossed his arms, settling against the headboard.

"For heaven's sake, you can wrap a towel around your waist until we get you in the tub, then I'll turn around so you can remove it and get in the water. There's no sense in lying around, itching from dirt."

"I'm not itching," he protested, although he knew it was true. The daily sponge baths she'd helped with provided at least some sense of privacy, covering his manhood more than would be possible in the tub.

She narrowed her eyes, not believing the lack of a bath in close to two weeks didn't bother him. "I'll bring in the tub and heat the water while you decide." Feeling confident the allure of a warm bath would change his mind, she left the room, closing the door behind her.

Within minutes, Lena returned, setting the washtub on the floor of the bedroom. After several trips, she'd filled it with water, then located the soap and a clean towel, looking at him with a self-satisfied smirk. "Are you ready?"

Hell no, he thought, looking from the tub to her, knowing there was little chance he'd be able to hide his body's reaction to her behind a towel.

"Give me the towel," he growled, reaching out his hand. Refusing her help, he struggled with the covers before slipping off his long johns, the exertion from this small act causing beads of sweat to form on his brow. He wrapped the towel around his waist. "All right. Let's get this over with."

Lena placed an arm around his back for support and helped him stand. Still unable to hold his body erect, Gabe bent forward, holding the towel in place with one hand.

"All right. Now lift one leg into the tub. I'll support you." Lena's expression transitioned into one of supreme concentration as she braced herself for his weight. To the surprise of them both, he climbed into the tub with little effort. "Excellent. Now sit down. I don't want to leave until you're in the water."

He glared at her, his grip tightening on the towel.

"Fine. Take the towel into the water with you. I'll get another one." Although she respected his right to privacy, the extreme amount of modesty he showed surprised her.

He nodded, accepting her help as he lowered himself, letting out a sigh at how good the warm water felt, even though it only came up to within a couple inches of the stitches above his abdomen.

Lena turned her back to him. "Do you need my help?"

"No. I can do it." He pulled the soaked towel from around him and held it in the air. "Here."

Not turning around, she glanced over her shoulder, then grabbed the dripping cloth. "I'll get a dry one while you wash. Call me when you're ready to get out."

Gabe thought he might never be ready to leave the warm water. Soaking the small washrag with water, he let it sluice over his shoulders and back, careful to keep as much moisture as possible away from the wound. Doc had told him it looked good, but the external appearance could be deceiving. He needed the injury to heal inside, which was where he felt most of the pain, a deep, almost burning sensation that turned into a dull, throbbing ache. Each time he moved, he felt as if he might be tearing skin, even though Doc had told him it was all part of the healing process.

He finished washing, then leaned back in the water and closed his eyes. Lena's soft humming drifted through the crack in the door and he found himself following the melody. It sounded like a lullaby his mother used to sing, but he couldn't place it. The thought caused him to wonder if she'd ever thought of leaving the saloon business behind, marrying, and having children. A picture of her pregnant, hands rubbing her belly, flashed through his mind. Then, before he could stop it, another image of her lying naked on his bed with a contented grin took hold. A groan escaped his lips as the fantasy became more distinct and his body hardened.

Gabe thought he had a difficult time keeping her from his thoughts before the shooting. She now occupied his mind most of each day, an occurrence he'd never encountered with any other woman. Most days, all he wanted was to reach out and draw her to him, discover if her full lips and soft curves felt as good as they did in his dreams.

He let the image play out as he continued to soak in the now tepid water. In his daydream, she reached her hand toward him, beckoning him to join her on the soft bed, then reached both arms above her head, stretching leisurely. The visions produced another low growl, causing him to clench his hands to stifle the desire scorching through his body.

"Gabe?"

So caught up in his own yearning, he almost missed her soft voice.

"Gabe, are you ready to get out?" He could hear the door creak open, soft footsteps moving toward him.

Clearing his throat, he leaned forward, resting his arms across his bent knees. "Yes," he rasped, trying to clear his mind, but he found her presence only made it worse. Taking a deep breath, he grabbed the towel she held out to him. Determined not to ask for help, he set the towel aside and placed his hands on each side of the tub, using them to leverage himself up. Noah had built the tub for him. Although heavier than most, it also provided a more rigid frame.

Using his arms, he pushed himself up, clenching his jaw at the sharp pain. A part of him welcomed the discomfort because it took his mind off the woman standing next to him. He muttered a curse as he felt his legs weaken, then her hand wrapped around his arm to steady him. She stood at his back, doing her best to keep her eyes level and not let them drift to the uncovered lower part of his body.

"Are you all right?" Her voice sounded unsteady and thick, and she wondered if she should be asking herself the same question.

When he nodded, she bent down to retrieve the towel. "Here."

He secured it around his waist and a firm arm circled his back.

"Let's get you out of the cold water."

The next few steps came easier. Within a few paces, he found himself at the edge of the bed. Feeling her arm around him, he closed his eyes tight, attempting to push away the temptation to pull her onto the bed and wrap his body around hers.

When he turned to face her, desire roared to life, more intense than any of the images he'd created. Her arm dropped from his waist, but she didn't take a step away. Reaching out his hand, he stroked his knuckles down her cheek, watching her lips part and hearing her sharp intake of breath. Her eyes flared as he moved his hand to her nape, drawing her to him, lowering his mouth to hers. A soft brush of his lips against hers felt like setting a burning torch to dry timber. The spark turned to a roaring blaze as his mouth captured hers, his arms tightening around her.

Forgetting his injury, he moved his hands to her face, holding her in place, his tongue tracing the outline of her lips, then delving inside. A sigh escaped her as she clung to him, pulling him closer.

"Lena, are you in here?" Nick's voice broke the spell. They jumped apart at the same time, Gabe mumbling an oath, and lowering himself to the bed, pulling the covers over his legs. "Are you in with Gabe?"

Taking a deep breath, she took a step backward, and turned toward the tub. "Yes. You can come in. In fact, I could use your help," she said.

He pushed the door open and took in the scene, not noticing the flushed look on either face as he spotted the washtub. "I'll get a bucket and start emptying it." He disappeared into the other room, leaving Lena and Gabe to look anywhere except at each other.

When Nick returned, he went right to work, filling the bucket and tossing the contents out the back door. "I thought I'd sit with Gabe a while, let you take some time off."

Her senses still reeling and her body pulsing, she flashed a look at Gabe, then turned toward Nick. "Yes. I need to stop at the millinery and general store." Without another word, she walked into the front area, picked up her reticule, and walked into the fading mid-afternoon sun.

Chapter Five

"Can I help you?" Al, the bartender at the Wild Rose, looked at the stranger across the bar. It had been a slow Saturday afternoon and he'd begun to wonder if everyone had gone to the Dixie.

"A whiskey, if you please."

The moment he heard the words, Al knew who stood across from him. They'd been waiting for the owner of the gold claim to make his way into Splendor. Tall and lean, he fit the description provided by the miners who frequented the Rose.

Setting the whiskey down, Al rested both hands on the bar. "I don't believe we've met. I'm Al. You must be new to Splendor."

"William Randolph Carlyle. I've only been into town once to file my claim." He tipped the glass toward Al, then took a sip, gazing around the saloon. Most tables were empty, still waiting for the onslaught of Saturday night cowhands. "It appears I'm too early for a game of cards."

"I expect they'll be crowding in before long. Saturday nights are the busiest."

The words were barely out of Al's mouth when the swinging doors slammed open and several men from the Pelletier ranch walked in, taking seats at two tables.

"Hey, Al. Can we get a round of drinks here?" Bull Mason glanced around, not seeing either of the usual girls who served the men. "Where are Belle and Dinah?"

"They'll be down in a bit." Al grabbed a bottle and glasses, setting them on a tray as Belle walked down the stairs and scooped it from the bar.

"Evening, Bull." Since she had arrived in town, Belle had tried several times to get Bull upstairs. Although always polite, he'd never taken her up on it. She'd finally given up.

"Belle. You're looking lovely, as usual." Accepting the bottle, he filled his glass, then passed the bottle around.

"You have any coffee back there, Belle?" Travis Dixon, another of the Pelletier top hands, rarely came to town with the others. Like Bull, he never accepted offers from any of the girls, preferring to relax and joke with the men.

"I'll get you some, Travis. You know, we have a new girl. She came in on the stage from Big Pine a few days ago. Amos hired her right off before she had a chance to see the Dixie." The Wild Rose had opened when Splendor first became a town, having no competition until Nick and Lena opened the Dixie. They now vied for customers and saloon girls.

"What's her name?" Bull asked, taking a sip of whiskey.

"Dolly."

Bull choked on his drink, hoping it wasn't the same woman Gabe visited whenever he went to Big Pine. It would make things mighty interesting if it were, especially now with Lena looking after him.

"You all right?" Travis slapped him on the back.

"Fine," he coughed again. "Just wondering if it might be the same girl I met in a saloon there a while back."

"Could be. I understand she's been in Big Pine for quite a spell." At the sound of footsteps on the stairs, Belle glanced over her shoulder. "Here she comes now."

Bull shifted enough to see her. Sure enough, it was the same woman.

"Good evening, gentlemen. I'm Dolly." Her gaze traveled from one man to the next until it landed on Bull. "I do believe we've met before."

"Yes, ma'am. Bull Mason."

"I remember now. You're a friend of Sheriff Evans'. Will he be in tonight?"

"He's a little laid up. Got shot a few days ago and has some mending to do."

"Nothing serious, I hope." Her face lost all humor. She liked Gabe, enjoyed their conversations when he visited her in Big Pine. She knew nothing would ever come of it, but she still cared about him.

"Could've been, but the doc took good care of him." Bull picked up his cards, attempting to end the conversation.

"Well, I'll have to stop by and give him my regards. Let me know if you boys need anything."

"How does she know Gabe?" Travis asked as he studied his cards, throwing down two.

"Don't know for certain," he lied, not wanting to mess in his friend's business. "I'm out." He tossed down his cards. "I believe I'll see how Gabe is doing." Nodding at Dolly, he left through the back, heading straight for the house behind the jail.

"Didn't he ride into town last night to check on him?" one of the ranch hands asked.

"Yep." Travis placed his cards on the table and scooped up his winnings, having a pretty good idea why Bull wanted to check on Gabe again.

Carlyle watched as first one barmaid, then another spoke with the men at one table. He'd been looking for the right game to join, deciding to take the empty chair vacated by the tall, broad-shouldered man.

"Gentlemen, I see you have an open spot. May I join you?"

The men glanced at each other, shrugging.

"Suit yourself." Travis scanned the expensive clothing, noting the revolvers resting on each hip as he sat down. "You just get into town?"

"Yes and no. I came into town on business earlier in the week. This trip is for pleasure." His mouth curved into a vague smile as he picked up his cards.

"Well, I hope you find good fortune."

"I have no doubt I will."

"Dolly? In Splendor?" Noah chuckled at the news. He'd taken over for Lena an hour before and now waited for Abby to bring their supper over from Suzanne's.

"Yep. I thought Gabe would want to know before he walked into the Rose and saw her," Bull said.

"Or before she shows up here at Gabe's place." Noah had met her the same way Bull had. On a trip with Gabe to the territorial capital. Attractive and congenial, without the heavy makeup worn by most soiled doves, he could see Gabe's attraction and willingness to travel a day's journey to keep his life private.

"Think he'll visit her at the Rose?"

"Doubtful. Of course, that doesn't mean he won't be friendly toward her."

"Who are you talking about, Noah?" Abby walked in carrying the food Suzanne prepared. "Hello, Bull. Will you join us for supper? We have plenty."

He'd already eaten, but the thought of Suzanne's cooking had his mouth watering. "Don't mind if I do, Abby. I'll grab plates."

Abby set the food on the small dining table and glanced at Noah. "How's he feeling?"

"I feel fine." Gabe's voice had them turning toward the bedroom door where he clung to the wall, steadying himself.

"What are you doing out of bed?" Abby reprimanded. "You're going to tear those stitches and start bleeding. Noah, Bull...help Gabe back to bed."

"No. I'm tired of lying in there day and night. I need to move around." His eyes lit up at the sight of the food. "Smells good." He released his grip on the wall as Noah stepped to his side.

"Stubborn fool. You could've called me to help."

He looked at Noah, his eyes narrowing, his voice low. "I have to do this."

Noah nodded, knowing he'd feel the same if the situation were reversed.

The four crowded around the small table, filling their plates and eating in silence. After a while, Gabe sat back to rest.

"How has it been going with Lena?" Abby thought it sweet of her to volunteer to help.

"Fine."

She grinned at his short response. "Has the doc told you how much longer until you can go back to work?"

"Too long. Maybe one more week, although I told him I'm fine now."

No one responded to his ridiculous assertion. They all knew he'd never be able to do his job properly when he couldn't even make it out of the bedroom without pain.

"Is Lena fine with staying until you're healed?" Abby asked.

"That's what she said, even though I told her I didn't want her to come back."

"What? You didn't say such a thing, did you?" Abby's wide eyes signaled her shock at his apparent lack of tact, a trait she had always admired in him.

Gabe shifted in the seat, trying to relieve the discomfort he felt at sitting in a hard chair. "I did. She doesn't belong here and I don't need her help. Lena's a saloon girl, not a nurse." He grimaced at the harsh way he'd treated her during her time helping him, then hid a grin when he remembered her uninhibited response when he took her in his arms.

Abby pushed up from the table, hands resting on her hips. "That's the most ridiculous comment I've ever heard you make. Besides, she isn't a *saloon girl.* She runs the business with Nick. There's a big difference." Grabbing the empty plates, she strode the short distance to the sink, mumbling to herself.

Bull leaned toward Gabe, lowering his voice. "There may be someone else who can come by and help."

"That so?" Gabe's brows drew together as he waited to hear who Bull had in mind.

"Dolly's working at the Rose now. Came in on the stage this week."

Gabe's expression changed at the mention of the saloon girl he'd visited for well over a year. Although he knew other lawmen who didn't care how the town perceived their personal lives, he'd been careful to keep his activities in Big Pine private, preferring not to give the few local gossips reason to talk.

"What's your point?"

Bull stared at him as if he'd gone daft, his voice lowering to a whisper. "No reason for Lena to come by each day when Dolly would be willing to do the same."

"It's not a bad idea," Noah added, watching as Abby glanced over her shoulder at them.

"You may be right." Gabe both dreaded and looked forward to the hours Lena spent with him. It would be more enjoyable if she came by choice, not out of a sense of obligation. Bull and Noah were right. It would be best to let her get on with her own activities. Besides, it would only be for a few more days. "Bull, do you mind asking Dolly if she can come by tomorrow for a spell?"

"I'll do it now, before I ride back to the ranch. What about Lena?"

"Leave that to me. She won't have any problem with it." At least that's what Gabe told himself.

"Of course I understand, Gabe. I'll just wait around until he gets here so I can let him know what Doc told me." Lena worked to control the disappointment at not having this to look forward to each day. After his churlish behavior the day after he'd kissed her, she knew this might happen. For what must have been the hundredth time, he mentioned he no longer needed her help, but she'd ignored it. Now, as a dull ache grew in the area of her heart, she knew he'd been serious.

Before their kiss, they'd settled into a comfortable routine, their bickering giving way to a friendly truce. He'd even told her a few stories of growing up in New York with Noah, while she'd been careful to offer little about herself. She'd gone to sleep each night anxious to see him again the following morning. It now became obvious he didn't feel the same.

He grimaced, knowing he'd left out the fact the replacement would be a woman. "I'll explain everything, Lena. You don't need to stay."

"But I'd like to. He may have questions you won't be able to answer. Besides, I'd like to meet him."

"Trust me, you won't need to explain anything. I have it handled. I don't want to keep you from your work any longer." Gabe cringed at the thought of Lena meeting Dolly. Although they shared the same profession and he admired them both, he felt a strong sense of unease at Lena meeting the woman he'd shared time with over the last year. He knew Dolly wouldn't bring it up in front of her, but Lena was a bright woman. She'd quickly figure it out.

"You know Nick doesn't need me until evenings, so you're not keeping me from my work. I have..." Her voice trailed off at the light tapping on the door. "That must be him now." She walked out of the bedroom toward the front door, plastering a smile on her face before grabbing the knob and pulling it open. The sight nearly knocked her backwards. "May I help you?"

Dolly showed no surprise at the woman who opened the door. Bull had been forthright in who she'd be replacing, so unlike Lena, her smile was bright and genuine.

"I'm Dolly. Gabe asked if I could come watch after him for a few days. You must be Miss Campanel. I've heard so much about you...I feel as if I know you."

Lena's irritation grew as her eyes wandered over Dolly. If he'd wanted *that* kind of attention, she would have been glad to send Deborah or one of the other women over. No matter how much she'd grown to care for Gabe over the past months, she knew men had needs. To her regret, she wouldn't be the one providing them.

She looked over her shoulder into the bedroom, finding Gabe hidden from view by the door standing ajar. Although acute regret gripped her, she had no choice but to let Dolly inside.

"Um, why don't you come in? He's had breakfast, so there won't be much to do until dinner, unless..."

"Don't you worry about that. I'll have no problem helping him to the privy or anything else he needs. I understand you've been here a good week and need to get back to your own work." She touched Lena's arm. "I'll take good care of him."

Lena had no doubt about that.

"I'll just get my coat and reticule, then be on my way. If you need anything, I'll be—"

"Oh, I know where to find you. I'm told you're one of the owners of the Dixie."

Starting for the door, Lena stopped to face Dolly. "Yes, I am."

"Well, I admire you. If business doesn't pick up at the Rose, perhaps I'll come knocking on your door."

Although she wanted to, Lena found it difficult to dislike her. Truth was, she'd have no problem finding her a place at the Dixie if she wanted it.

"Nice to meet you, Dolly."

"Miss Campanel." Dolly nodded as Lena disappeared outside. She closed the door, draped her coat over a chair, and walked into the bedroom, believing she just might have found a new friend in town.

At the sound of pounding on the door, Dolly set down her dime novel. After saying no more than a dozen words to her the entire morning, Gabe had fallen asleep after dinner. Three days had passed since she started tending him and she felt comfortable doing what he needed. She just hoped he'd visit her at the Rose after he got back on his feet.

"What can I do for you?' she asked the man standing outside, holding a package toward her. She could see his face turn a light shade of red as he looked her over and pulled off his hat.

"Ma'am. I have a package for the sheriff. Is he in?"

"He is, but he's sleeping. I'll be happy to give it to him." She held her hand out.

Bernie Griggs looked past her, unable to see into the bedroom. "If it's all the same, I'd like to hand it to him myself." He speculated at the contents, knowing their importance to Gabe. "No offense, ma'am."

"None taken, Mr...."

"Griggs. Bernie Griggs. I run the Western Union office and handle the mail for Splendor."

"I'm Dolly. I came in on the stage a few days ago."

"You must be the new girl at the Rose. Al mentioned you." He walked past her as she stepped aside, waving him in.

She pushed the bedroom door open enough for Bernie to see Gabe asleep.

"I'll just place it on the table, if you don't mind."

Nodding, she watched as he set it down, took a quick look at Gabe, then walked to the door.

"He knows where I'll be if he needs to send a reply. Nice to meet you, Miss Dolly."

She'd no more than closed the door when sounds from the other room told her Gabe was trying to get out of bed. "Hold on. Let me help you." Dolly slipped an arm behind him as he pushed himself up.

Standing, he took a couple steps, then shrugged off her arm. "I can make it, Dolly."

He hadn't changed from the trousers and lightweight shirt Lena had helped him into days earlier. A brief pang of regret coursed through him as he remembered the look on her face when he'd told her someone else would be helping. He didn't think he'd hurt her, but now he knew different. The kiss they'd shared changed everything. He felt it himself, seeing the wounded expression which crossed her face.

She'd wanted to stay more than he thought, but it didn't matter. He needed to find a way to stop his growing attraction to her, as well as his body's response. The kiss had been a mistake. She now had no doubt about how her presence affected him. Staying would only complicate their tenuous friendship, forcing him to acknowledge his feelings. He had no desire to accept that realization.

"Let me help you down the steps, then you can be on your own."

The back door led from his bedroom to the privy, not more than twenty feet away. He'd been handling that small trek alone the last two days, another reason it had come time for Lena to relinquish her vigil to Dolly. From the way he felt, he wouldn't even need Dolly after today.

She waited until he finished, then helped stabilize him as he took the steps back up into his bedroom and maneuvered the short distance to the bed.

"Do you mind getting Doc Worthington over here? I'd like him to check on my wound, see if he'll cut me loose."

"Anxious to get back to work, Sheriff?" Dolly grinned, believing any doctor would probably tell him to give himself more time. From what she'd heard, Gabe had been fortunate. The bullet had torn a lot of flesh, but hadn't penetrated any major organs. Still, he'd lost a considerable amount of blood, and there might still be a chance for infection.

"More than you know." The look on his face told her how much he needed to get out of the confines of the small house and back on the street.

"I'll head over there now."

As soon as the door closed, Gabe slipped into a clean shirt. Dolly had given him a shave that morning, trimming his hair the day before. If Doc gave his blessing, he'd be back at the jail by late afternoon. Cash or Beau had stopped by every day, telling him of the happenings around town, letting him know they had it all under control. He didn't doubt that. He just wanted out.

The package Bernie brought by contained a copy of his uncle's will, as well as answers to the questions he'd asked the attorney. According to the lawyer, Gabe had more choices than his father realized—or wanted him to know. Gabe didn't fault him. He knew his family wanted him home. The longer he stayed in Splendor, the less chance it would happen.

"Dolly tells me you're ready to get back on the job," Doc said as he walked through the door and into the bedroom.

"That's right. Today, if you give your consent." He needed to send a response to the attorney, then meet with Horace Clausen at the bank.

"Let's see what we can do."

For the next fifteen minutes, Doc pressed and probed, asked questions, and checked Gabe over until it seemed he hadn't missed a square inch.

"Well?" Gabe asked, watching Doc put away his supplies.

"No matter what I say, you're going to do what you want, right?"

"Pretty much." Gabe smiled, glad he didn't have to lie about his intentions.

"The wound is healing well. You take it easy, wait a few days before riding, and you should be all right."

"Thanks. I'll be over to square things up later today."

"No hurry. Come over when you have time."

"Guess you won't need me any longer." Dolly picked up her wrap and reticule before walking up to where he still sat on the bed. She leaned over, placing a kiss on his cheek. "You come and see me when you're up to it." At the door, she turned, narrowing her eyes at him. "I wasn't going to say anything about this, but changed my mind. You talk in your sleep."

He looked up, his eyes widening. "Should I worry about what you heard?"

"Nope, but you should be aware of one word you mumbled over and over."

"And that was?"

"Lena."

Chapter Six

Gabe muttered curses all the way to the telegraph office, wondering if he'd called Lena's name while she sat by the bed, watching him. He told himself if she had, she would've assumed he was calling for her help and nothing more.

"You doing all right, Sheriff?" Bernie looked up from dumping the latest mail delivery onto the counter.

"A good deal better than a week ago. Any other mail for me?"

"Nothing besides the package I left a few days ago."

"That's what I'm here about. I need to send a response."

"Figured you would." Bernie picked up paper, handing it to Gabe. "Let me know when you're ready."

It didn't take long for him to scribble the message. He now knew he'd have to make a quick trip to New York, finalize a few details regarding the estate, meet with the hotel managers, and visit his parents. His three brothers lived within a few miles of the home they all grew up in. As the oldest, Gabe had felt a sense of duty to continue the business—until the war had changed his thinking. Now, the thought of settling back in a big city held no appeal.

He slid the paper and a few coins across the counter. "Here you are."

"I'll get it right out."

His next stop would be the jail to let Cash and Beau know he'd be back on the job the following day. Afterwards, he'd visit Noah to tell him he didn't need to bring his supper any longer. Instead, he'd treat him and Abby to supper at the boardinghouse tonight. He knew he should do the same for Lena and Nick, but he didn't know if she'd accept, even if Nick did.

Nick had come by most days, giving Lena a break. Gabe had shared a little of the news from New York with him, as well as more of his background growing up. Nick had talked of his plans for two other businesses in Splendor, hinting he'd like Gabe to be a part of one or both. At the time, Gabe still didn't know how his uncle's estate would all work out, or if he'd have choices. The news from the attorney indicated he would. Now he and Nick would be able to talk in earnest.

Gabe had just left the livery when a covered wagon, followed by a buckboard, made its way up the main street toward him. He waited as they pulled to a stop in front of the livery.

"Noah! Looks like you may have some customers."

Noah walked outside, wiping his hands down his apron as the drivers of both wagons jumped down and approached him and Gabe.

"Afternoon, Sheriff. I'm Lewis Gibson and this is my son, Franklin." They shook hands with Gabe and Noah, then motioned them to the back of the covered wagon. Lifting the back flap, he nodded toward a piece of machinery. "This is my printing press. I plan to open a newspaper."

"We've heard rumors someone planned to start one. Are you here to speak with Horace Clausen, the banker?" Gabe asked.

"Yes, but we need some work on the wagons first. Would you have time to look at them?" His gaze landed on Noah.

"Show me what's wrong and I'll get started." It didn't take Noah long to see the problems. "Why don't you move them both behind the livery? Where are you planning to stay tonight?"

"At the hotel, if there is one." Lewis put his hands on his hips and looked around, spotting the boardinghouse across the street.

"If Suzanne has room, the boardinghouse is your best bet. You'll like her cooking, too," Gabe said, beginning to feel his stomach protest at the lack of food.

"I believe that's where we'll go first, Franklin. We can meet with Mr. Clausen in the morning."

Franklin nodded, then climbed onto the buckboard and pulled it to the spot Noah indicated, doing the same with the covered wagon.

"The bank is right up the street," Gabe indicated to Lewis. "Welcome to Splendor."

Lewis walked up the boardwalk as Gabe continued to Suzanne's. It wouldn't be long before Noah and Abby joined him. He'd have a cup of coffee and wait for them, hoping for a chance to see Nick before he left for the Dixie. If all went right, there would be some changes in Splendor, and he'd be playing a big part in them.

Lena sat on her bed, rereading the letter from Isabella Boucher. They'd been best friends since they were children, growing up in the saloons where their mothers worked. Just as with Lena, Nick had taken care of Bella after her mother had died in a freak carriage accident.

They'd both escaped a life of prostitution. Bella met, and against all odds, married a wealthy and much older businessman from Philadelphia. Even though she had been thrilled for her friend, it had broken Lena's heart when the carriage drove away. Her own escape had come through Nick's offer to bring her into the business on one condition—she would never sell her body for money.

At the knock on her door, she placed the letter in her lap. "Yes?"

"It's Nick. Are you ready to go to supper?" he called through the door.

"You go ahead. I'll be down in a few minutes." Picking up the letter, she read the last two paragraphs again.

Isabella had been ill, but all seemed to be going well now. Little Jackson talked up a storm and couldn't wait for a chance to travel west to see Lena. Her stomach clenched at the thought. It had been too long since she'd seen him, and from Bella's comments, he'd grown at least a foot.

Folding the letter, she opened her bureau drawer and added it to the stack already tied with a bright red ribbon. Taking a deep breath, she checked herself in the mirror and grabbed her coat.

The sound of male voices and female laughter greeted her as she entered the dining room. She spotted Abby first, glad she'd be able to share supper with another woman. Nodding at Noah, her gaze traveled to the man next to him. Deep in conversation with Nick, Gabe hadn't yet noticed her. An undefinable emotion passed through her as she watched him, touching a finger to her lips, remembering their kiss. For perhaps the hundredth time over the last few days, she felt a stab of disappointment.

At the sound of someone approaching, Gabe tore his gaze away from Nick to see Lena on the other side of the table, her eyes locked on his.

"It appears you are feeling much better. Seems Dolly's presence agrees with you." She sent him a meaningful look as Nick stood to pull out her chair.

"Dolly?" Abby's eyes furrowed in confusion.

"I doubt you've met her. She arrived in Splendor just a week ago." Lena smoothed her skirt, willing herself not to take any further notice of Gabe, his quick recovery, or the reason for it.

"I'll have to seek her out and introduce myself. Where is she staying?"

"At the Rose where she works." Lena's comment wasn't meant to shock, yet she saw the surprise in Abby's widened eyes.

"Oh..." Abby bit her lip, her brows scrunching together. "Well, I suppose I should wait to introduce myself until she comes into the bank then." She cast a puzzled glance at Gabe, the meaning of Lena's original comment becoming clear.

Noah saw Abby's cheeks flare with color. He hid his amusement by focusing on Suzanne approaching with heaping plates of food.

"Sorry to take so long. As you can see, we have a nice crowd tonight." She set the plates down. "I'll bring yours right out, Lena."

"No hurry, Suzanne. There's time before I have to be at the Dixie." She turned to Abby, ignoring Nick and Gabe as they continued their conversation, drawing Noah into their discussion. "Have you seen baby Patrick recently?" Dax and Rachel had brought him to Abby and Noah's wedding reception, but Lena hadn't spent much time around him. By the time she joined the women, he'd fallen asleep in his mother's arms, snuggling into the soft blanket.

"Rachel brought him into town late last week. I believe you must've been tending to Gabe." Abby sent him another pointed look, still irritated he'd replaced Lena with a new girl from the Rose. Even though she worked at the Dixie, everyone knew Lena wasn't one of the soiled doves. "He's growing fast. It won't be long before he'll be walking all over the place."

Lena thought of Isabella's letter and the mention of Jackson. He'd be six now. From Bella's previous letters, she knew he was smart and active, keeping her friend busy and challenged by his unending questions.

"I expect they'll be at church on Sunday if you want to see him." Abby knew neither Lena nor Nick attended, except for the occasional reception or town party. "Or we could ride out on Saturday morning for a visit."

"Saturday would be wonderful. Do you have a buggy?"

"No, but I can saddle Hasty and Joker for us." Abby's eyes lit up at the thought of a ride. Noah hadn't had much time to spend with her in weeks, so she'd taken the occasional ride to her old ranch to see how Luke and Ginny Pelletier were doing.

"It sounds wonderful. I haven't ridden in such a long time. The last time wasn't such a good experience—"

"That's because you reined up and didn't give your horse his head to jump the fence," Nick chuckled, turning to the others. "She had a new mount. He could've made it if she hadn't panicked."

"I did no such thing," Lena protested. "It felt as if he started to stumble, so I reined back—"

"And flew right over the top of him. Scared the daylights out of me, but all she suffered were a few scrapes and bruises." Nick took a bite of his meal, shaking his head at the memory.

"And ruined my new red dress, crumpled my hat, and tore my riding gloves. It was a disaster." She grinned at Nick, remembering how worried he'd been.

"Where are you planning to ride?" Gabe asked, studying Lena, no humor in his voice. Through his whole conversation with Nick, he'd fought the urge to stare at her. He hadn't seen her since Dolly arrived, hoping the change would help him get Lena out of his mind. It didn't work.

"To visit Dax and Rachel on Saturday. Lena wants to see Patrick." Abby missed Gabe's questioning look. He never figured her for a woman with an interest in children.

"I'll go with you."

Lena's head swiveled toward Gabe, surprised at his offer.

"There's no need. I'm certain Abby and I are quite capable of making it there and back without incident." Lena touched her napkin to her lips, then placed it back in her lap, gripping it in her hands.

"Most likely, but I'm going anyway. What time?"

Lena let out a sigh. Spending a Saturday with him would mean she'd have to be cordial, and that wasn't what she felt toward him right now.

"After breakfast. Does that suit you, Lena?" Abby suggested, ignoring Gabe, already knowing he wouldn't change his mind.

"Sounds wonderful."

"I'll meet you ladies at the livery." Gabe pushed his chair back and stood. "Nick, why don't we talk again next week? I'd like to hear more about your ideas."

Before Nick could respond, the door slammed open, Cash taking quick strides to their table.

"Gabe, you might want to see what's going on at the land office. There's trouble between some of the miners. Beau's there now, trying to hold off a fight."

Cash nodded at the women, then followed Gabe outside.

The land office comprised no more than three hundred square feet in a building next to the Dixie. On a normal day, three or four men might visit the office. Today, people spilled out onto the boardwalk, their shouts carrying onto the street as tempers flared. Gabe and Cash pushed their way through those standing outside to see two groups squared off in front of the counter.

"What's going on here, Otis?" Gabe's hard voice rang out, silencing most of the men.

"Seems we've got us a dispute on a few gold claims, Sheriff." Otis Ivie ran Splendor's land office, while his brother handled the assay office.

Gabe turned toward the crowd, noting Beau standing in one corner and Cash in the other, both with their hands resting on their guns.

"Anyone who isn't here about the disputes needs to step outside." He waited as men mumbled to each other, continuing to stand their ground. Gabe rested his hands on his hips. "Let me put this a different way. If you are *not* one of the supposed owners of a claim in question, I want you to get out of here. Now."

This time, the majority of the men headed outside, grumbling as they went, not walking more than a few feet from the building.

"Now, tell me what's going on, Otis."

"Well—"

"I'll tell you what's going on. Those men are trying to steal our claims." He pointed to four men standing against one wall. "We caught 'em moving stakes and we want 'em stopped." An older gentleman with a long, graying beard, slender face, and deep-set eyes glared at the men a few feet away.

"That's a load of crap, Sheriff. We were staking our claim, not moving theirs." The man standing near the wall crossed his arms, a smirk on his face.

"That's a damn lie," the older miner threw back. "These men work for Carlyle. They got orders to do whatever is needed to move us off the mountain. Well, we ain't budging."

Gabe looked between the two groups, then addressed the man with the complaint. "Anyone else see them move the claim?"

"My partners here..." he nodded to the men next to him, "and our other partner still at the claim. All four of us caught 'em."

"Otis, you have a recording for the claim by these men?"

"I sure do, Sheriff. Got it right here." Otis held it out for Gabe.

Scanning the document, it seemed plain to Gabe that the four partners filed a valid claim a few weeks before.

"Is the location on this claim accurate?" he asked the miner.

"Yes, sir. We've been real careful about all this."

Gabe nodded, then looked at the group near the wall. "Have you men filed a claim yet?"

Several looked at the ground before one spoke up, not looking Gabe in the eyes. "We've been meaning to file, but couldn't get to town."

He handed the document back to Otis and took a step toward Carlyle's men. "Seems to me you'd be better off getting out of here and working the claim Carlyle already filed." Gabe looked at Cash, then Beau, then back at Carlyle's men. "You have a dispute in the future, you see me or one of my deputies. Don't be bringing a wagon full of supporters to a fight you can't win. Now, get out of here." He stepped in front of the miners as the gunmen left the building, congregating outside with the others. "Do all those men outside work for Carlyle?" he asked the miner.

"Him and his partner. They're buying up land and bringing in men faster 'n we can pull gold from our claim. We just want what's ours, Sheriff. Nothing more."

"You have a name for this partner?"

"No, sir. From what I heard, he arrived at their claim last week."

"I've got it here, Sheriff," Otis said, holding up the document to the claim Carlyle filed. "Says his partner's name is Thomas Pennington."

"You boys ever hear of a man named Pennington?" he asked Cash and Beau.

"No. Doesn't sound familiar." Beau looked at Cash, who shrugged.

"Have you met him yet, Otis?"

"I have not. Carlyle signed his name to the claim." Otis filed the document in his cabinet. "I'll let you know if he shows up."

"I'd appreciate it. Cash and Beau, see that the gunmen get out of town. I don't want them starting up trouble. I'm going to the Dixie to speak with Nick. He may have heard something about the other partner." He offered the miners a grim smile. "You men watch yourselves. These recent gold strikes have tempers running real high around here. It would be best if at least two of you are at the claim at all times."

"Thanks, Sheriff. We've been thinking the same."

Gabe walked into the Dixie, spotting Nick at the far end of the bar, Lena talking with Deborah near the piano. She shot him a quick glance, then turned her back to him. He needed to speak with her, although he had no idea what he'd say regarding his decision to replace her with Dolly. He knew what Lena assumed. She couldn't be more wrong.

"Gabe. Let me buy you a drink." Nick signaled Paul for another glass, keeping his eyes on a table full of men who'd become more boisterous as the evening progressed.

They touched glasses, Gabe downing his in one gulp, trying his best to watch Lena without Nick noticing.

"You know, she wasn't too happy about the way you sent her off."

"She had no business being there in the first place." *So much for keeping my interest in her to myself,* Gabe thought.

"And why's that?"

Gabe didn't answer, picking up the bottle of whiskey and filling his glass.

"I know why Lena keeps ignoring what's going on between the two of you. I just don't understand why *you* do."

Gabe took a sip of his drink before looking at Nick. "What's her reason?"

"You'd have to ask her." Nick leaned his back on the bar.

Gabe mumbled a curse, then chuckled at the situation. "What's your relationship with her?" He'd never come out and asked, although he'd heard the same rumors as everyone else.

Nick's lips turned up at the corners. "I wondered why you never asked. She's like a sister and always has been."

"And that's it?"

"If you're asking if I've ever slept with her, the answer is yes...when she was little and woke up screaming from another nightmare, or when she ran a fever so high I thought she'd burst into flames."

"And the men she's been with—"

"Now you're crossing the line." Nick's hard voice cut off whatever Gabe had been about to say. "If you're thinking she's like the rest of the women in here, you'd be mistaken." Anger radiated from him. "She's my family. Do you understand that?"

Gabe hadn't believed it until now. He knew Nick was fiercely protective of her, but now his staunch defense of Lena made Gabe feel like a fool. Never in his life had he asked these questions about a woman. He'd never cared enough to dig into their past and understand them—until Lena.

"I understand." He finished the whiskey, setting the glass on the bar. "Tell me about Carlyle. And don't say you've never met him."

Nick debated on how to respond. Gabe needed to know at least some of the history, but nothing more. "If he's the same Carlyle with the gold claim, and I assume he is, we knew him in New Orleans. He hadn't been in America for long and didn't know many people. He told us he gave up his title in England to come here, insisting he had considerable wealth stashed away in a safe place." Nick's jaw worked as he thought of how he'd taken advantage of their friendship. "I made the mistake of taking him into my confidence. One night, he experienced a tougher than normal stretch at the tables, losing a tremendous amount of money. The next morning, all the money and valuables stored in my safe had disappeared, as did Carlyle."

"Did you report him to the authorities?"

"I did. They took little action, claiming we didn't see whomever took the money and had no other proof to the thief's identity. In my mind, it didn't take a genius to know who robbed us. We never saw him again." Nick glanced at Lena, knowing she'd seen Gabe come in and had chosen to avoid him.

"Is that why Lena reacted as she did to learning he'd come to the area?"

"Perhaps. They'd become friends. She took his betrayal hard." Nick wouldn't say more, leaving the rest up to Lena. He turned back toward the bar, lowering his voice as his eyes locked on Gabe. "I'm warning you as a friend. Don't go after her if you aren't prepared to see it through. I'd hate to be the one to put you back under Doc's care."

"Don't feel you must ride out with us, Gabe. Lena and I will be fine on our own." Abby tightened Hasty's cinch, then checked Joker's one more time.

"I'm certain you would be, but I'm still going." He walked Blackheart to the front of the livery, then mounted, waiting as Lena closed the boardinghouse door behind her and walked across the street to join them. He swallowed a tight knot in his throat as he watched her hips sway in a riding skirt similar to a few he'd seen back east before the war. Although still full, the material draped from her small waist and rounded hips before touching high-topped riding boots.

Tipping his hat, he saw her nod, her lips tipping up without offering the wide smile he'd become used to seeing when she came to his home. She headed straight to Abby, taking Hasty's reins. Talking softly to the horse, Gabe watched her stroke his neck in long, fluid movements, his body tightening at the sight. Forcing his gaze away, he adjusted his position in the saddle, trying to still the immediate discomfort. So focused on controlling his body's reaction to her, he didn't notice they'd ridden up beside him, reining to a stop.

"Are you ready, Gabe?" Abby asked, following his gaze up the street, seeing nothing.

"Uh...yeah. Let's go."

He let them ride ahead, content to keep watch on the trail from the back. Abby had been right about the trip being simple with little chance of threats along the way. An easy ride would get them to Dax's ranch in less than an hour.

"How are Luke and Ginny doing at your old place?" Lena asked Abby, lifting her face toward the warmth of the sun. She'd been to the Tolbert ranch a few times after Abby's father died, offering to do anything the young woman needed to get beyond the drastic change in her life.

Giving up her job at the bank for a short period, Abby had run the ranch, as well as the various businesses her father owned, before deciding to offer the ranch to the Pelletiers. She kept all the other investments, which she could manage with Noah's help. Within days, the sale had finalized, and Luke and Ginny moved into her old home. The Pelletiers now owned the largest amount of property in western Montana. It had been a good decision.

"They love the house. Ginny's making changes, which is what should happen. I wouldn't be surprised if they start a family soon."

At Abby's mention of a family, Lena glanced behind her to see Gabe a short distance away. She caught her lower lip between her teeth, thinking of how she had felt with his arms wrapped around her—safe, even as the contact sent chills through her body. He'd been right to send her away. If she'd stayed, there was no guarantee she wouldn't weaken under the intensity of her own desire and his ministrations. She had too much at stake, too many secrets he wouldn't understand. She couldn't allow herself to fall in love. Getting close to a man like

Gabe Evans would do nothing except complicate her life and lead to heartache.

Chapter Seven

"I can take them out real easy, boss. Just give me the word." Rance Stillwell, the gunman hired by Carlyle and his partner, Thomas Pennington, had been watching several nearby claims. The majority consisted of between one and four miners, leaving little room to keep watch for claim-jumpers.

"Do whatever you need to." Carlyle pulled a thin cigar from his pocket and lit it.

"Short of killing," Thomas added, sending a look to his partner.

"He'll do what needs to be done to protect our claim," Carlyle shot back, then glanced at Stillwell. "No killing unless they refuse to leave."

"I'll take care of the—"

"Spare me any details, Stillwell. It doesn't matter to me how you handle each situation, as long as it gets done and we take over the claim." Carlyle drew on his cheroot, letting the smoke waft into the air, filling the small cabin.

Carlyle's men had built four structures. Two served as residences for Pennington and himself, one served as an office, and the last held supplies. His men lived in tents, using the nearby stream for baths and laundry. They took meals in the largest tent, congregating there at the end of the day to play cards and drink the small amount of liquor Carlyle allowed in camp. He provided enough whiskey to relax them, but not enough to hinder their work.

Stillwell nodded. "I'll get started."

Pennington watched him leave, uncomfortable with Carlyle's desire to steal claims from other miners. He felt their own claim held enough promise without resorting to intimidation or killing.

"We should buy them out, not try to run them off." Pennington took a seat and crossed his arms.

"I tried. They're not interested."

"Then we should concentrate on our own claims and ignore them. I'm not comfortable using men like Stillwell."

"Getting soft, Tommy?"

"I prefer to believe I'm taking the smart approach. The sheriff suspects us of attempting to grab the claim of the four miners north of here. It won't be difficult for him to connect Stillwell to us. I'm not interested in killing men for claims that may have little to no value. That was not the plan when we came here from San Francisco." Pennington stood and paced to the window, looking out the dirt-encrusted glass to see workers scurrying about.

Willie and Tommy became close friends in England, both third sons with little chance of obtaining title or wealth. They'd traveled to America, using their supposed social standing in England when it benefited them. Otherwise, they ignored ties to their homeland and family.

At first, the two stayed in Boston, finding success using their considerable gambling skills. Ready to see more of America, they moved to New York. Tommy met an actress and decided to stay, while Willie continued to New Orleans. His luck there ran out at the same time Tommy and his actress lover parted ways. They traveled across the country, discovering the bawdy bay town of San Francisco was a perfect fit—until Willie became obsessed with gold fever.

"Plans change, Tommy." He unfurled a map and pointed to a large area surrounding their claim. "We want to control claims in this section. There is a chance veins could intersect. If that happens, we'll be buried in disputes. The smart decision is to eliminate the risk now."

"As long as Stillwell does whatever he can to dislodge them before he resorts to killing. We don't want a murder to come back to us."

"Stillwell will be the one who hangs, not us. No one will be able to connect his actions to us, and he'll leave the territory as soon as his job is done."

Thomas didn't like it, but the order had already been given. "What about our plans to open a gambling hall in Splendor?"

"Rumor has it the Wild Rose is losing money fast and the owner, Amos Henderson, is thinking of selling. We'll speak with him on our next trip." His lips quirked into a wry grin at the decision they'd made to bring men to Splendor to work their claims, then open a saloon where they could spend their wages.

"Have you learned anything about the Dixie?"

Willie knew quite a bit about the other establishment, shocked when he'd discovered who owned it. He thought the chances of him ever crossing paths with Nicholas and Magdelena again were slim. Thinking back, he wouldn't mind another go-around with the beautiful woman who'd captured his interest in New Orleans. It had been a real shame when he'd decided to cast her aside in favor of the large sum of cash and jewelry they kept in their safe. Now he had another chance. The more he thought of his goals, the more he believed she could play an essential role in helping him achieve what he wanted. Wealth had a place, but what he craved had been taken from him in England by the order of his birth—namely power and social standing.

"It's booming. The owners seem to have a magic touch when it comes to saloons and gambling halls. Perhaps a visit is in order. It doesn't hurt to learn as much as possible about the competition, right, Tommy?"

"Patrick is beautiful, Rachel," Lena whispered, holding the baby in her arms as she rocked back and forth. "He's grown so much since I saw him last."

"He never stops eating," Rachel laughed, enjoying the look of pleasure on Lena's face. "It is much more work than I'd ever imagined. He never wants to sleep. Dax keeps telling me to sleep whenever he goes down for a nap, but there's always so much to do." She sighed, thinking of all the work waiting to get done.

"The work will get done. It's more important to take care of yourself than worry about a clean house or laundry. He's little for such a short period of time. You don't want to be so exhausted you miss it."

"It sounds as if you've had some experience," Rachel said, watching Patrick's eyes flutter open.

Lena looked at her. "My closest friend has a young boy. I've been able to visit them many times." She bit down on her lower lip, remembering how much Jackson grew between each visit. Her heart twisted at the memory. There were some things in life you couldn't get back.

Gabe stood a few feet away, talking with Dax, listening to Lena at the same time. She appeared so content holding Patrick, letting him grasp her fingers as she rocked him. Not for the first time, he wondered if she'd ever wanted to settle down and have children of her own.

"Here you are." Abby brought out a tray filled with cups of coffee and spice cake. "Rachel, I'm surprised you have even an extra minute to bake with this little man always wanting attention."

"You learn to make time. Taking care of him and keeping the house in order are what take up most of each day. Ginny often rides over when Luke is working with Dax. She's a huge help. And I have Lydia," she said, referring to the oldest of the orphans. At almost twenty, Rachel wondered how much longer they'd have her before love and marriage took her away. "I don't know what I'd do without her. She often watches Patrick when Ginny isn't able to come over."

Holding Patrick to her chest, Lena stood. Seeing Gabe look her way, she took a few steps to stand in front of him.

"Have you had a chance to hold him?" Her eyes sparkled when she saw Gabe's eyes widen.

"Uh...no." Gabe backed up a few inches when she held Patrick out to him.

"You won't break him. Place your arms under him and pull him to your chest."

"Go ahead," Dax encouraged. "You may have a few of your own someday, and this will give you an idea of what it's like."

"Not me. Noah and Abby plan to have a houseful of children. That'll be enough for me." Even though he protested, he held out his arms, letting Lena transfer Patrick to him.

The room quieted as they watched Gabe. Most of Rachel's female friends had held the baby at least once, but fewer men wanted the experience. Luke, Bull, Travis, and Dax were the only men, besides Doc Worthington, who'd held him. Now Gabe joined the list.

"What do you think of him?" Lena asked, watching over his shoulder, seeing Patrick's eyes focus on Gabe's.

He glanced at her, his mouth twisting into a smile. "I'll be more impressed when he's old enough to ride and help with chores."

"Amen to that," Dax chimed in, although no one could mistake the love he had for his son. "Why don't you hand him back to Lena and I'll show you our newest colt?"

Gabe gave Patrick back to Lena, his gaze locking on hers for a brief moment, feeling something pass between them. Her lips parted, seeming to sense what he had, then she stepped away.

It didn't take long to follow Dax to the barn. Talking in his smooth southern drawl, Dax talked of the delivery, as well as their plans for the horse breeding program. However, most of his words faded into the distance as Gabe thought of the unexpected sensations which passed between him and Lena. He'd never experienced such a profound sense of yearning, almost painful in its intensity. From the bewildered expression in her eyes, he felt certain she felt it, too.

"Are you ready to head back to the house?" Dax asked, clasping Gabe on the shoulder.

"Sure." He shoved his hands into his pockets and walked toward the house, trying to sort out the mixed feelings rumbling around in his mind.

"When are you going to do something about her?" Dax asked.

Gabe's brows furrowed as he glanced over at his friend. "Who?"

Dax rubbed a hand on the back of his neck, then stopped and turned toward Gabe. "Lena. And don't tell me you have no idea what I'm talking about."

He didn't want to talk about her or any feelings he might harbor for her. At no time in his life had he ever envisioned himself married and having a family. Even with their substantial resources and constant stream of nannies, as the oldest of four brothers, he'd always been looked upon as being responsible for those younger. Never one to shirk his duties, Gabe did what his parents expected. When he left for college, he swore it would be a long time, if ever, before he accepted the responsibility of a wife and children.

"Lena's a beautiful, smart, compassionate woman. Any man would be fortunate to claim her—

any man except me. Truth is, I'm not interested in a relationship, no matter how attracted I am to her."

Dax watched him, noting that Gabe never made eye contact, letting his gaze settle on the mountains to the west.

"You sure about that?"

"No doubt. Marriage isn't for me. Never has been."

Dax nodded, not believing a word of it. Most men felt the same until they met the right woman. Gabe could be as stubborn as any man he'd ever met. Nevertheless, from the way he looked at Lena, Dax would give him a few months at most. A man could only hold out for so long.

"Are you certain I have the money to hire another person, Nick?" Suzanne studied the numbers again. She'd had one person work for her over the years. Ginny Pelletier helped clean rooms in exchange for a place to live and meals for her and her sister. It had worked well for both of them until Ginny met and married Luke.

"If you hire another person, you'll be able to add more tables, expand your menu, and be available to talk with your customers. It may hit your savings for a short period, but then you'll see your income rise."

Suzanne watched as he adjusted the patch over his left eye. She'd never asked how he came to wear it, not wanting to broach an uncomfortable subject.

"I'd like to continue doing the cooking." She folded her hands in her lap, thinking about who she might be able to hire to wait on the customers.

"You'll want to hire a cook so you can be available to take care of all the other duties." He held a hand up when she started to object. "You can still plan the meals and help in their preparation, but you need to have time to run the dining room."

"All the women I know, who can prepare descent meals, aren't looking for work. They're tending to their families."

"There's no reason you can't hire a man. That's what most of the ranchers do when there's no woman on the place. I'll bet you'd have a good number from which to choose."

"Maybe, but those ranch cooks are stubborn and set in their ways. I'll need someone who'll do the job *my* way." She scrunched up her face, thinking of the pigheaded men she'd met who handled the cooking chores on the trail and for the bunkhouses.

"Then we look until we find the right person."

She looked up at him, her brows lifting in surprise. "You'd help me find someone?"

"I'd be glad to help you, Suzanne. Whatever you need." He settled his hand over hers for a moment before pulling away. Clearing his throat, he stood and grabbed his hat. "I'd better get to the saloon before Lena wonders where I am." His voice held a slight huskiness Suzanne had never noticed before. She found herself wondering if he felt any of the jitters or heart-pounding sensations she did when they were close. "Perhaps we can meet for coffee when you're finished serving breakfast tomorrow. We can talk about finding your new cook then." A hesitant smile tipped the corners of his mouth before he turned to leave.

Suzanne finished the last sip of her coffee, watching as he walked out. He'd been living in the boardinghouse for close to a year. They'd become friends, had coffee once or twice a week, and on occasion, even shared a late supper when business slowed at the saloon. She looked forward to those visits, perhaps more than she should.

Pushing herself from the table, she grabbed the documents, planning to study them more after the supper crowd left. Doubts still plagued her, even though Nick felt certain of her abilities. It felt good to know someone understood a little of the fears she faced as a widowed businesswoman. She owned the building and everything in it, feeling certain Horace Clausen would grant her a loan. Nick had also offered, but Suzanne would never accept money from him, even as a loan. Walking into the kitchen, she set to work on the final preparations for supper, her mind focused on finding someone who could replace her in the kitchen. It might be a long search.

"I hope you will consider our offer, Mr. Henderson. It could be quite a while before you find anyone who can pay more." Carlyle finished his whiskey, placing the empty glass on Amos' desk before standing.

Thomas had remained silent during most of the discussion. He'd taken one look at the well-worn saloon and almost walked out. It was several steps below the ones he'd owned in San Francisco. However, one look at the meticulous records Amos kept changed his mind.

Amos didn't have an interest in selling due to the need for money. It had to do with his desire to travel, see more of the country before he got too old to enjoy it. He felt no rush to sell. Instead, he'd take his time, put word out in Big Pine, and see what kind of response he got. Neither Willie nor Tommy wanted that to happen. They'd made a generous offer and would push until Amos accepted it.

"Nice to meet both of you." He shook their hands, a trickle of unease passing through him as they turned to leave. "It might be a while before I make a decision."

"Take your time, but I'm certain you'll find no one who will match our offer." Willie led the way outside, then stopped as he scanned the main street. "We'll give him a week, then visit again."

"And if he still isn't certain?" Tommy asked.

"We'll send Stillwell to make sure Henderson sees the advantages of selling to us, and the disadvantages if he doesn't," Willie smirked. "Regardless, the saloon will be ours within weeks." Hearing the music from the Dixie, he started across the street. "It's time to visit what will soon be our competition."

Nick set aside the paperwork on his desk as the noise level in the saloon increased, knowing he'd have to make his presence known before the mood of the patrons got out of hand. He'd been grateful when Gabe insisted he have Cash, Beau, or himself in the saloon most nights. The Dixie attracted a wilder crowd than the Rose, younger and prone to grab their guns to settle any dispute. More often than not, the jail filled with its customers, sleeping off the effects of too much alcohol. Gabe didn't spend much time on lesser crimes. There simply wasn't room in the jail when the circuit judge came through town just once every couple months.

Opening the door into the saloon, Nick saw every table filled with men playing cards, drinking, or joking with the girls. Faro, seven up, and poker were the most common card games. The previous spring, he and Lena had made the decision to ship in a roulette table. Soon, they would add keno, a game Nick had played in Houston, and a craps table, making them the first in the territory to offer those games.

They talked of expanding to the abandoned building next door, until Lewis Gibson had made the decision to lease it to the newspaper. Now they'd be forced to enlarge their space by relocating the office and storage rooms, then pushing out the back. With the increase in population, the changes would soon pay for themselves.

Taking his usual spot at the end of the bar, he ordered a whiskey and let his gaze wander over the room. Nothing drew his attention until the doors swung open and a man he hadn't seen in close to seven years walked in, his eyes connecting with Nick's. Knowing Carlyle would visit the Dixie at some point, he'd prepared himself for this moment. By the way his eyes widened and skin paled, Carlyle didn't know who owned the saloon. For a few minutes, Nick held the advantage. He knew it would be short-lived.

Nick never let his gaze leave Carlyle's as he and another man stepped up to the bar.

"Whiskey for my partner and me." Willie tossed coins on the bar, then turned toward Nick. "It's been a long time, Nick."

"Not long enough. Finish your drink and leave. We don't cater to those who can't be trusted." Nick watched Willie's face harden as a hand moved to his gun. "You may be a scoundrel, but even *you* aren't foolish enough to start something with two deputies nearby." Nick nodded to a corner where Cash and Beau sat at a table, their attention focused on him and Carlyle.

"Of course not. I understand your anger, even though it's directed at the wrong person. I heard about the theft of your money, but if you're thinking it was me, you are mistaken." Carlyle picked up his whiskey and took a slow slip, his gaze moving up the stairs to the balcony above.

"She's not here," Nick growled, his eyes narrowing.

"Pity. But we both know if you're here, she's close. Give her my regards, would you?"

Nick fumed at the thought of Carlyle getting anywhere close to Lena. He glanced at the second man standing on the other side of Willie, listening to their exchange.

"And you are?" Nick asked.

"Thomas Pennington. William and I are partners in the Devil Dancer mine." He stretched out his hand, which Nick stared at before tossing back the rest of his drink.

"I'll give you the same message. Finish your drink and leave. Neither of you are welcome at the Dixie."

He glanced at the stairs, hoping Lena didn't choose this moment to walk down. She'd been tending to Deborah, who'd taken ill with some form of stomach ailment. Doc had left a couple hours before, cautioning them to keep her in bed until the symptoms subsided.

Carlyle finished his drink, setting the glass down. Pennington did the same. "It was a pleasure to see you, Nick. Perhaps we'll encounter each other again." The superior tone of Carlyle's voice grated on him, but he stayed quiet. Getting them out of the saloon had become his top priority.

"It's doubtful as you won't be coming back in here." Anger seethed through him as the doors closed behind them. He worked to control his fury, not wanting Lena to know of Carlyle's visit. It would be a false hope to believe Carlyle wouldn't come back, if for no other reason than to see Lena. He tightened his hand around his glass, the pressure almost shattering it.

"Was that Carlyle?"

Nick turned to see Cash beside him. "And his partner, Thomas Pennington."

"They sure didn't stay long." He signaled Paul for a beer. "Did you have anything to do with their leaving so suddenly?"

"I told them they weren't welcome in here." Nick spotted Lena coming down the stairs. "We'll talk about it later."

Cash noticed Lena and clamped his mouth shut. "Good evening, Lena. You look wonderful tonight."

"Why, thank you, Cash. This dress came in on the stage today, all the way from New York." She smoothed her hands down it, feeling the silk, and admiring the deep blue color. "Deborah's doing better," she said, answering the unspoken question she saw on Nick's face. "She wanted to get dressed and work tonight. I told her if she came downstairs, we'd fire her on the spot."

"Tough lady," Cash joked, knowing her threat was real. They didn't allow sick girls to work, insisting they recover before offering entertainment to the men.

Lena smiled at Cash's comment. It hadn't been easy for her to clamp down her natural tendency to nurture and overlook behavior which might prove harmful. At first, she'd wanted to be friends with all the girls. Now she knew better. Being the boss meant distancing yourself from those who worked for you, being careful not to let the bond get too strong. She'd made mistakes over the years, but what needed to be done was now ingrained in her.

The man at the piano launched into to a fast, jaunty tune, belting out the words. Before long, several miners had joined him, along with two of the saloon girls. As they swayed back and forth to the music, Lena's attention went to the swinging doors, her breath catching as Gabe walked in.

She'd never seen him so decked out. Black trousers, jacket, shirt, boots, a tapestry vest of blue silk, matching ribbon tie, and black hat. His appearance gave the impression of a man going to an important function, or perhaps courting someone. Her stomach clenched at the thought of him showing an interest in another woman. She knew several single or widowed women in the area who'd jump at the chance to be with him. If her life were different, she'd be included in that group.

Without any hesitation, he walked up to her. "Good evening, Lena." His gaze wandered over her, appreciation clear in the way his eyes darkened. "You look stunning."

She swallowed, hoping to clear the lump in her throat. "Thank you, Sheriff. You look...remarkable." Her voice came out as no more than a whisper.

"I thought we agreed you'd call me Gabe," he said, his eyes sparkling. Shifting his stance, he cast a look at Nick. "If you can spare her, I'd like to have a few words with Lena. In private."

Nick's eyes sparked in amusement. "It's up to the lady."

Turning toward Lena, he tilted his head, the question clear in the way his eyes met hers.

"Yes. I can spare a few minutes."

Accepting the arm he offered, he led her out the swinging doors, surprising most of those who noticed them.

"What do you think that's all about?" Nick asked Cash, who looked as confused as he felt.

"I have no idea. I've never seen him so gussied up." Cash took a slow swallow of his beer. "Guess I may just have to stick around a while." His brows rose, already enjoying the unexpected entertainment.

Chapter Eight

Stepping into the cool night air, Lena's heart raced at the feel of her arm through his, as well as the surprise at the unexpected invitation. She didn't want to read too much into it, preferring to think of it as a stroll with a friend.

"I believe fall may be my favorite time of year. It reminds me of New York with the changing colors and crisp air." Gabe smiled at her, taking the boardwalk to the opposite end of the street, placing a hand over hers.

"I've been to New York. It's a fascinating city and so different from New Orleans. Although it seems similar to Philadelphia where my friend, Isabella, lives."

"Do you ever get a chance to visit her?" Gabe asked, slowing their pace, wanting to prolong their walk.

"Not as often as I'd like. She's quite busy with her social functions and raising Jackson."

"Jackson?"

Lena bit her bottom lip, not wanting to go into detail. "He's six and growing fast. Perhaps they'll visit me out here someday. Do you miss your family, Gabe?"

He pondered the question a few moments. Although he thought of his parents and brothers, he'd never considered that he missed them. With the death of Uncle James, he believed he'd be traveling east in the near future to settle details on the estate. While there, he'd take a few extra days to spend time with his family.

"There are times I miss them. My brothers bickering amongst themselves, Mother chastising them for being too rowdy."

"How many brothers do you have?" Lena asked, interested in anything she could learn about him.

"Three. All younger."

A pang of longing passed over Lena. As an only child, Isabella had been her one playmate. "Sisters?"

"No, just the three brothers. And you?"

"No siblings. Just Nick and Isabella."

As much as he loved his brothers, the idea of growing up in a quiet home held a certain appeal. As he'd gotten older, the time he spent at home decreased because of work at his uncle's hotel and friendship with Noah. His mother tried to get him to spend more time with his brothers, but the next oldest was four years younger. In Gabe's opinion, they had little in common.

"Does Isabella have any other children?" Gabe asked as they came to a stop in front of the boardinghouse.

"Um...no. Just Jackson."

Gabe looked through the windows to see a few diners still eating. Making a quick decision, he turned to Lena. "Do you have time for a slice of Suzanne's pie and coffee?"

"I think Nick can handle the saloon a little while longer."

"Well. Hello, you two." Suzanne flashed a smile at them when they walked through the door, nodding to a table up front.

"Pie and coffee for each of us please, Suzanne." Gabe held out Lena's chair, then took a seat across from her. "Did I already tell you how nice you look tonight?"

"Why, yes, I believe you did." The smile she flashed at him created a pool of heat deep in his belly.

He waited to explain his reason for bringing her here until Suzanne set down their plates and cups. Taking a sip of the steaming liquid, he thought of what he needed to say, hoping she'd understand. As he waited, she took a bite of pie, her eyes lighting up.

"I don't believe I've ever had better pie than the ones Suzanne makes." She took one more bite, then picked up her cup. "I believe it's time for you to tell me why you wanted to speak with me tonight."

Her straight-forward comment surprised him, even as the corners of his mouth tilted up into a tight smile.

"Can't a man take a pretty woman for a walk?"

"Yes, most men can. However, I don't believe you to be that kind of man. You seem to have a purpose for every action." Taking one more bite of pie, she set down her fork and waited.

"All right. It's about the time you spent helping with my recovery. I wanted to thank you and let you know how much I appreciated all your help. Even though you didn't volunteer, I'm grateful for the time you spent at my place." Gabe took another sip of coffee, hoping what he said came out right.

"I see." She hesitated a moment to collect her thoughts. They might never have another opportunity to sit and talk about their time together, so she wanted her words and their meaning to be clear. "You're a stubborn man, Gabe...strong and proud. I know how difficult it was for you to accept help. As the sheriff, you've always gone beyond what most people expect, and we're all grateful to have you. There's no need for thanks. It was the least I could do to express my appreciation."

"And if another man had been injured, would you have offered your help to him?" He could see a slight amount of pink tinge her olive-colored skin as she thought about his question.

"I've never asked myself that question, so I don't know. Perhaps, depending on the circumstances. Cash, Beau, maybe a few others who had no one else to help." Clasping her hands in her lap, she straightened her spine, knowing he searched for some answer, but not sure what.

He pushed the plate away and leaned forward, resting his arms on the table.

"And would you have offered them the same degree of help you gave me?"

She caught her bottom lip between her teeth as his probing became clear. It had nothing to do with her cooking, cleaning, or helping him with his daily needs, and everything to do with their kiss. That's what weighed on his mind, the same as it had on hers since the day it happened.

She thought of her life—growing up in a saloon, working in the Dixie every day. In all that time, two men had drawn her attention. Willie Carlyle and Gabe Evans. Willie had turned out to be a scoundrel of the worst sort, while Gabe had shown himself to be the opposite. Other than Nick, she knew of no finer man. If she could ever love again, it would be Gabe, but circumstances had intervened long ago. She had more to consider now than the opportunity for love. Not that a man like him, raised with wealth and advantage, would be interested in more than a casual relationship with a woman of her background.

"If you're asking if I would have allowed one of them to kiss me, the answer is no."

He stared at her, his expression hooded. Standing, Gabe reached into his pocket, tossed money on the table, then pulled out her chair, reaching his hand toward her.

She made no comment as they stepped onto the boardwalk and turned toward the Dixie, her arm once again through his. The excitement of being with Gabe diminished at the knowledge nothing would ever come of their friendship. There were confidences she'd never share with him. He'd never understand the choices she had to make and that knowledge made her feel lacking.

Every shop between the boardinghouse and the Dixie had closed hours ago. Other than the lights from the Dixie and the Wild Rose across the street, the walkway was bathed in darkness. As they continued on, Gabe's arm tightened, drawing her closer to his side.

He said nothing as they approached the last shop before the saloon. Turning toward her, he touched her cheek, running the knuckle of a single finger along the curve of her jaw. He lifted her chin, locking his gaze with hers, then lowered his mouth. Brushing his lips in a light stroke across hers, the brief touch he intended turned heated as she moved her hands up his arms, holding tight, and leaning into the kiss.

Cupping Lena's face, his mouth began to ravage hers, seeking entry. Her lips were warm and moist, tasting of apples and coffee. Letting his hands move to her shoulders, he wrapped them around her back, aligning their bodies. Heat fused them and he felt her writhe against him, as if she couldn't get close enough.

"Lena," he whispered, his lips trailing a line down to the hollow of her neck. His splayed hands on her back pulled her tight before one drifted down the curve of her waist and soft fullness of her hips.

"Gabe..."

Her voice echoed through his mind as she tried to push away, but his body wouldn't respond. A vague impression of her thrusting against him as she repeated his name broke through and he eased away.

His eyes locked with hers as he took a deep breath, trying to calm the turmoil he felt. One touch of her lips to his and he was lost, unable to form a simple thought. Never had a woman's touch affected him so.

"My apologies, Lena. That shouldn't have happened." He stepped away, even as desire continued to draw him to her.

Although right, his words pierced what she still allowed herself to think of as hope. The kiss shouldn't have happened, no matter how much she wanted it to and how perfect it felt. She had a life, responsibilities he knew nothing about. A relationship with any man was out of the question.

Besides, she doubted he would have taken such liberties with any other woman, at least not one who worked in a saloon. When he found the right woman, she'd be someone he'd be proud to have by his side for everyone to notice. To her regret, Lena knew she'd never be that woman. Touching a hand to her face, feeling her heated skin, told her how easy it would be to forget everything and surrender to the desire she felt for Gabe. But Lena knew the cost of such a reckless action.

"You're right. We must forget it ever happened." Smoothing her hands down her skirt, she straightened and walked past him, disappearing into the Dixie without looking back.

Gabe wanted to call her back, but what would he say? The more time he spent around her, the more his arguments against a relationship dissolved. His deeply held conviction to leave marriage and providing heirs to his younger brothers faded into the distance when he thought of having Lena as a permanent part of his life. At that moment, he couldn't remember a single reason why he'd been so adamant about keeping his bachelor status.

No matter how inappropriate it seemed, Nick knocked on Suzanne's door, hoping she hadn't yet gone to sleep. All evening he'd been thinking about a possible solution to finding someone to replace her as the cook at her boardinghouse. It took a random comment from one of Luke Pelletier's ranch hands for the solution to appear.

"Suzanne, are you awake?" He knocked again, trying not to wake any of the other boarders.

The door flew open, Suzanne still pulling her wrapper tight around her waist, attempting to brush strands of hair away from her face.

"What is it, Nick? Are you all right?" Instead of being upset at his late summons, her face lined with worry as her eyes searched his.

Nick's lips parted as he took in the sight before him. Her bare feet, braided hair draped over her shoulder, and sleep-glazed eyes made her look no more than a young woman of twenty.

"Nick?"

"Oh, yes. I'm sorry to wake you, but I have information on someone who might be available to take over the cooking." He took a slight step back as doubts about waking her for a discussion that could wait until morning assaulted him. As a rule, he always thought his actions through and didn't act on impulse. Standing in the hall, watching Suzanne shiver in her gown and wrapper, forced him to accept there may be other reasons he pounded on her door so late.

Her eyes squinted as she tilted her head, her lips slanting up at the corners. "Of course. If you believe it's important enough to discuss tonight, I'll make us some tea and we can talk in the kitchen. Let me get my coat."

He stood aside as she headed for the stairs, still closing the buttons of her coat. Other than sliding into silk slippers, she'd taken no time to freshen her appearance, an act which would've been unheard of by most women he knew. The girls in the Dixie obsessed about their appearance. Suzanne possessed none of this vanity.

Pulling down cups from a shelf, he watched as she boiled water and lifted tea leaves from a sealed container. It remained one of her personal indulgences, offered to friends who visited, and not appearing on the menu. Pouring hot water into the cups, she handed him one, then took a seat at the table.

"Don't keep me in suspense, Nick. Tell me your thoughts."

He sat across from her, idly stirring the tea with a spoon. "I overheard two of the Pelletier men mention the cook at Luke's place."

"Fanny Dobbins."

"Right. They said she told Luke and Ginny she'd like to find a place in town, live closer to the shops and church. They're going to move Hank and Bernice Wilson from Dax's over to Luke's to take over for her."

The older couple had worked at the ranch for years, ever since the original owner started it. Hank had been the foreman while Bernice cooked and cleaned. When Bernice took ill, they'd given up their jobs, but stayed on at the ranch at Dax's request. Her health had improved at a slow, steady pace, and now she wanted to get back to work. Since Rachel had Lydia to help her, moving them to Luke and Ginny's made perfect sense.

"I had heard about Bernice wanting to get back to work, but thought it would be to help Rachel."

Nick could see Suzanne's eyes begin to sparkle at the thought of having Fanny work for her. They'd be perfect together.

"What do you think?" Nick asked, sipping his tea, grimacing at the weak flavor.

"It's a wonderful idea. I've known her for years and she's always mentioned living in town someday. I wonder if she still wants to work."

"There's one way to find out." He set the cup down, leaning his arms on the table. "I'll ride out tomorrow morning and talk with her. Of course, you're welcome to come—"

"No," she interrupted. As much as she wanted to be the one to approach Fanny, she couldn't leave her boarders. "You go ahead. I don't have an empty room in the place right now." Her lips drew into a thin line at the realization she had no place for Fanny to live. "There may be no room for her if she *does* accept."

"Leave that to me." He pushed back from the table, holding out his hand to Suzanne. "Now, get some sleep. I'll head out after breakfast tomorrow."

They walked upstairs, stopping at her door.

"Thanks, Nick. I appreciate your help with this."

"Whatever you need, Suzanne." He leaned down and gave her a quick kiss on the cheek, then disappeared into his room a few doors down the hall.

"It's settled then. You can start at the boardinghouse whenever you're ready." Nick sat in Luke Pelletier's study, Fanny on one side with Ginny beside her. They hated to lose her, but the offer to work for Suzanne made them feel better about her leaving.

"Hank and Bernice will be moving over here the end of the week," Fanny said, looking at Ginny. "Is it all right with you if I leave?"

"Whatever you want, Fanny. We appreciate you've stayed this long." Ginny placed a hand on Fanny's arm.

After Abby's father died, Fanny had moved back to Splendor to help her. She had no intention of staying when the woman she had helped raise married Noah and moved to town. However, after a few months, Fanny had grown used to being back and liked the Pelletiers.

"When you're ready, I'll bring a wagon out to take you to town." Nick glanced at Luke. "I wonder if we might speak in private."

Ginny and Fanny took the hint and both stood, Fanny looking at Nick. "Thank you, Mr. Barnett. Please tell Suzanne how much I look forward to working with her."

"I'll be sure and do that." Nick waited until they'd closed the door before turning to face Luke. "I'm in the market for some land and thought I'd start with you."

Not too long ago, the two men had a misunderstanding about Ginny, which could've led to ongoing resentment. They'd worked it out and now got along fine.

"Do you want to run cattle, raise horses?" Luke asked.

"Nothing so grand. I'll have a few horses, but not to breed, and enough acres where I can get away from town, have my privacy. Maybe enough so Lena can have a place nearby." He leaned forward, resting his arms on the desk. "The truth is, even though I'll continue with the Dixie, plus maybe open some other businesses, I'm getting tired of town life."

"I can't blame you. It's good to have a place to get away. Noah and Abby stay at his cabin most Saturdays and Sundays, and...well, I might not go into town on Sundays if Ginny and Rachel didn't insist." He grinned at how his life had changed since they'd married. All for the better. "Dax and I have twenty acres not far from where the road splits. A lot of trees and boulders, so it's not suitable for our needs. There's a creek, so you shouldn't have trouble digging a well. Would that do?"

"Sounds about perfect. Do you have time to show it to me?"

"Let's go."

The land stretched across what appeared to be more than twenty acres. A winding creek set one border, while tall boulder formations lined the north, separating it from the southern end of the Pelletier property. As they rode through it, Nick located two level plots of ground, perfect for home sites, with enough land for barns and other outbuildings.

He reined up his horse and slid to the ground, walking around one flat plot as Luke stayed atop Prince and watched. After a few moments, he returned and swung into the saddle.

"How much?"

Checking herself in the mirror once more, Lena draped a coat over her arm and picked up her reticule. She'd slept through breakfast and now her stomach growled. Suzanne would have something left in the kitchen, if only bread and jam.

"I wondered if you were coming down today." Suzanne glanced over her shoulder, then back at what she worked on in the sink. "Would you like some eggs?"

"Coffee and toast if it isn't too much trouble."

"None at all. Take a seat and I'll get it for you." She motioned to the table where most people congregated when they visited her in the kitchen.

"Has Nick already left for the saloon?" Lena stirred a little sugar in the cup Suzanne set before her, then took a sip.

"Actually, he rode out to Luke's place to talk with Fanny."

Lena's brows knit together. "About what?"

"Taking over the cooking for me. Nick believes I can afford it."

"That's a wonderful idea. You might even be able to take some days off." Lena had never known anyone who worked as hard as Suzanne. Seven days a week from sunup until she finished cleaning after the last customer left, with a rare break to eat. "I'd think Ginny would miss her, though."

"Fanny wants to move to town, and they have someone to take over for her." Suzanne explained about Hank and Bernice. "I just don't know where she'll live. All my rooms are full, and I don't expect anyone to move on for quite a while."

"She can stay in my room. I'll stay at the saloon until a room opens up."

"Absolutely not. I'm certain there'll be another solution." Suzanne turned her attention back to the potatoes in the sink, not hearing the front door of the restaurant open and close.

"Suzanne, are you back here?"

Lena flinched at the sound of Gabe's smooth, deep voice. She hadn't seen him since the night they'd taken their walk, but she'd thought of little else. Gripping her hands in her lap, she resisted the urge to put a finger to her lips, a normal reaction whenever she thought of him.

"In the kitchen, Gabe."

"I have a favor to..." His voice trailed off as he stepped into the kitchen to see Lena at the table.

"Hello, Gabe."

He stared at her a moment too long, causing Suzanne to glance over her shoulder at them. The look on their faces didn't surprise her.

"Hello, Lena." His voice sounded unsteady, his eyes uncertain as they narrowed at her. "I thought you'd be at the saloon by now." He fingered the brim of his hat, rotating it in his hands.

"What favor did you want to ask me?" Suzanne dried her hands on her apron.

Tearing his gaze away from Lena, he shifted, not wanting to state his request in front of her. "Uh...I can come back later."

"You're not interrupting us. Just tell me what you need."

"A pie," he blurted out. "I wondered if you might have an extra one I could buy." He cleared his throat, hoping Suzanne wouldn't ask why he needed a whole pie.

"I have an extra apple pie. Will that do?"

He nodded, reaching into his pocket for money and setting it on the table next to Lena.

"Who's the lucky person?" Suzanne handed the pie to him, tilting her head to one side.

He shot a quick look at Lena. "It's for Dolly. A thank you for helping me."

The air left Lena's lungs, although she kept her face blank. Of course he'd want to thank her. Dolly had spent considerable time at his home, helping him with who knew what. The knowledge bothered her so much more than she wanted to admit.

"Well, that's nice of you. I hope she likes it." Suzanne untied her apron and tossed it next to the sink. "I need to grab a few items for supper. I'll be right back." She stepped through the back door, letting the wind push it closed.

Lena stood, taking her empty cup to the sink. "It was good to see you again, Sheriff. I hope Dolly likes the pie." She walked past him and toward the front door.

"Lena?"

"Yes?"

He closed the distance between them, stopping a few inches away. "I enjoyed the other night. If you'll allow me, I'd like to take you to supper. Soon."

Her eyes widened, surprised he'd asked. She needed to decline, not encourage him or allow her own feelings to blossom any further.

"It's not a good idea, Gabe. You already thanked me for helping you. There's no need for more."

"This would have nothing to do with thanking you." He gripped the pie in both hands, thinking of placing it on the table, then thought better of it. If he did, it would be too easy to reach out and touch her. "You're a beautiful, smart woman who I want to get to know better. Unless you have no interest..." His voice faded away as his eyes searched hers. He knew their kisses affected her as much as they did him. She'd gripped him tight, responding to his touch in a way no other woman ever had. Gabe needed to know if there could be more.

"It's not that."

"Then what is it? Is it because I'm a lawman, I fought for the North, what?"

She let out a long, audible breath, flinching from his unwavering gaze. "It's none of those. It's just..."

"I can't believe how much the wind has picked up." Suzanne let the door slam behind her, dropping the vegetables she'd gathered into the sink.

Gabe's attention had swung to Suzanne when she entered. When he turned back, Lena was gone.

"You didn't need to do this, Gabe." Dolly's face split into a wide smile as she accepted the pie.

"I should have gotten it for you sooner." He glanced around, noting one other customer sitting alone at a table in the corner, paying no attention to them.

She stretched up on her toes to place a kiss on his cheek. "You know, there's another way you can thank me," she whispered before taking a step back.

Gabe didn't want to think about Dolly's offer and had no intention of taking her up on it. "You know my feelings on that. It's why I traveled to Big Pine." He chuckled as she stuck out her lower lip in a pout. "You'll have plenty of customers."

"I hope we can at least stay friends."

"There's no reason we can't." He'd liked Dolly from the first night he'd seen her standing at the most prominent bar in the territorial capital. Different than the other women, her relaxed manner and more natural appearance attracted others to her. She made it easy for him to talk, not pushing and asking few questions. A few nights with her and he'd return to Splendor with an improved outlook, ready to resume his role as sheriff. "How about a drink?"

"Sounds good." She grabbed a couple glasses and a bottle of whiskey from Al, joining Gabe at a table near the new piano Amos had shipped to town.

"Is the piano drawing a bigger crowd?" He sipped his drink, glancing up when another man entered and walked to the bar.

"It would if we had someone who could play it as well as the fellow at the Dixie. I heard Nick and Lena brought him in special from Denver." She shifted in her seat, resting an arm over the back of her chair. "Nick came over and talked to me about leaving here and working for them."

Gabe's brows shot up at the news. He thought Nick had all the women he needed. "What did you tell him?"

"I told him it would be unfair to Amos if I left so soon. He paid my stage fare, so I owe him." She glanced over her shoulder, not wanting anyone to hear, and lowered her voice. "I may change my mind in a few months, but I'd still want to pay him back. Now, tell me about you and Lena Campanel."

The request surprised him. No one knew about his feelings for her, not even Noah—or he had never *acted* as if he knew. "I don't know what you mean." He tried to keep his voice even.

"No? A few nights ago, when business slowed down, I stepped outside to get some fresh air. The Dixie seemed full and the piano music blared outside, but the street had little activity. Except for one couple who came out of the boardinghouse. They walked up the street, then slipped into the darkness several feet before the saloon. I don't think they considered the full moon." She glanced at Gabe, raising her eyebrow. "Should I continue?"

"No need." He leaned his arms on the table and stared into his glass. "No one knows. I want to keep it that way."

"I hope you know me better than that."

Gabe winced at the twinge of disappointment that crossed her face. He let out a breath and sat back. "You're right. I do." He narrowed his gaze at her. "What you saw is all there is, Dolly. Nothing more."

"Although you'd like there to be."

His jaw worked, but he remained silent. Any feelings he held for Lena were private and not open to public debate.

Both turned at the sound of the doors opening.

"I thought I might find you here, Gabe." Cash walked up, grabbed a chair and spun it around, taking a seat and resting his arms on the back. "Hello, Dolly."

"Cash. Well, I believe I'll excuse myself. It's time for me to freshen up. I expect it will be busy tonight."

They watched her sashay away and climb the stairs. "You planning on picking up where you left off in Big Pine?"

"Nope. You interested?"

"Not me. I'm partial to one of the girls at the Dixie." Cash signaled Al for a glass of whiskey.

Gabe raised his eyebrows at the comment.

"I don't have the same problems with bedding a working woman in Splendor that you do." He shrugged, swallowing some of his whiskey. "That's not why I came looking for you. Do you remember those four miners who came to town complaining about Carlyle's men trying to jump their claim?"

"I do."

"Appears he went after a claim owned by two other miners. One of them rode in a few hours ago. Seems Carlyle and his partner may have hired a gunslinger to try to negotiate sales of gold claims. If the miners refuse, he threatens them into signing their rights over. The gunman shot and killed this man's partner. The remaining partner signed his rights away rather than suffer the same fate."

"He get a good look at him?" Gabe asked.

"Good enough, but he refuses to stay around and help us find him. He came here to let us know it's happening."

"How can he be certain Carlyle and Pennington hired the man?" Gabe crossed his arms. He'd been concerned about this exact situation since the day at the land office when gunmen tried to intimidate several miners into walking away from their claim.

"He can't, but who else could it be, Gabe?"

"You're right. Let's go talk to this fella again." Gabe started to push his chair back.

"Can't. He's already gone."

Gabe cursed at losing the one connection they had tying claim jumping, and now murder, to Carlyle.

"Beau said you two might be in here." Bernie Griggs stopped next to them, holding out a telegram. "This came for you." He handed it to Gabe and waited.

Gabe read the short message twice, a grin touching the corners of his mouth. "I want to send a reply." He took the stub of a pencil Bernie handed him and scribbled a note on the back. "Here you are. Thanks, Bernie."

"Good news, I hope," Cash said as Bernie headed back to the telegraph office.

"You remember I mentioned my uncle passing?" Cash nodded. "The message had to do with his estate. I may not have to travel back to New York as I first thought." Standing, he tossed money on the table. "I'm heading to the Dixie to speak with Nick, then I'll meet you and Beau at the jail. It may be time for us to pay Carlyle and Pennington a visit."

Chapter Nine

"He's riding in now." Thomas Pennington pushed open the door of the shack they used for their office and stepped outside. "We expected you days ago." He rested his hands on his hips, glaring at Stillwell.

"I had some trouble. Nothing for you or Carlyle to worry about. The matter is settled." Stillwell slid from his horse, slapping his hat on a post to dislodge the trail dust, then followed Pennington inside. Carlyle stood, pushing aside the papers he'd been studying.

"You've got two new claims if you want them." Stillwell tossed two signed documents on the table, then stalked to the potbelly stove, filling a cup with coffee. "One doesn't appear to be worth your time to file. The other one has promise," he sneered, grimacing at the taste of the rank liquid.

"Tell us about each one." Carlyle leaned a hip against the table, crossing his arms.

"First one is about eight miles south. One miner. I gave him the price you offered and he agreed to sell the claim. The second one is closer to your camp. Took me a few days to spot the two miners who are working it. Neither had an interest in selling."

"What changed their minds?" Pennington asked.

"One of them came down with a powerful ache in his gut." Stillwell chuckled at his little joke. "The other one decided he didn't want to continue on his own."

"Might as well take them both. No telling what our men could find on the claims." Pennington lowered himself into a chair. He didn't like the methods men such as Stillwell used to get their way, and Carlyle wasn't any better when he wanted something.

"I'll ride to Splendor with a few men in the morning. What about the four miners north of here?" Carlyle asked Stillwell.

"I'll find them tomorrow. There'll be a resolution by sunset." Stillwell walked to the door, tossing out the remainder of his coffee. "I'm going to find some grub, then sleep. I'll be gone by the time you get up in the morning."

Pennington waited until he left before turning toward Carlyle. "We can't have him killing off all the miners who won't sell. I say we send him on his way and deal with the others ourselves."

Willie waved him off. "He's the quickest way to get what we want, and he's good at covering his tracks. The sheriff and deputies in Splendor won't be able to tie us to him."

"Perhaps, but are you willing to take the risk? How many of the claims are worth killing over?"

"Don't know. The one north is the biggest besides ours—"

"And the sheriff already knows we want it. He'll be expecting us to force their hand." Pennington stood and paced the cramped space. "If you're determined to use Stillwell, I say we wait, file these two claims, and let the dust settle before we send him north."

"Do you believe a few weeks will make any difference? I say we let him go, get this over with, and concentrate on working the claims." Even though still early in the day, Carlyle grabbed a bottle of whiskey out of a wooden crate and poured some into a cup, handed it to Pennington, then poured another for himself. "Those four miners have a claim that should've been ours. I see it as taking back what belongs to us."

Tommy had heard this argument several times. Before he arrived, Willie worked the Devil Dancer claim with a group of men who'd followed him to Montana. Four of them split off within a few weeks, headed north several miles, and found gold. In Willie's mind, what they found should've been his. Pennington disagreed, but he'd had no success changing his partner's mind.

Although he'd never spoken of it, Tommy noticed the way Willie had changed over the years, becoming obsessed with power, and at times, certain women. His actions had become more extreme with each passing year, turning to violence to solve disputes.

Letting out a sigh, Tommy swallowed the whiskey, knowing there'd be no reasoning with Willie. "You just better make certain there's no way of tracing his work back to us."

"Our men won't talk. Besides, they don't know why he's in camp. The man is like a ghost, which is safest for everyone." Willie tipped his cup toward Tommy, then finished off the contents. Picking up the documents Stillwell had left on the table, he held them in the air. "Within a week, we'll have a third claim to add to these. After that, we'll send Stillwell on his way."

Gabe saw no one in the Dixie, except Paul cleaning glasses behind the bar. He looked up from his work long enough to nod.

"Is Nick around?"

"In his office."

Gabe walked to the end of the bar and into a small alcove, then knocked before opening the door. "You got a minute?" he asked, noticing Nick pull off a pair of spectacles before lowering the patch he wore over his left eye.

"Have a seat." Nick gestured to a chair.

"Word has it you and the Pelletiers struck a deal to buy some of their land."

Nick didn't answer as he leaned forward, grabbing a bottle and two glasses from a tray at the corner of his desk. He filled one glass, glancing at Gabe, who shook his head.

"News travels fast." He took a sip of his drink, then sat back. "I decided the time had come to plant more permanent roots." Nick spent a few minutes describing the land and his desire to build a house, purchase a few horses. "It's time to enjoy some of the money I've made."

"Do your plans include sharing your new home with anyone?" Gabe had noticed the way Nick looked at Suzanne and wondered how deep his feelings went for her.

He stared at Gabe, although his face remained impassive. "Perhaps." Finishing his drink, he set the glass aside. "I'm guessing my land purchase isn't what brought you in here this early, though."

"It's time we talked about the hotel you want to build." Gabe set his hat on the desk.

Nick's eyes showed his surprise for a moment. He'd heard the rumors that Gabe had taken the sheriff's job on a temporary basis until the town could find someone permanent. A year later, he still wore the badge.

"Sounds as if you've decided to stay around a while."

Gabe hadn't thought of it in those terms. He'd taken his future a day at a time, trying to live each day the best he could without looking too far ahead.

"Guess I have."

Nick turned his back to Gabe, opening a file cabinet behind his desk and pulling out several papers. He slid them across the desk.

"Drawings for the hotel I plan to build in the open lot next to the newspaper office. I already own the land." He noticed Gabe's brows lift. "Horace Clausen told me about it a few months ago. I bought it, even though the timing wasn't right for a hotel then. It is now."

Gabe studied the detailed drawings. The design had been patterned after the grand plantations of the South. Three stories with a wraparound veranda, the details would require craftsmanship few were capable of providing. He read the notes, which included the number of rooms, Splendor's first upscale restaurant, and many of the amenities common in East Coast hotels.

"If we start now, it will be ready to open when the snow melts in the spring."

"Fifty-fifty." Gabe's face was unreadable, although his words weren't.

"Lena will be a partner."

"Then you split your fifty with her. It's the only way I'll do it." Gabe wouldn't budge on this.

Nick had been an equal partner in his businesses, most with Lena and some with others. He trusted each partner with his life. If he couldn't, he'd walk.

"It will be a substantial investment."

"I know."

Nick studied him another minute. Satisfied with what he saw, he walked around his desk, extending his hand. "Glad to have you, Gabe."

"No. I will absolutely *not* be a partner with Gabe in a hotel. Not now or ever." Lena's normally serene face lit with anger at the news of Nick agreeing to allow Gabe into their business. "What can he add that we don't already have?"

"Investment money and a background in the hotel business." His voice remained calm. Nick let her irritation at his decision continue until she ran out of words. "What is it about Gabe you don't like?"

"It's not that I don't like him." *Far from it,* she thought. "I just don't see the need to add another person. Haven't we done fine on our own?"

"We can do better. We need an additional investor and someone with expertise in areas where we're weak. Gabe offers both."

Lena lowered herself into a settee in the parlor of the boardinghouse. When she'd left after breakfast and Gabe's invitation to supper, she'd spent time in the general store and millinery, then returned to her room. Glad she didn't need to be at the saloon for another hour, she'd laid down. It seemed as if mere seconds passed before a pounding on the door woke her. Nick stood in the hall, anxious to tell her his news. She felt petty, unable to show the excitement he expected.

"If you believe it's the right decision for us, I'll go along with it. I hope we're not sorry, though." Tying a bonnet on her head, she picked up her reticule. "I'd better get to the saloon before some altercation breaks out amongst the girls."

The group of women they employed were good at what they did. They also had a particular talent for frustrating each other, especially when it involved being favored by a particular customer who'd taken more than one to bed. It amazed Lena how women with little regard for marriage could become so possessive with one of their customers, as if they owned the exclusive right to him.

Nick opened the door, stepping aside for her to pass. "I'll be over in a bit. I'm going to see if Suzanne has any dinner left."

He watched as she strolled up the boardwalk to the saloon, wondering about her strong aversion to having Gabe as a partner. On numerous occasions, she'd expressed her admiration of the sheriff, how well he did his job, and the level of trust the townsfolk bestowed on him. Then he thought of Gabe and their conversation several nights before at the Dixie when he'd asked several probing questions about her. Nick had responded with a warning to treat her with care if he decided to go after her. Perhaps he'd already made his move. By Lena's reaction to having him as a partner, he figured it was a damn good possibility.

Heading into the kitchen, he peeked into covered pots still sitting on the stove. Reaching for a bowl, he ladled in a generous amount of stew, then cut a large square of cornbread. He'd just sat down when Suzanne bustled through the back door, her arms laden with vegetables. She didn't notice him as she set the food into the sink.

"The last of the garden," she mumbled to herself.

"What did you say?"

Gasping, a hand flew to her throat as she spun around. "My gracious, Nick. I didn't see you." The smile she sent him spoke of the humor in the situation. Spotting the bowl, she moved forward, seeing it already full of stew. "I would've been happy to warm it up for you."

"It's delicious as it is." As if to prove it, he scooped up another large spoonful. "Best you've ever made." He finished the last bite of cornbread, then pushed the plate away. "I'll be bringing Fanny to town in a couple days."

"I know and I couldn't be more thrilled. Although I *am* concerned about where she'll live. I thought the gentleman in the upstairs front corner room would be leaving, but he informed me last night he's staying at least through the end of the month."

"She's staying in the house near Gabe's place behind the jail."

"She is?" Suzanne's voice rose in excitement. "I didn't know there was an empty place in town."

"There wasn't until a week ago. Abby Brandt owns quite a bit of property around town and decided we needed more places for new people to live. Noah hired a few men and they've already built two places, with three more halfway completed. They aren't fancy, but have all that's needed."

Suzanne's eyes locked on his, although she said nothing.

"What?" He stood, walking over to her.

A look passed over her face he couldn't quite decipher. He took her hands in his, rubbing his thumbs over them.

"I've lived in Splendor for over fifteen years. You've been here less than two and know more about what is happening." She glanced up at him. "It seems I'm missing so much."

His gaze softened. "Fanny coming to work for you will give you time to get out, enjoy the town and your friends. All you need to do is take advantage of it."

"Thanks, Nick."

"For what?"

"I never would've had the courage to make the changes if you hadn't encouraged me."

"All you needed was a little nudge, nothing more. In your head, you already knew what needed to be done." He released her hands, tapping a finger to her forehead. "You're a smart woman, Suzanne. You're going to be quite successful—more than you already are." An unexpected sensation had ripped through him at her closeness and the feel of her hands in his. He knew he needed to leave, give them both some space. "I'd better return to the saloon." On impulse, he bent down and placed a kiss on her cheek, then stepped away.

"I'll save some supper for you, Nick."

Nodding, he settled his hat on his head and left.

Gabe stared at another game of solitaire, his eyes beginning to cross. He didn't know how many rounds he'd played in the last two hours. Fifteen, twenty, maybe more. If he thought she'd accept, he'd make the short walk to the Dixie and invite Lena to supper.

She must know by now about the partnership he and Nick agreed on. He sure would've liked to have been in the room when she learned about it. His gut told him she wouldn't have accepted it with ease.

His stomach growled. A few months before, he would've stopped by the livery, convinced Noah to join him for supper, then they would have walked to the Dixie or Rose for cards and drinks. Now, his friend spent almost every night with his bride. Gabe didn't blame him. Abby couldn't have been more perfect for him.

With Cash and Beau making the rounds, he had the freedom to head to the boardinghouse for supper. Fall decided to descend on Splendor, with temperatures dropping into the forties in the evenings. Grabbing his coat, he slipped it on, adjusting his hat, then closed the door behind him.

Hearing the piano music from the Dixie, he felt drawn toward it, but tried to resist the urge to find Lena. Taking a few steps, he stopped in the middle of the street.

"Ah hell," he groaned and changed directions, heading straight for the Dixie.

She stood alone at one end of the bar, staring at an untouched glass of whiskey, her fingers drumming away in a pitter-patter only she could hear. So absorbed in what occupied her mind, she didn't see Gabe walk up, order a drink, or set it down next to hers. Fascinated, he leaned one arm on the bar and watched her.

A noise, a change in light, a movement across the room—Gabe didn't know which—caused Lena to stir, then look up, gasping at how close he stood, as well as his amused gaze.

"Good evening, Lena. Everything all right?"

"Well, yes...of course. Why wouldn't it be?" Picking up her drink, she took a swallow, letting out a sigh as the amber liquid warmed her throat.

Another letter had arrived from Isabella. She'd recovered from her illness, only to watch as her husband, Arnott, fell victim to the same ailment. Twenty-five years her senior, he'd suffered from respiratory problems since childhood, and the doctor's concern seemed extreme, frightening her. At her husband's direction, the doctor told her little about his condition, which fueled her anxiety to a fever pitch. She wanted to seek the advice of another doctor, one who would discuss his condition with her, but her husband refused—a tactic he almost never used with Isabella. She'd decided to wait, forcing herself to believe he'd pull through and all would be back to normal soon.

At least Jackson had emerged unscathed. She'd sent him to her husband's sister, who lived a few blocks away. Once Arnott recovered, he'd return home. Then they'd plan a visit west. Even though it would be months off, the excitement Lena felt at their visit consumed her.

Gabe continued to watch as she fingered the rim of her glass, her face softening as a thought passed through her mind. He wondered what consumed her and if she'd share it with him.

"Have you had supper?"

She glanced up, her brows drawing together. "Um...no. I must have forgotten."

"Good. Then let me escort you to Suzanne's."

"I don't believe—"

He touched a finger to her lips, silencing her. "I won't keep you long. We'll eat, then I'll bring you back." Letting his hand drop, he searched her eyes, hoping to see agreement. "I want to spend some time with you, Lena."

Her lips parted a fraction. "You do?"

"Of course. I believe it would be good to get to know each other better. After all, we're going to be business partners. I assume Nick mentioned our agreement."

Even though foolish, those weren't the words she wanted to hear. She should've been glad his intentions had to do with solidifying a relationship which had the potential to make them thousands. Instead, she couldn't help the stab of disappointment racing through her at knowing his purpose wasn't more personal.

"Yes. Nick told me of the partnership."

"Then you'll join me for supper?"

Picking up her glass, she finished the contents, and set it on the bar with more force than intended. "Why not?"

Walking over to Nick, who sat at a table with Bull, Travis, and a few other Pelletier men, she whispered in his ear. He shot a look at Gabe, his eyes narrowing into a warning he assumed the lawman understood. The gesture had been lost on Lena, who accepted Gabe's arm as they left the saloon.

Neither spoke as they walked down the street and entered Suzanne's, taking one of the many open tables before ordering the nightly special. Gabe watched her fidget with her skirt, then the napkin, and wondered what troubled her.

"Are you certain you're all right?" he asked as her gaze met his.

"Do you remember the friend I mentioned who lives in Philadelphia?"

"Isabella? I believe you said she'd been ill."

"Yes. Now her husband is sick and no one will speak with her about it. The doctor refuses to give her any information, and her husband has rejected the idea of getting another opinion. She sent Jackson to his aunt's until Isabella's husband recovers, but the tone of her letter told me she's worried he won't make it." Her gaze slipped to the table and her clasped hands, then back up. "She's so devoted to him. I don't know what she'll do if he doesn't improve."

Her blue eyes were full of anguish. Without thought, he reached across the table, taking her hands in his.

"Have you thought of going back to be with her?"

"I sent a telegram yesterday, suggesting a visit." She stared at their joined hands, loving the feel of his callused skin and the way his touch always caused her blood to heat and heart to pound. As disturbing as it all was, she didn't want to let go, lose the connection with him.

"It's possible I may have to travel to New York. If so, I'd be honored to accompany you to Philadelphia." He'd done all he could to avoid a trip back east. Now, if Lena traveled with him, he found himself eager to make the trip.

She continued, as if she hadn't heard his offer. "Isabella mentioned coming out here with Jackson once her husband improves. It's doubtful he'll join them. He's always so busy with his many business interests." She squeezed his hands before slipping hers away and clasping them in her lap, immediately missing his touch.

"Then it appears there's nothing more you can do except wait to hear from her. Perhaps the next message will be good news."

They remained silent through most of supper, making casual talk about the increase in miners coming to town and the influx of farming families still escaping the effects of the war. Neither had any appetite for dessert, so after laying money on the table and thanking Suzanne, he looped her arm through his.

"We still didn't speak of the hotel or our partnership," Gabe said, drawing closer to the saloon. "I suppose that means we'll need to find another time to have supper." The smile on his face sent her pulse racing. She knew she should decline.

"I'd like that, Gabe."

The urge to pull her to him, kiss her until they were both wild with need consumed him. Knowing it would be the worst move he could make, he ignored the warning, leaning down to brush his lips with hers.

"Goodnight, Lena."

She couldn't deny herself one more kiss. Tilting her head up, she braced herself on his arms, and touched her lips to his before giving him a warm smile. "Goodnight, Gabe." She turned and walked through the swinging doors of the Dixie.

Chapter Ten

"It's done." Stillwell tossed the document onto the desk, crossing his arms. He'd ridden in early, hoping to get paid and ride back out well before mid-morning.

Carlyle picked up the paper, a feral smile crossing his face when he saw what the gunman had given him. "What happened?"

"All four partners were at the site when I rode in and offered them the price you set. They huddled for a while, then the oldest came back with a higher figure. You'd given me enough cash, so I agreed. They signed and that was it." He sounded disappointed it had gone so well.

Pennington walked inside, brushing the dust from his clothes, and stomping mud-encrusted boots on the floor. Carlyle handed him the paper, explaining what had happened.

"Too easy," Pennington commented. "Makes me wonder if the claim has played out."

"They were working it when I rode up."

"It's done now. When will they be off the land?" Carlyle asked, glad to have the three claims in their possession.

"I'd expect them to be gone within days. There's nothing to hold them there."

Carlyle placed a strongbox on the table, opened it, and took out the two claims Stillwell had secured days before. "It's time to file all three of them. You want to ride in with me, Tommy?"

"I'm ready to leave when you are."

"My work here is done. I'll be riding out—unless there's more you want me to handle." Stillwell filled his glass again, tossing it all back.

Carlyle pulled a stack of bills from the strongbox. "What we agreed to for the work you've already done." He handed it to Stillwell. "However, I want you to stay around for a few days. We may have another job for you."

Stillwell scratched his stubbled chin. "All right, but I expect pay for days I sit around."

"Fair enough. We'll know more once we return from Splendor."

"I'll be camped in the usual place. Come and get me when you're ready." Without another word, he pocketed the money and left.

Strolling to the window, Carlyle watched as Stillwell mounted his horse and rode from their camp, then he turned toward Tommy. "That went better than expected."

"Except we may have three worthless claims."

"Doubt it. Those miners don't have the equipment or men we do to work the claims. We'll send some people to the large one in a few days, see what they find." Willie thought of what he wanted to get done in Splendor.

"Let's get going. I'm hungry for cooking that isn't my own, maybe stay in town long enough to take the pretty young woman at the Rose up on her offer. It's been a long time." Tommy's face brightened at the thought of spending time with a warm and willing woman.

Willie had other ideas. First, he'd finish business, then take another look around town. Lena couldn't hide from him forever. He'd find her, apologize for the way he'd left New Orleans, then use his considerable charms to get back in her good graces. From there, he believed it wouldn't take much to get back in her bed, making her more amenable to the demands he planned to make.

"It shouldn't take long to load her belongings and return." Nick climbed onto the seat of the wagon. "By sundown, you'll have a new cook and a small measure of freedom."

Suzanne stood by the wagon, still not quite appreciating how her life would change with Fanny's arrival. She'd be paying a portion of the rent for the house and wages she still didn't know if she could afford. But her faith in Nick outweighed her concerns.

"If the place wasn't so full…"

"I have time to do this. We'll be back in no time." He smiled, slapping the reins to get the wagon moving.

She stood with her arms crossed until the dust disappeared. Nick had been joking, but she *would* miss him. He'd been an unexpected blessing in her life.

"Has he left?"

Suzanne turned to see Lena standing behind her, a hand shading her face from the morning sun.

"Yes. I doubt it will take long before he's back. How about some breakfast?"

"I already helped myself to coffee and some of the spice cake on the counter. I didn't think you'd mind."

"Not at all, Lena. I make it to be eaten." Suzanne followed her back inside, then got to work with the morning cleaning, both unaware of the men who sat astride their horses not fifty yards away.

"Is that her?" Tommy asked, leaning forward in the saddle.

"Yes, that's Magdalena Campanel." His voice thickened as he watched her disappear inside.

She'd been beautiful when they'd been together, but now, almost seven years later, she was stunning—one of the most magnificent women he'd ever seen. And he'd walked away from her. If he were being honest, he knew nothing would change if he had it to do over again. Money and a good time were all he wanted back then, and he'd gotten both with Lena, although he doubted she'd think the same. His mother once told him he'd been born flawed, entered the world without a shred of remorse for his actions, no sense of right or wrong. At the time, he didn't believe her. Now he did, accepting the man he'd become.

"Now what?" Tommy asked, nudging his horse into a slow walk.

"I do believe I'm in need of breakfast and a cup of coffee. You?"

"Sounds fine to me."

Walking inside, Willie spotted Lena at a table near the back, reading what appeared to be a dime novel while sipping coffee. She didn't look up at their approach.

"Excuse me. Are these seats taken?"

Lena's stomach knotted at the familiar voice, the sound grating on her senses, encouraging her to jump from her seat and flee. She wondered if ignoring him would have any impact. The scraping of chair legs across the floor gave her the answer.

Lowering the book, she pinned him with an unwelcoming stare. "You aren't welcome at this table, Willie. I suggest you find a place where you may converse with people of your...persuasion."

"And what persuasion would that be, my dear?" His smooth, accented voice sent chills through her, and she fought the urge to pick up her coffee and fling it in his face.

"The reptile kind. Those who slither, then hide in their holes when they can't face real life." She slipped her book in a pocket, then stood. "I'll make sure Suzanne knows she has customers." Hemmed in on one side by the wall and the other by Willie, she turned sideways, trying to push past him.

"There's no need for you to leave so soon." He reached out a hand, grasping her arm, and hauling her toward him. "We have so much to catch up on." Stale breath, smelling of smoke and old whiskey, washed over her, causing her stomach to churn.

"Sorry you had to start without me, Lena. I was held up at the jail." Except to those who knew him, Cash's deep, southern drawl might sound congenial. However, his temper had flared the moment he stepped inside to see Lena in obvious distress. A thin, mental barrier now stood between his temper and the need to thrash the two men who stood over her. His gaze bored into the man holding Lena, daring him to make a move.

"Cash, darling. I'd begun to think you weren't coming."

Willie's hand fell from her arm at the sight of the badge. He had no desire to tackle the law, especially someone this threatening.

Lena stepped around Willie toward Cash, moving behind him.

"Why don't you find Suzanne, see if she needs some help?" Cash took a step toward Willie.

She nodded, knowing he wanted her out of the way while he spoke to them.

"I don't believe we've met. I'm Cash Coulter, one of the deputies in Splendor." His gaze never faltered, nor did he extend his hand.

"William Randolph Carlyle. And this is my partner, Thomas Pennington. We're the owners of the Devil Dancer mine west of here."

"I've heard of it, and you." Cash looked over his shoulder to make certain Lena had disappeared in the back. "It might be wise if both of you kept away from Miss Campanel. I believe she's made her desires clear."

"On the contrary. Lena and I are old friends from New Orleans." Willie smirked as he crossed his arms.

Cash couldn't help but wonder at the mental capacity of the man. "You may have been friends in the past, but from what I can see, she wants nothing to do with you now. Of course, I could go ask her. That way there will be no mistake."

Willie dropped his arms as his bluster faltered. "No need, Deputy. I'm certain it's a misunderstanding, one that may be resolved once she agrees to speak with me."

"I wouldn't count on it, Carlyle. From what I've seen, she's a pretty good judge of character, and the way she looked at you, she's found you lacking. My suggestion is you two find another place to take your meals when you come to town." Cash stepped aside, a clear indication the conversation had ended.

Willie and Tommy edged past him, not glancing back as they left the restaurant.

"Cash, are they gone?" Lena's voice shook as she moved into the parlor to peek out the front windows, seeing Willie ride in the direction of the bank.

He stepped up behind her, seeing her shake. "I gave them a reason to leave and not return. Do you want to tell me about them?"

Sitting on a settee in front of the window, she took a deep breath. "I don't know the one man, but Willie and I met long ago. He left New Orleans abruptly, taking most of my jewelry and a good portion of Nick's and my money with him. We could never prove the thefts were his doing, so the law didn't go after him. I'd hoped to never see the man again."

"Seems he wants to have a chance to talk, explain himself."

A mirthless laugh escaped her lips. "The man is a viper, Cash. He has no concept of good and bad. I've been told evil men are incapable of seeing the foul stench within themselves. Willie Carlyle is one of those men." She stood, grabbed her coat from a nearby hook, and started outside.

"Hold on. I'll walk you to the Dixie." Cash moved beside her, keeping her on the inside of the boardwalk during the short walk to the saloon. "You know, Gabe will need to know about today, as will Beau."

"Yes, I know. I'll tell Nick what happened, too." She looked over her shoulder as she pushed open the door of the saloon. "Be wary of him, Cash. The man isn't to be trusted."

"Any trouble while I was gone?" Gabe tossed his hat on the desk and hung up his coat. He'd left early, not disclosing his destination to either Cash or Beau. Until they took on the badges to help bring down a group of rustlers who plagued the area, he'd been the sole lawman for months. Both had stayed on, but Gabe still hadn't learned to share much about his whereabouts with either of them.

"The owners of the Devil Dancer mine rode in this morning."

"That so. Did you meet them?"

"In a roundabout way." Cash continued to study the wanted posters before him. He would've bet he'd seen one with Carlyle's image not long after he put on the badge. "William Randolph Carlyle and his partner, Thomas Pennington. I walked into

Suzanne's as Carlyle tried to *persuade* Lena to speak with him."

Gabe's head snapped toward Cash as his eyes flared. "And?" he ground out, hands fisting.

"I let them know Lena didn't want their company and they weren't welcome in the boardinghouse. When Carlyle objected..."

Cash didn't get any further as Gabe snatched his hat from the desk and grabbed his coat, slamming the door on his way out.

"That didn't take long," Beau chuckled as he reached out his hand. Cash dug in his pocket, pulling out a coin and handing it to his friend.

"Hell, I thought he'd at least wait until I finished explaining." Cash resumed his position over the desk, scanning the posters, promising himself to stop making wagers with Beau. He always lost.

Gabe wasted no time finding Lena. She sat alone at a table in the corner of the Dixie, a cup of coffee in front of her, a glass next to it. He took slow steps, not wanting to alarm her.

"A little early for whiskey, isn't it?" He nodded toward the glass as he took a seat next to her.

"It's brandy, and yes, it is a little early." Her hand trembled as she picked up the coffee and brought it to her lips.

"Cash told me you had a visitor."

A shaky breath escaped her as she set the cup back on the table. "A man I knew many years ago paid me a visit."

"William Carlyle."

Her gaze shot to his. "How did you know?"

"Cash mentioned it. Nick also told me Carlyle might ride into town looking for you. He told me what happened in New Orleans."

Shock and something else Gabe couldn't decipher crossed her face, then disappeared. "You mean the way he robbed us?"

"Was there more?"

"No...nothing else."

His instincts told him there was, but he wouldn't push...at least not yet. "What did he want?"

"I don't know. As soon as he approached the table, I tried to leave. That's when Cash walked in."

"Does Nick know?"

"He left this morning for Luke Pelletier's place to bring Fanny back. She's going to be the new cook for Suzanne." Lena's tormented gaze lifted to meet his. "He'll be furious and might go after him. I don't want that to happen."

"Then I'll tell him. I might be better able to impress upon him the need to come to me, Cash, or Beau if Carlyle causes trouble." He leaned forward, resting his arms on the table. "Are you certain there's nothing else about him you want to tell me?"

Lena knew Gabe wanted to help, protect her from the man, yet there wasn't any more she could share that would aid him. Her own personal hatred of Carlyle, the way he'd used her and then walked out, would remain her secret. Besides, it had nothing to do with what happened in Splendor.

"There's nothing more, Gabe."

"Well, then, come on. I'm taking you out of town for a while." He stood, reaching out his hand.

She thought of refusing, staying safe within the walls of the Dixie. Then she looked into Gabe's face. He wanted to be there for her and she was going to let him. Lacing her fingers through his, she let him lead her outside.

"You'll need a warm coat, and I want Suzanne to pack us a lunch." He pulled her hand through his arm. "There's a place I want to show you a few miles from town. I doubt you've ever been anywhere near it. It's at the south end of the Pelletier ranch and has the most beautiful view you've ever seen."

His deep voice comforted her as they walked, and she found herself beginning to relax.

"What if I like it so much I won't want to leave?"

His low chuckle warmed her blood. "Then I guess we'll just have to figure out some way to make it happen."

Chapter Eleven

"Forget about her, Willie. There are plenty of women who won't fight you and aren't protected by some overzealous lawman." Pennington stood with Carlyle at the bar of the Rose. His partner hadn't budged from this spot in over an hour, nursing a third drink after tossing back two in succession. Tommy didn't like the angry gleam in Willie's eyes as he shot back the whiskey in his glass.

"I don't care how many people guard her. She's who I want." His voice came out in a growl as he filled his glass again.

"Only because she doesn't want you. Once you've had her, you'll do what you do with all the women you've taken. Why bother when you've already been in her bed?"

Willie turned toward him, a look Tommy had never seen in his eyes before, ominous in its intensity. "She will be with *me* or no one. She's mine, always has been. I'll not let another man have her." The absolute certainty in his voice had Tommy taking a step away.

Tommy set down his empty glass. He'd been watching a card game at a nearby table with an empty seat. "We'll continue this conversation when you're sober. It's Saturday afternoon and I'm going to enjoy myself."

Willie looked up from his numbed state. A part of him knew Tommy was right. He wanted Lena even more because she'd spurned him, but a part of him wanted to discover if she might be the cure that would heal him—turn him from a man without a conscience to one who could learn to love and offer compassion. He knew he couldn't squelch this obsessive feeling until he'd had her again.

Whether he found salvation in her arms wasn't the main reason for wanting her. She held property and status as a businesswoman, even if it was tied to the saloon. Marrying her would help him gain the power he craved.

"Bartender." Willie's hard command had all heads turning in his direction, including Tommy's. "More whiskey. A bottle this time."

Tommy looked around the bar, spotting one of the girls standing near the staircase, her eyes fixed on Willie. Laying down his cards, he walked toward her, leaned down, and whispered in her ear, then pulled some bills from his pocket.

It took a couple more glasses of whiskey and a little coaxing from the woman, but Willie finally followed her up the stairs. By the looks of him, and even though the sun hadn't begun to set, Tommy figured it would be well into tomorrow before he showed his face back downstairs.

"This is so beautiful. And it took such a short time to get here."

Gabe had helped Lena down from Joker, the horse Noah had loaned him, watching as she turned in circles, looking in all directions. He'd been coming to this bit of unspoiled land for months, discovering something new each time. He figured his feelings for the place would never change. It was the only spot he could envisage himself growing old.

"How did you ever find this place?"

"In a way, it found me." He walked both horses toward a large pine, not releasing the reins. "Last winter left the ground soaked for months. One Sunday, I'd had enough of slogging around in town and saddled Blackheart, riding northwest without a destination in mind. I don't know why, but the trail called to me. It felt as if a magnetic pull dragged me up this hill, even though I had to ride through thick brush at times. Then I heard it."

"What?"

"Rushing water. I followed the noise and it led me here, to this exact spot."

Lena looked around again, listening. "I don't hear any water."

"Come here." He took her hand, leading the horses and her along another path, ending near several large boulders. Dropping the reins, he pulled her to him, wrapped an arm around her waist, and skirted the rocks, pointing down.

"Oh, my gracious. A waterfall!" She turned her face toward him, her bright eyes glowing with excitement.

"It's much larger and louder in the spring when all the snow is melting. It's beautiful, no matter the time of year."

"Gabe, it's spectacular. I've never seen any other place to compare." She turned toward him, and without thinking, wrapped her arms around his waist, looking up into his eyes. "Do you know who owns it?"

The sight of her glowing face and full lips inches from his severed any remaining control he possessed. Ignoring her question, he lowered his head, giving her a chance to pull away before capturing her mouth in a scorching kiss. Drawing her into his chest, he deepened the contact, moaning when her lips parted for him.

Heat seared through his body with an intensity he'd never experienced before, causing him to tighten his hold. Pulling back, he stared into her eyes, seeing something hot and dark that set his skin on fire. He bent his head, covering her mouth once more.

Blood thundered in her ears as she became heedless of everything around her, except the feel of his body pressed against hers. His lips consumed hers as he let them glide along her chin to the delicate skin of her neck, all the while his hands leaving trails of fire along her back. It felt as if he were everywhere, yet she still didn't feel close enough.

Wrapping her arms around his neck, she drew him down as his mouth moved to the hollow of her neck, then lower still. She moaned as his hands slipped to her hips, holding her tight against him.

"Lena?" It was a request, a plea, his voice raspy and strained.

She dropped her arms and looked into his eyes, glazed and darkened with passion. Walking the few steps to her horse, she untied the blanket and laid it on the ground. Looking at him, she lowered herself to it, then extended her hand. "Please, Gabe."

Dropping to his knees, he held her face between his hands, searching her eyes. "Make certain this is what you want because there's no going back. I won't give you up once I've had you." He lowered his mouth, brushing hers, then pulled back. "Do you understand?"

"I don't want any other man..."

With that simple statement, he wrapped his arms around her, lowering her to the ground, finding all he'd been searching for in this one woman.

"Lena, sweetheart, you need to wake up. We have to start back." Gabe kissed her forehead, then feathered kisses along her cheek before seizing her mouth. Making love twice hadn't been enough, but he had no choice except to get her back home before darkness made it impossible to see the trail.

Lena's eyes opened to slits, closed, then sprang wide as she saw who leaned over her. Recognition came in a slow wave, accompanied by a sleepy smile.

"Do we need to leave?"

"Unless you want to spend the night out here." Gabe kissed her again, lingering until he pulled away on a quiet groan, convincing himself they had to go. "Our next time won't be on the hard ground."

"No?" She pushed up, grabbing his hand.

"It shouldn't have happened this way." He picked leaves from her hair, then did the same with his own, missing her wary expression.

"Do you regret it already?"

Grabbing her shoulders, he turned Lena to him. "Not for an instant. It's just...you deserve better than the hard ground in the middle of nowhere."

"I'm not complaining." She reached up, giving him a kiss, noticing how the sun had already begun to disappear behind the western mountains. "You're right, though. We'd better start back."

The return ride took longer, darkness settling across the trail as they joined the main road. Both remained silent as the time ticked by, neither broaching the subject they knew hung between them.

Gabe reined to a stop at the livery, dismounting, then helping Lena, letting her body slide down his, feeling the heat rise again. Taking her mouth in a slow kiss, he moaned when she broke the kiss and stepped away.

"I need to get to the Dixie before Nick sends men looking for me."

"He knows you're with me. I asked Noah to tell him we were going on a ride."

She didn't know how she felt about Nick knowing about her time with Gabe, but she let the thought pass. "Still, he'll worry if I'm not back soon."

Gabe caught her arm as she turned to leave. "Let me put the horses away and I'll walk you over."

A smile spread across her face. "There's no need. It's close." Hesitating a moment, she glanced up. "Will you be by tonight?"

"Couldn't keep me away."

Brushing the horses, Gabe's mind kept prodding him about what needed to be said between them. He didn't even know how she felt about him—other than her declaration of wanting no other man. Her uninhibited reaction to their lovemaking had left him wanting more.

He'd been concerned about being her first, but she'd surprised him by admitting there'd been one other man years before. She refused to give his name, but Gabe knew it had to be Carlyle. The knowledge didn't dissuade him. He wanted her, would always want her, even if he wasn't her first.

"Where'd you ride?"

Gabe hadn't heard Noah come up beside him. "The waterfall." Tossing the brush in a bucket, he grabbed Blackheart's harness as Noah grabbed Joker's, leading them to their stalls. Closing the gates behind them, Gabe let out a deep breath. "Do you have any coffee left?"

"You know I never let the pot go empty." Noah motioned him toward the back of the blacksmith shop.

"I'm surprised to see you here. I thought you and Abby would be up at your cabin." Taking a seat on an old, well-worn bench, Gabe accepted a cup of the steaming liquid.

"We would be, except Dax put in a big order for some tools they need right away. Anyway, she's not feeling well, so I had her go to your place to sleep for a bit. Didn't think you'd mind." Noah had been worried about her inability to sleep, poor appetite, and nausea for several days.

"Not at all. In fact, why don't you two stay there tonight? I'll bunk down here."

"Thanks. I believe we'll take you up on that." Noah cradled the cup between his hands. "I've never known you to be serious about anyone."

Gabe glanced up from where he studied the contents of his cup. "Who says I'm serious about Lena?"

"You saying you're not?"

He didn't respond right away, thinking of the secrets he knew she kept. "She's got secrets and damned if I can get her to talk about them."

Noah let out a robust laugh. "Hell, all women have secrets. It's the way they're made." Noticing Gabe's stone-still expression didn't change, Noah leaned forward, resting his arms on his legs. "You thinking what she isn't saying is serious?"

"Must be, or she wouldn't keep it quiet." Draining his cup, he set it aside. "I'm going to the Dixie for a while. See you in the morning."

Crossing the street, he heard the usual loud voices and laughter coming from both saloons. Spotting horses with the Pelletier brand outside the Rose, he took a detour, seeing Bull, Travis, and a couple other ranch hands playing cards at one table.

"Pull up a chair, Gabe." Bull signaled Dolly for another glass. "You just missed Cash."

Gabe nodded for Travis to deal him in. "He mention having any trouble tonight?"

"Nope. Said it's been real quiet. Then again, it's still early." Saturday nights could be wild or quiet, depending on the mood of the cowboys and miners. "He mentioned something about a bank robbery in Big Pine. Sheriff Sterling thinks it's the same gang that rode through Colorado and Wyoming," Bull said. "Sterling is certain they're heading our way." He tossed down some cards and leaned back.

Gabe played one hand after another, winning more than losing, while contemplating what needed to be done to protect the townsfolk from another danger. Seemed they were destined to always face one vulture or another in the isolated frontier town.

"Did Cash say where he was headed?" Gabe asked.

"Doing the rounds, then heading to the Dixie to meet with Beau." Bull stood and stretched. "I think I'll make my way over there and try my luck on the roulette wheel."

"I'm on my way over there myself." Gabe nodded at Travis and the others as he followed Bull to the door.

"Leaving so soon?"

He turned at the sound of Dolly's voice. They'd spoken of her decision to move to Splendor and his feelings about it. She'd already figured out they'd just be friends, his time in her bed ending when she stepped off the stage.

"I need to find Cash."

"Well, come back later for a drink—if you don't have other plans." Her gaze darted around the saloon, landing on a man at a table filled with men Gabe recognized, except for one. Something about her suggestion seemed more like a plea.

"Anything wrong, Dolly?"

"Probably nothing. Just a feeling I have about a man at that table." She nodded toward the man Gabe didn't know, then rubbed her hands up and down her arms as if to ward off a chill.

"Who is he?"

"Thomas Pennington. His partner is William Carlyle. They own the Devil Dancer mine."

"Maybe I should go over and introduce myself."

She held out a hand to stop him. "Forget I said anything. It's probably nothing. Have a good night, Gabe." Moving to the bar, she leaned against it, her gaze still focused on the table.

Gabe watched her a moment longer, not liking the wariness on her face, yet knowing she knew where he'd be if anything happened.

He spotted Cash at the Dixie right off, a wave of jealousy consuming him when he saw his friend's arm around Lena's waist. She threw her head back, laughing at something he said, then moved from his hold, her eyes locking on Gabe.

Noting the firm set of his jaw and hard eyes, she moved toward him. Memories of what transpired a few hours before were still fresh as she stopped before him, offering a tentative smile.

"I hoped you'd come by."

"Seems you've had no problem keeping yourself occupied." His gaze shifted to Cash, then back to her.

"Jealous, *mon cher*?" She slid an arm through his, unmindful of the curious eyes watching them.

"Do I need to be?"

Her face became serious, the humor gone. "No, Gabe. My interest is in just one man."

He looked down at her, his thoughts concealed behind stormy eyes. "Good." Taking a slow breath, he stepped away. "I have to speak with Cash, then I'll buy you a drink."

"All right. I'll be waiting."

Gabe shook his head, wanting to dislodge the jealousy which possessed him the moment he saw Cash touching Lena. She was his, no one else's, and he wanted every man within a hundred miles to know it.

Joining Cash, he wasted no time asking about the message from Sterling.

"They held up two banks in Big Pine, taking all the cash from each, then disappeared. The message said it happened yesterday. If it's who Sterling believes it is, they did the same in Wyoming and Colorado. Hit two banks, then vanished."

"Did he try to find them?"

"Couldn't find a trace...not one track." Cash filled his glass, then one for Gabe. "What do you want to do?"

"Does Clausen know?" Gabe asked, referring to the president of Splendor's only bank.

"No. It's Saturday and the bank is closed. Besides, I wanted to talk with you first."

"I'll speak with Clausen and several other businessmen on Monday morning, let them know trouble may be on its way. I'd like you and Beau to ride out to the ranches closest to town, see if they have any men they can spare for a few days to help us keep watch. My guess is if the outlaws are coming this way, they'll hit us soon."

Cash leaned forward, lowering his voice. "Clausen's holding a good amount of gold in the bank. What will you do if the gang hits town while Beau and I are gone?"

"I'll tell Noah, Nick, and a few others to be alert. We'll do the best we can." Gabe swallowed his whiskey in one gulp. "I need to spend some time with my lady." He sent Cash a meaningful look.

"I wondered if you were ever going to make a move." Cash sent him a knowing smile.

"Just so we're clear...I've made it."

Chapter Twelve

"Get out of my face, Tommy." Willie groaned as he sat up, rubbing his eyes, which felt as if they contained a fistful of sand. Glancing at the bed, he saw the sleeping form of a woman. "What the hell happened last night?" His voice felt raw and his head spun.

"I'd think it's obvious." Tommy opened the curtains, letting in the early morning sun.

"It's not, so tell me." Willie stood, groaning, bracing himself on a nearby dresser as he searched for his clothes. The woman never budged from her position under the covers.

"Here." Tommy grabbed a pair trousers off the floor and flung them at Willie. "You finished one bottle and started on another before following your companion upstairs. You've been up here ever since."

"What day is it?" He began to topple to the side as his leg missed the pants, then righted himself.

"Sunday. Time for us to ride back to the mine."

Willie's stomach grumbled as he slipped into his shirt and boots. "I've got to get something to eat first."

"After yesterday, the boardinghouse is out of the question. I'll see if the bartender can rustle us up something." Tommy opened the door, then turned back, glancing at the still sleeping woman. "She's paid for."

Willie tucked in his shirt, taking a last look at the woman. He couldn't think of her name, but didn't care. One whore was the same as another.

Joining Tommy at a table, he tossed back the whiskey in front of him, hoping it would remedy his pounding headache.

"This is the best I could do." Al placed two plates of eggs in front of them. "You're lucky I was up. Next time, I suggest you go to the boardinghouse."

Tommy slid a plate closer to Willie. "Eat this."

The smell of eggs had Willie gagging, pushing the food away.

"Get something in your stomach so we can head out. You won't have enough strength to stay on your horse if you don't."

Willie cursed before relenting. After a few bites, he sat back, rubbing his temples.

"I can't say we can spare them, but Bull and Travis are our best men. You're welcome to use them if it will help keep Splendor safe." Standing on the bottom rail of the corral, Dax and Cash rested their arms on the top, watching Bull try to wrestle a new gelding into submission. Both Travis and Bull possessed soft hands when it came to breaking horses, a skill few men enjoyed. Besides Luke, they were critical to the success of the Pelletier horse breeding program.

"I hate to take your best men." Cash winced as Bull landed on his backside.

"It may be good to get him out of here before he hurts himself," Dax joked, watching Bull grimace as he climbed back on the horse. "Sheriff Sterling has no idea who these fellows are?"

"He sent us another message this morning. Appears they might be a group of ex-confederates. From what he knows, there are a couple brothers in the gang. Doesn't help us much."

"It's somewhat better than being hit by surprise. At least you can be ready for them." Dax jumped to the ground. "Travis is over at Luke's. I'll let Bull know to get his gear ready."

By late-afternoon on Monday, Cash, Bull, and Travis returned to Splendor, Beau riding in an hour later with Gil Murton. Three additional men weren't much, but at least they were the best. Within an hour, they had a plan for keeping watch outside of the bank, making certain Sally Phelps and Abby would be safe inside.

Finishing the meeting, several of the men decided to have supper at Suzanne's while Noah took off to check on Abby. The last couple nights, the two had stayed at Gabe's. She hadn't improved either Sunday or today, staying bundled up, drinking tea, and trying to force down some food. Noah had already decided to take her to see Doc Worthington, then leave for their cabin. He'd return in the morning, leaving her with Suzanne if she hadn't improved.

The men had encouraged Gabe to come with them to the Rose, but he declined, deciding to pay a visit to the Dixie. He knew it went against all his actions in the past, but he wanted Lena in his bed every night. And not just for a few weeks or months. So far, he'd held his thoughts inside, not willing to voice them out loud.

Approaching the Dixie, he heard none of the usual laughter or music, and saw few customers. Nick's usual spot at the bar was empty and he saw no sign of Lena.

"Quiet tonight," he said to Paul as the bartender slid a drink to him.

"Always is early in the week. If you're looking for Nick, he's in the office." He nodded to the door behind him. "Been holed up there most of the day."

Gabe wandered back, needing to speak to Nick about the new hotel. As he knocked and pushed the door open, he found him studying the drawings. He glanced up, motioning Gabe to join him.

"I'm not certain starting before the snow is a good idea. We may not have enough time to get the place closed up to stop damage from the winter storms."

Gabe walked around the desk to stand behind Nick, scrutinizing the plans. "If we start soon, there may be enough time to close up the bottom floor. We can resume work again at the first sign of spring and be able to finish before the snow falls next year."

Nick didn't respond, searching for a way to make the suggestion feasible. "With a few minor changes, we could make it work. What about men? Are there enough to get this started right away?"

"More than enough. We've had such a large influx of people coming west to rebuild their lives after the war, new people are moving in every day. Add to that the influx due to the gold strikes and we shouldn't have a problem finding good men. That's why Noah built those extra houses and plans to build more. He already has a waiting list. A lot of men are looking for work."

"Nick, I wondered—" Lena stopped as she saw who stood next to him. A smile broke across Gabe's face in an instant, causing her chest to tighten.

"Hello, sweetheart."

Gabe's endearment surprised her, and Nick even more. His gaze shifted from her to Gabe, then back to Lena, although he kept his thoughts to himself.

"Hello, Gabe." Her attention lingered on him a few moments before she stepped inside and closed the door. "I saw Cash and several other men at the boardinghouse. It seems you may be expecting trouble."

"That's one reason I came by here. I wanted to ask you and Nick to keep watch for a group of five or six men, probably in their twenties, with southern accents. It's believed they've hit several banks, the last ones being in Big Pine." He continued to explain what he knew, asking for them to send word if they saw a group who fit the description. "Don't make any moves on them. If it's the same gang, they've already killed, and I doubt they'll hesitate to kill again."

"And the other reason you came by?" Nick asked, his gaze narrowing on Gabe.

He looked at Lena. "To ask Lena to supper."

"I'd love to have supper with you, but I need to speak with the girls first."

"Take your time. Nick and I are still discussing plans for starting the hotel now rather than waiting until spring."

"Then I should stay. After all, what you two discuss also concerns me." She moved next to Gabe, feeling the heat from his body radiating toward her, like a blast of warm air from Noah's forge. Never had she felt this much pull to one man, not even Willie.

Nick explained what they'd discussed. "If we're able to gather enough men, we could start early next week. That gives us perhaps two months before the first heavy snows. I've already alerted Silas at the lumber mill that we may need to purchase materials soon."

Lena couldn't help the tense feeling pulsing through her. Although their time together yesterday had been wonderful, she found herself waiting for him to tell her it had been a mistake.

"So you already planned to start now?" Gabe asked Nick.

"I'd thought about it. Your suggestion to move forward hardened my belief we should start while we still can."

"Then I'll ask around tomorrow, see how many men we can round up. You know, Bull used to work with his father constructing large projects back home. He's in town to help keep watch for the outlaws. We might as well put his time to good use. His insights would be invaluable as we lay out the building."

"Ask him to meet with us in the morning." Nick stood, crossing his arms. "Lena, why don't you take care of business upstairs? There are still a few issues I need to speak with Gabe about before you leave for supper."

"Why don't you join us, Nick?" Lena asked, missing the warning look Gabe shot Nick.

"Thanks, but I believe I'll grab some food a little later." He waited until she closed the door behind her, then rounded on Gabe, his voice taking on a hard edge. "Do you want to tell me what the hell's going on?"

Gabe knew this discussion would occur at some point. Might as well get it behind them. "I'm courting Lena. Are you going to object?"

"Not if you're serious about her. It won't end well between us if you take advantage and break her heart."

Silence settled between them as each considered the consequences if a relationship between Gabe and Lena soured. As business partners, the aftermath could destroy what appeared to be a successful venture.

"I'd never trifle with Lena, if that's what you're implying. On the contrary, I'm quite serious about her. Beyond that, I can make no promises."

Taking a breath, Nick considered his next words. "She's been hurt in the past."

Gabe had already figured that out, but kept it to himself. "It's not my intention to hurt her."

The door burst open, Lena entering, a coat over her arm. "Are you ready?"

Nick glanced at Gabe. "I believe we're finished here."

"Wonderful. All of a sudden, I'm starving." Lena's warm smile hit both men in the gut, but for totally different reasons.

The tables in the boardinghouse were empty when Gabe and Lena entered. They selected a back table, sitting so they faced the front. He reached over, intertwining her hand with his.

"Gabe, someone will see." Her protest held no conviction as the corners of her mouth tipped up.

He glanced around, throwing his head back and laughing. "There is no one here to see us."

"Suzanne and Fanny." Her olive skin darkened as heat infused her body. She doubted a full minute went by without her reliving what happened between them near the waterfall.

"I guarantee you they won't say a word to anyone." If anyone in Splendor could be counted on to keep confidences, it was Suzanne and Fanny.

Lena glanced up, seeing Suzanne approaching with two plates.

"I brought you the roast beef and vegetables. The stew is gone, but there are still plenty of biscuits and pie." Her eyes lit up, noting Lena pulling her hand from Gabe's grasp. "I'll be back out with coffee."

The room stayed quiet, except for the sound of their knives and forks clicking on the plates. After several minutes, Gabe broke the silence, deciding he needed to be clear about his feelings.

"You need to know I have no intention of letting you go. I never thought I'd say this, but you've changed my mind about what matters."

Her hands began to shake. She cared about Gabe, maybe even loved him, but anything more than what they already had was out of the question. There were too many obstacles from her past that couldn't be changed. She found herself praying he didn't say what she feared most.

"How could one afternoon with me change what matters to you?"

"One afternoon didn't. What happened between us yesterday came from months of getting to know you and wanting you. I never saw myself settling down, marrying, or wanting a family. But I want all of those with you."

She waited, her heart pounding as fear knotted inside her. Wondering if she should stop him now before he said the words which could change everything between them, she reached toward him, taking his hand in hers.

"Please, let's not discuss this tonight."

Gabe hesitated, staring at her in confusion, trying to make sense of her request. "You don't feel the same." Disillusion tinged his voice.

She squeezed his hand, not letting him pull away. "Like you, I've always believed I'd live out my life without marrying. Whatever is happening between us is new and I need time to understand it.

Can't we enjoy what we have without making decisions so soon?"

Struggling with confusing emotions, Gabe straightened his spine, his face turning from one of hope to cool detachment. "If that's what you want."

Her spirits plummeted at the way he closed himself off. He pulled his hand from hers, reaching into his pocket to leave money on the table. "It's getting late. I should get you back to the saloon."

Every step away from Suzanne's created more distance between them. Gabe didn't say a word, his eyes focused straight ahead, his face set as if chiseled from granite. As they neared the doors of the Dixie, Lena pulled him to a stop.

"I want you, Gabe. I just need time. Can you understand that?"

He didn't, but he already loved her. Their hours near the waterfall had been the culmination of months of wanting Lena. The thought of losing her tore at his heart. Remembering Nick's warning about her being hurt in the past made him want to find the man and beat him senseless. He'd do anything to ease her pain.

"If you need time, that's what you'll get." He leaned down, kissed her cheek, then stepped away. "Goodnight, Lena."

The night settled into a comforting routine for Lena, although she struggled with boredom from an almost deserted saloon. Two men wandered in an hour after her return, had a couple drinks, then left.

"Go home, get some sleep. There's no need for us both to be here. I'll be closing the place within the hour." Nick had watched Lena since her return, noting a face devoid of any trace of joy. He wondered what happened between her and Gabe to cause such a change, making the decision to speak with her in the morning after she had a chance to rest.

"All right. I'll see you in the morning."

Slipping into her coat, she stepped into the cool air, staring at a sky blanketed in millions of stars. She never grew tired of the clear night skies, feeling as if she could reach up and grab a handful of the sparkling gems.

Not tired enough to fall asleep, she wandered the boardwalk, turning away from the boardinghouse. She walked toward the church, crossed the street, and strolled toward the road behind the bank. It had been a long time since she'd roamed the town at night and saw no one.

Paying no attention to where she walked, she found herself standing outside Gabe's home, struggling with emotions that pulled her in too many directions. One dim light glowed from within. Taking one step, then another, she found herself at his front door, her heart drumming a painful beat in her chest. Lifting her hand, she knocked twice, then stepped away.

A moment later, the door swung open. Gabe stood in front of her, feet bare, his unbuttoned shirt pulled from his trousers. His eyes widened in surprise.

"Lena? What are you doing here?"

Her tongue darted out, licking lips that had gone dry at the sight of him.

"I just..." She swallowed, trying to find the words. "The way you left..."

He stepped outside, shielding her with his body, guiding her into his home. Closing the door, he turned Lena toward him, seeing distress and anguish on her face. Pulling her close, he wrapped his arms around her, stroking her back as he kissed her temple.

"Talk to me, sweetheart," he whispered in her ear. Her arms wound around his neck and she buried her face in his shoulder.

"I want you, Gabe, and don't want to lose you. I just..." Her agonized voice speared through him.

Pulling back, he stared into her pleading eyes. "We'll do this however you want, sweetheart. If you need time, I'll do my best to give it to you." He leaned down, taking her lips in a passionate kiss, then pulled away. "I'll take whatever you can give me."

She dropped her head to his chest, a soft sob escaping.

Placing a finger under her chin, he lifted her face to his, lowering his mouth once more. Within seconds, the kiss turned from a soft caress to fierce urgency, their hands roaming over each other at a frenzied pace. His lips touched the corners of her mouth before trailing down the silky skin of her neck to trace a path along her collarbone, then back up.

Holding her close, he let his hands roam up and down her back before settling on the soft curves of her hips. She didn't protest when he lifted his hand to slide her gown off her shoulders, kissing the sensitive area below her ear, then going lower.

Tightening her hold around his neck, she tangled his hair in her fingers, moaning into his mouth as heat roared through her body. Snuggling against him, she pushed one leg between his, feeling the hardness of his muscles against the softness of hers. A moan escaped as she aligned her body with his.

The sounds of her desire were like liquid fire racing through him. He could wait no longer. Without breaking the kiss, he scooped her into his arms, taking the few steps into his bedroom, kicking the door closed behind them.

Chapter Thirteen

Gabe felt a strange sense of peace as his eyes opened. Feeling the soft curves of her body draped over his, he refused to move, not wanting to break the spell. He wrestled between the need to get her home before Nick discovered her missing, and began a search, and his own desire to keep her locked within his embrace.

His hands roamed her bare skin, igniting an almost unquenchable thirst for her. He had to stop before need overcame common sense.

"Lena?" He touched his lips to her forehead. "Lena, darlin', you need to wake up."

She groaned, her body not wanting to emerge from the warmth surrounding her. As she awoke, her hand began to play with the crisp hairs on his chest before moving lower. Grasping her wrist, he pulled it back up, capturing it against his heart.

"If you do that, we'll be here until afternoon," he chuckled, his warm breath washing over her.

She let out a deep sigh, wishing they could stay in his bed all day. "All right." Lena pushed herself up, turning to sit beside him, not shielding herself from his view.

The lump in his throat wouldn't dislodge as he took in the sight of her. He'd never get used to her beauty. It would be hell keeping the image from his mind as he tried to concentrate on his work.

Getting up, he reached out a hand. "Come on. I'll get you home before anyone sees you."

She knew he was right, even though every instinct urged her to stay. Accepting his hand, she slid off the bed on shaky legs, wrapping her arms around his waist. The feel of his rough skin against her sensitized body triggered a desire she felt helpless to ignore. Accepting the consequences of anyone spotting them, she dropped her arms and slipped into her clothes.

Within minutes, they'd stepped into the darkness, both grateful for the dense cloud cover. Gabe reached behind her, pulling the hood of her cloak over her head in an attempt to shield her face. Walking with quick, quiet steps, they made their way between the jail and Wild Rose, then crossed the main street toward the boardinghouse side entrance. Gabe turned the knob, breathing a sigh of relief when it opened.

"Tonight, Lena," he breathed as his lips descended on hers. "Come to me again tonight."

"Yes." She broke the kiss and dashed inside, closing the door on a quiet click.

He waited until his heart slowed, then took a breath before shoving his hands in his pockets and returning to his house. Never had he felt such a sense of immediate loss, and never before had he slipped around in the dark with a woman, trying to hide his actions. A mixture of desire, guilt, and his conscience warred within him. He didn't know how long he'd be able to go along with her request to give themselves time while keeping their relationship outside the bonds of marriage. It ate at him in a way he couldn't reconcile.

Looking around, he noted a few lights flickering through closed windows, knowing it wouldn't be long before the street would be crowded. If they'd waited any longer, the odds were someone would have seen them, exposing her to ridicule she didn't deserve. He had a great deal of thinking to do about their future. In the meantime, he would do what he'd told her and take whatever she would give him.

"Are you certain you're all right? You look as if you haven't slept in days." Nick held the cup between his hands, bringing it to his lips as he peered over the rim at Lena. Although she seemed more relaxed than he'd seen her in weeks and her face held a slight glow, her eyes were tired and she moved slower than usual when she'd entered the dining room.

Not looking at him, she focused on the plate of eggs in front of her. "I awakened several times and it took a while to fall back to sleep." *Both true*, she told herself, her chest tightening at the memory. "But I'm fine. What will you be doing today?"

"Gabe and I have a meeting with Clausen at the bank. Afterwards, we hope to meet with Bull to review the plans before getting the word out we need men. If all goes well, we should be able to start as early as Friday." Nick set his cup down, deciding to share one other piece of news. "I've bought land from the Pelletiers."

She looked up, her brows rising. "Whatever for?"

"I felt it time each of us had some property where we could build homes, have our own lives, a sense of permanency. All we've ever done is move from one town to the next, never setting down roots. I'd like to change that. Besides, we can't live in the boardinghouse forever."

Her throat constricted as hope settled in her chest. A home is what she'd always dreamed about, never voicing her desire for fear of ruining any chance of ever obtaining it. She'd always left the decision of where and how they lived up to Nick, pushing her own needs aside. He'd been her anchor, saved her from a life as a prostitute, and made her a wealthy woman by most standards.

She glanced up at him, unable to hide a broad smile. "Where is this land?"

One look at her face told Nick he'd made the right decision. "At the southernmost end of their property, a few miles from town. Luke said it's not suitable as ranchland, but it's perfect for two houses with barns. There are over ten acres apiece, and a stream runs through the property. I'm anxious to show it to you."

She set down her fork and tossed her napkin on the table, ready to leave that instant. "Why not today?"

Nick laughed, glad he'd made her smile. "I'll tell you what. We'll ride out there tomorrow morning, right after breakfast. Perhaps Gabe would like to go with us."

A warning flared through her. Had he seen her return with Gabe before sunrise? "He's awfully busy, but we can ask."

"Good. I'll mention it to him when we meet at the bank." Swallowing the last of his coffee, he stood. "I see no need for you to come along, unless you want to."

"No, you go ahead. I may lie down a while. I do feel a little tired." *And sore*, she thought, wondering if it wise to go through another night with Gabe without letting her body recover. Her lips tilted up, knowing nothing could keep her from seeing Gabe again tonight.

"I'll see you at the Dixie then."

Staring at her half-eaten plate of eggs, she felt a sense of peace for the first time in many years. Nick had made the decision she prayed he would—to make Splendor their home. And now she had Gabe, who had agreed to her request they keep their relationship unofficial, at least for right now. There were risks to both their reputations, but her fear of him learning her secrets outweighed the perils of being discovered. She'd known other couples who'd continued down this path for years, never feeling the necessity to marry. They'd just need to be careful and all would be fine.

"Amos is taking too much time deciding on our offer to purchase the Rose." Tommy watched as one of their men walked toward the mine, his arms loaded with tools.

"Perhaps we need to sweeten the deal, or provide another incentive for him to accept. I believe it's time to have Stillwell pay him a friendly visit. The man has nothing else to do and we're paying him to sit around."

"I don't want him threatening Amos. At least not outright. Just showing his face and gun might be all that is needed. We don't want the town to go against us before we've had a chance to settle in." Tommy thought of his night with Dolly, wondering if she looked forward to seeing him again.

"What about the whore at the Rose?" Willie knew Tommy had spent a night with Dolly, and he knew his friend's particular tastes. "Do you have plans to see her again?"

A feral smile appeared on Tommy's face. He'd enjoyed her. Perhaps he'd gotten a little rough, but she didn't fight him too much. The blood was her own fault. If she'd just done as he asked, he never would've had to hit her. Anyway, the bruising would heal in a few days.

"Her name is Dolly, and yes, I believe I will be seeing her again."

"If Stillwell doesn't get any action before then, I'd suggest you use a little *gentle persuasion* to get her to speak with Amos. Remember, as an owner, there'd be no reason you couldn't have her whenever you liked." Willie understood Tommy better than his friend knew. Finding a woman willing to share his particular tastes wasn't easy. If Dolly turned out to be one of those women, it would be a huge incentive for Tommy.

"I can definitely use persuasion. How gentle it is will be up to her." He cast a glance at Willie, his face darkening even as the smile remained.

"Good. I'll send Stillwell in tomorrow, give Amos some serious incentive to think about our offer. We'll ride in on Friday. By then, he should have enough time to make the right decision."

Tommy hoped Willie was right. They didn't need any more blood on their hands.

"Where's Dolly?" Gabe asked Al as he walked into the Rose. He had a little time to waste before meeting Nick, but he'd heard she'd taken ill. It triggered a memory of her acting a little off on Saturday night. He'd ignored it at the time.

"I don't know much, except she hasn't come out of her room since Sunday morning. Amos spoke with her, and when they were finished, he stormed out and came back with Doc."

"Sunday, huh? And she hasn't been down since?" Gabe asked. Two days didn't sound right to him. From what he knew about her, she almost never took a day off.

"That's right."

"Do you mind if I go upstairs, see if she'll talk to me?"

"Go ahead. All she can do is run you off." Al turned his back to Gabe, finishing preparations for the day's business.

Taking the steps two at a time, he knocked on her door. Getting no response, he knocked again.

"Dolly, it's Gabe. Open the door." He could hear the sounds of sheets rustling, then footsteps.

"You'll have to come back another time. I'm not feeling well." Her strained voice carried through the door.

"Nope. I want to talk with you now." His instincts told him something wasn't right.

"Please. Just come back another time."

"You can either let me in or I'll get the key from Al. Your choice." It didn't take more than a few moments for the knob to turn and the door to open a crack. What he saw shocked him. Her right eye was almost swollen shut, with bruising down her face and around her neck. "Open the damn door." His hardened voice startled her into doing as he asked.

She stepped back, clutching her stomach as she lowered herself to the bed.

"Who did this to you?" It wasn't so much a request as a demand.

"It doesn't matter. I allowed it to happen and I'll deal with it."

"The hell you will. Does Amos know about it?" He loomed over her, spotting the remnants of dried blood on her sheets.

"Not all of it. Doc Worthington does, though. Amos brought him over thinking I had some kind of stomach ailment."

"And you told Doc not to say anything, right?" He had a hard time keeping his anger in check and his voice level.

She didn't look at him as she nodded. Gripping both hands in her lap, he could see her tremble, either out of fear or the cold. He crouched in front of her, taking her hands in his.

"Tell me who did this, Dolly."

Frightened eyes met his and he knew she'd been threatened.

"I can't. Please. Just leave this alone."

They'd been friends for over two years. He'd shared her bed countless times, and even though he'd never experienced any of the feelings he had for Lena, he still felt a strong need to protect her.

"I'll speak with Amos. You're not to have any guests up here until we figure out who did this."

"No! I have to work." Her objection came out as a panicked plea.

"I'll take care of it with Amos until this is resolved."

"I can't and won't take your charity. This is my mess, not yours."

"You forget I'm the sheriff in Splendor. Any citizen who's been beaten as you have *is* my business. If you won't give me the name of the man who did this, I'll find out myself. You can either choose to help or make my job harder." Gabe crossed his arms, watching her expression change from firm resistance to reluctant defeat.

"Thomas Pennington."

If he hadn't been listening, he would've missed her whispered response.

"Carlyle's partner? The one you pointed out to me the other night?"

"Yes."

"All right." He pulled a chair over, taking a seat and leaning forward. "Tell me exactly what happened."

"All I need is your signature here, Gabe, then we'll be finished." Harold Clausen handed Gabe a copy, showing him as a fifty percent owner. The new attorney, Del Utley, finished them within hours of being asked. So far, Clausen thought Utley a welcome addition to Splendor. "I'd be happy to file these for you with Otis at the land office."

"Thank you, Harold. I'd appreciate it."

"The bank owns quite a bit more land around town if either or both of you have further interest."

"Who owns the property north of the boardinghouse?" Gabe asked.

Clausen chuckled as he glanced at Nick. "Up until three weeks ago, the bank owned it. Nick is the new owner."

Gabe turned toward Nick. "That so? And what are your plans for it?"

"The town has one boardinghouse, which has been full for months. Noah and Abby are building small, family homes, but there's going to be a continuing need for rooms to accommodate workers, not just those who can afford to stay in our new hotel."

"You're thinking of building another boardinghouse?" Gabe wondered how a competing place would affect Suzanne.

"Not necessarily. I'd prefer to work with Suzanne to expand what she has and enlarge the restaurant."

"What has she said?"

Nick cleared his throat, sitting back in the chair. "Let's just say she's considering it. It took quite a bit of persuading to get her to hire a new cook. This might take quite a bit more coaxing."

Their attention darted to the office door as it swung open and Cash entered.

"Excuse me, gentlemen. Gabe, the visitors we're expecting may be riding into town. Bull spotted a group of five riders coming in from the north."

Gabe stood, adjusting his gun belt, then turned toward Clausen. "I want you to close now and stay closed until I say otherwise."

"I don't want to start a panic, Gabe. We can't stay closed more than a couple hours." Clausen grabbed his own gun belt from a hook on the wall, slipping it around his waist.

"It shouldn't take long to figure out why these men are here. And I want you to send Sally and Abby home."

"I'll make certain Abby leaves. It's doubtful Sally will, though. We've had warnings before and she's refused to go, but I'll do my best."

"Nick, can you keep Lena at Suzanne's?" Gabe asked.

"I'll try."

Gabe, Cash, and Nick stepped outside, hearing Clausen lock the door behind them. A group of horses were tied to the post outside the Rose.

"Where's Beau?" Gabe asked Cash as they took long strides toward the saloon, wanting to get a good look at the newcomers while Nick strode toward the boardinghouse.

"With Gil Murton inside the Dixie. Bull and Travis are at the Rose."

When they heard shouting coming from the Rose, they picked up the pace, coming to an abrupt stop and peering over the swinging doors.

Al stood behind the bar, a shotgun in hand while pointing at one of the new men who held a bottle of whiskey. "I told you already. Leave the money and you can take the bottle. Pay first, then drink."

"And I told you, old man, we'll pay when we're finished."

Cash shook his head and stepped inside, Gabe right behind him—both with their hands resting on the butt of their guns.

"Put the bottle down. Once it's paid for, you'll be welcome to it." Gabe walked closer, stopping several feet away.

"This ain't none of your business, mister." The stranger never took his eyes off Al's shotgun.

"Well, you see, it *is* my business." Gabe stepped in front of him, his back to Al, who lowered the gun and waited.

Eyes growing wide at the sight of Gabe's badge, he set the bottle on a nearby table, dug into a pocket, and extracted several coins. "Here."

"You pay the bartender. I'll stay right here and make sure no one steals your whiskey." He glanced at Cash, who leaned against the wall, his gaze trained on the men at the table.

Tossing the money at Al, the stranger grabbed the bottle, joining his friends.

"Took you long enough, Bobby." One of the men slapped him on the back.

"You boys new in Splendor?" Gabe asked, trying to memorize each face.

The five shifted in the chairs, getting a good look at him.

"We are, Sheriff. Heard you have a nice little town here." A man, who appeared to be the oldest in the group, stood and faced Gabe, his medium height requiring him to look up at the well over six foot tall lawman.

"You heard right, and my deputies and I aim to keep it that way. Now, do you have jobs around here or are you passing through?"

"Haven't decided."

Gabe's chuckle didn't change the harsh expression on this face. "I'd advise you to make a decision by tomorrow night. If you don't have work, I expect you to be gone before sunset."

"So you're saying this is our one night in town?" the older man snarled.

"That's what I'm saying, unless you have a good reason for staying. Have a good night, gentlemen."

Turning, Gabe and Cash walked out, not acknowledging Bull or Travis sitting at a table near the newcomers. With luck, the two might overhear something helpful while the men drank and played cards.

"What do you think?" Cash shot a look over his shoulder, taking a good look at the horses belonging to the men.

"I'd bet a month's pay they're the gang Sheriff Sterling warned us about. I want Beau and Gil in the bank. I'll ask Noah to get word to Bull and Travis that they're to keep watch on the men in the Rose. If they leave town, we let them go, but all of us need to stay close in case they return."

Gabe and Cash entered the Dixie, finding Beau and Gil at a table near the window. "Cash, fill them in while I go speak with Noah."

Gabe didn't say he planned to stop at the boardinghouse to make certain Nick kept Lena inside and away from the Dixie and the bank. It didn't take more than a minute to convey to Noah what he wanted, then continue across the street to Suzanne's. Inside, Nick and Lena sat together, finishing their lunch. Joining them, Gabe wasted no time describing the incident at the Rose.

"You're certain they're the ones?" Nick hadn't missed the way Gabe looked at Lena when he sat down, or the slight blush on her face.

"As certain as I can be with the information Sterling sent. Five riders, all new to town, with the look of gunslingers and not cowhands. I understand you'll need to be at the Dixie, Nick, but I'd like Lena to stay here until we figure out what these men plan to do."

"I'm sitting right here, Gabe. Why don't you ask me directly?" Lena's mouth shifted into a thin line. Crossing her arms, she waited for his response.

He studied her, wondering if she'd listen to him or not. "I want you out of danger. The best way to do that is to keep you off the streets and away from the saloon. I've already asked Horace to send Abby home. All I'm asking is for you to stay inside with Suzanne and Fanny."

"What about Nick? He'll still be in danger."

Gabe wrapped her hand tight in his. "He's prepared to deal with them. Do this for me, Lena. I've given them until tomorrow night to leave town. Within forty-eight hours, this will be settled one way or the other."

"And if they come in here?" She turned her hand over, lacing her fingers with his.

"Stay upstairs or in the kitchen with Suzanne and Fanny, although I doubt they'll cause trouble while they're eating."

"It's them all right." The three turned at the sound of Bull's voice. "The one called Bobby can't keep his mouth shut. We listened for a while. From what we could hear, all fought for the South, and they're not too pleased with the way Lee surrendered. When Travis and I left, they were arguing about whether they should ride out or stay to finish what they came here for."

Gabe walked to the window, watching as the five left the Rose, riding north and out of town, then turned back to Bull. "What's your gut tell you?"

Bull dragged a hand down his face. "I think they're going to hit the bank before you have time to prepare a defense. Beau and Gill are already there. It won't take long for the rest of us to get into position."

"Let's go." Gabe cast one more look at Lena, then followed Bull outside, determined to crush the gang and make Splendor their last stop.

Chapter Fourteen

The sun moved across the sky to signal midday without the outlaws making an appearance. None of Gabe's men moved from their positions. In another hour, Clausen would lock the doors, securing the money and gold in his vault. If the gang didn't show by then, they'd all take up their spots again in the morning.

Gabe's main concern centered on the townsfolk carrying on with their business while staying unaware of the potential danger. At least there were few ranch hands or miners in town this early in the week, and school had already let out for the day.

Moving from position to position, Gabe checked with each of the men until he got to Noah, who leaned against an outside wall on the balcony of the Dixie, his sharpshooter rifle beside him. If the gang tried to rob the bank, he had a clean shot. Whoever came out wouldn't escape.

"I've got a favor to ask you." Noah glanced at Gabe, needing to get this said.

"Anything, you know that."

"If the outlaws hit town and I don't make it—"

"What the hell, Noah? Nothing's going to happen to you."

Noah took a breath. "Abby's pregnant."

Gabe's jaw dropped open as understanding flashed across his face.

"Promise me. If anything happens—"

Gabe held his hand up. "You don't have to ask. I'll make sure she and the baby are taken care of."

Noah nodded, then turned his attention back to the street below. "Ah, hell," he muttered as a group of three wagons entered town from the south, obscuring his view of the bank. "Lousy time for the newcomers to arrive."

The wagons pulled to a stop along one side of the street in front of the bank. It was then that Gabe and Noah saw the extra horses tied to the back of two of them, a lone rider taking up the rear. Gabe recognized him as the oldest of the men in the saloon.

"It's them," Gabe hissed. "They've hidden inside the wagons. Look." He pointed across the street, seeing men jump from the wagons and rush into the bank. "I've got to warn the others. Keep your spot here. You'll have a better chance of sighting them from this balcony than anywhere else. When they come out, pick off the one riding at the back first. That will get us down to four."

Noah nodded, his face a mask as he focused on the task before him.

Dashing down the stairs and through the Dixie, Gabe spotted Gil peering out the window.

"Gil, the gang hid in the wagons. At least three are already in the bank. Go around back and find a position behind the church. You should have a clean shot when they come out."

Gil nodded, wasting no time in dashing out the door.

Gabe moved onto the boardwalk, searching for Bull and Travis, who'd hidden along the same side of the street as the bank, opposite where he now stood. Getting Bull's attention, he pointed toward the bank, hoping he'd seen the men jump from the wagons and disappear inside. At Bull's positive nod, Gabe signaled for him and Travis to move closer to the general store, which would put them within fifty feet of the bank. Gabe turned his attention to Cash, who'd taken a position outside the Dixie. If the outlaws rode north, he'd be their last opportunity to stop them.

Turning his head, Gabe's gaze landed on the driver of the first wagon and the two children sitting next to him. He wondered why they hadn't pulled away, leaving the robbers to their own fate. Focusing on the man's face, he could see fear and indecision as he glanced at his children, then back at Gabe.

He holstered his weapon and strode across the street to the lead wagon, hoping the outlaw waiting at the back of the third wagon would think he strolled out to welcome the newcomers. Stopping a few feet away, he noticed someone crouched behind the driver, his arm extended, holding a gun to the man's back.

"I'm Sheriff Evans. You must be new to town." His gaze locked on the driver, seeing sweat drip from the man's brow. He also noticed the gun move further into the wagon, the outlaw attempting to hide from Gabe.

"Uh...yes. We're new." The man's voice shook, his face ashen with fear. "I'm Elijah Smith and these are my two sons."

Gabe extended his arms, hoping the boys wouldn't hesitate. "Come on down, boys, while your father and I talk."

Looking at their father for confirmation, the first boy turned, jumping into Gabe's arms, followed by the younger boy. He set the boy down. "See that man?" he whispered, nodding toward Nick. "You two run toward him like the devil is after you."

He didn't have to say another word before they shot across the street toward the Dixie where Nick stood, holding one of the swinging doors open.

Straightening, Gabe again pulled his revolver from its holster, then moved a step closer to the wagon. From his position, he couldn't see the older outlaw at the back, but he could see the shadow of the outlaw hiding inside the wagon.

"If you need any work done on your wagon, the livery is at the other end of town. Noah Brandt is the proprietor—"

The sound of gunfire inside the bank had Gabe reaching up and yanking Elijah Smith to the ground. In a split second, the outlaw hiding in the back moved forward, aiming his gun at Gabe. No sooner had he shown his face than one well-placed bullet in his forehead slammed him backwards. Gabe looked over his shoulder and up, seeing Noah's quick nod as he swung his rifle toward the outlaw at the back of the wagons. Another shot rang out and the older outlaw toppled to the ground, unmoving.

Another blast of gunfire erupted as the bank door flew open. Three men, each carrying sacks of money, raced outside. They never had a chance. Gunfire from Cash, Bull, Travis, Gil, and Noah echoed down the street, and within seconds, two of the robbers lay dead. The third, the one they called Bobby, leaned against the outside wall of the bank, his gun at his side, bags of money in a pile at his feet.

"Put your gun down, kid. You don't want to end up like your friends." Cash moved toward Bobby, his gun trained on the young man's chest. "There's no need for you to die today." Cash shook his head at the others. He wanted to take this one in alive.

Bobby's eyes widened in fear as his gun arm began to rise, his hand shaking so hard, Cash knew he wouldn't be able to aim.

"Don't do it. You're the last one standing and there are too many of us for you to get away. Just drop the gun and this will all end." Cash moved a few feet closer, near enough to see the sweat on Bobby's brow.

Bobby's body trembled as he continued to raise the gun, aiming at Cash.

"Stop!" Cash yelled at the same time a bullet flew out of Bobby's gun, missing him by inches. Without further thought, Cash fired, hitting him square in the chest.

Gabe and the others moved forward as Cash knelt beside Bobby, seeing the young man's eyes slowly close. Checking his pulse, he knew there was no saving him.

Before Gabe could check the men who lay sprawled in front of the bank, Cash rose and pushed past him, dashing inside. His breath caught when he saw Clausen kneeling on the floor next to Beau, a hand putting pressure on a wound to his shoulder.

Cash dropped beside them, seeing a flow of red coming from his friend's back.

"Beau?" Cash gazed down, watching as Beau's eyes opened to slits.

"Did y'all get them?" Beau ground out, grimacing when he couldn't stop the sudden cough which racked his body.

"Get Doc. I think the bullet went straight through, but there's a lot of blood." Clausen continued to apply pressure to the wound.

"Bull went to fetch him." Gabe walked up, crouching next to the men.

Clausen shook his head. "Sally gave them the money and we thought they'd leave. The one who fired didn't give any warning before he shot Beau. He would've pulled the trigger again, but we heard gunfire outside and they scrambled out of here. Cowards, every single one of them."

"Let me have a look." Doc Worthington set his bag on the floor, making a quick check of Beau's wound. "From what I can tell, the bullet went clean through his shoulder. Take him to the clinic and I'll get him patched up."

"Bull and I can take care of him, Gabe."

"Thanks. I'll stop by the clinic after I learn what I can about the dead men. I'll need to send a message to Sheriff Sterling, letting him know he doesn't have to worry about the gang any longer. Doc, I know you'll handle the death certificates."

Doc nodded. "Line them up alongside the clinic and I'll check each one after I get finished with Beau. I'm telling you, Gabe, I don't believe I've handled so many gunshot wounds since the war." Settling his hat on his head, Doc followed behind Bull and Cash as they carried Beau across the street.

Gabe had already confirmed the oldest of the group and the man in the wagon were dead, Noah's clean shots leaving no doubt. Kneeling next to the one they called Bobby, he scrubbed a hand down his face, thinking the boy could be no more than eighteen and knowing Cash had no choice except to pull the trigger. *What a waste of a young life*, Gabe thought, moving to the next body. Confirming they all were dead, he began to go through their pockets, handing Gil and Travis the contents before glancing up at them.

"We'll take it all back to the jail, see if we can identify any of them and notify their kin."

"Do you honestly believe anyone's going to come looking for these thugs?" Gil asked, his eyes wide as he stared down at the still bodies.

"I know how you feel, Gil. Remember, though, each of these men was someone's son, brother, or husband." Gabe stood, noticing the townsfolk leaving the safety of their stores and homes to see the carnage. "In truth, it's doubtful anyone will come looking for them. I'll keep their belongings with a copy of the death certificate. We'll need to line them up on the side of the clinic so Doc can finish his work."

"I wonder what they did with the money they stole from the other banks." Travis bent down, dragging one of the bodies across the street.

"That's an excellent question, and one we need to try to figure out." Gabe followed Travis, tugging a body behind him, Gil doing the same.

"We'll get the other two," Noah said as he and Bull passed them. "Cash is staying at the clinic with Beau."

When they lay the last outlaw out on the ground, Gabe took one more look, thanking God the danger had passed with just one casualty. Heading straight into the clinic's exam room, he saw Doc still hovering over Beau, Cash standing a few feet away with his arms folded across his chest.

"How is he?" Gabe moved up beside Doc, watching him secure the last of the bandages.

"I'm fine and ready to head out of this place." Beau tried to sit, cursing when both Doc and Cash pushed him back down. "Hell, I had worse than this in the war."

"Doc?" Gabe asked.

"Same as with you, infection is the biggest worry right now. He can go to his place and I'll stop in to check on him for the next few days." Doc glanced down at Beau. "You're fortunate you're right-handed and the bullet went through your left shoulder. You shouldn't have any problem taking care of yourself, although you'll have a good deal of discomfort for a couple weeks."

All heads turned toward the door as it swung open, slamming against the wall as Lena entered. A hand flew to her throat when her eyes, wide with concern, met Gabe's.

"What's wrong, Lena?" He walked up, taking her hands in his.

Swallowing the fear that had lodged in her throat since she'd first heard the gunfire, she took a breath, glancing at the others.

"I heard the shots, but neither Suzanne nor Fanny would let me leave. When it stopped, I went to the Dixie. Nick told me you were here, and I thought…"

The concern in her voice overwhelmed him in a way he hadn't expected. He squeezed her hands. "I'm fine. Beau took a bullet to the shoulder. Doc's just finishing with him. Why don't I walk you back to Suzanne's?"

"No, no. You have work to do. Besides, it's past time I should be at the Dixie." Casting a tentative smile to the others, she dropped her hands to her sides as Gabe turned toward Cash.

"I'll be back in a few minutes to help you get Beau to your place."

"Hell, I'm not some damn invalid." Beau's face reddened as he shot a look at Lena. "My apologies, ma'am."

"I quite understand." Her face softened at his apology. She'd heard so much worse over the years.

Gabe held the door open, then wrapped her arm through his, staying on the side which shielded her from the sight of the bodies next to the clinic.

"We were lucky. Beau is the only casualty, and as long as Doc keeps watch for infection, he'll heal fine."

"And the robbers?"

"All dead." He blew out a breath as they stopped outside the Dixie. "It could've been much worse. They used those wagons to hide. We wouldn't have suspected anything, except one of the outlaws stayed on his horse at the back of the third wagon. Don't know why as it signaled their presence, but I'm glad it happened that way. You'd best get inside." He lifted her hand to his lips and pressed a gentle kiss to the palm, feeling the slight tremble that coursed through her. "I'll come by later."

Gabe pounded on the telegraph office door, knowing Bernie would still be in the back at this hour. If he wasn't, Gabe would check the house behind the office.

Bernie threw the door open, stepping aside as Gabe entered. "I figured you'd be by tonight."

"I need to get a message to Sheriff Sterling to let him know we got the outlaws." He scribbled out a quick note, including a few questions he hoped Sterling could answer. "I'll be at the jail, then the Dixie before heading to my place. If there's a response, come and get me, no matter the time."

Bernie read through it, then started tapping out the message. "I'll do that, Sheriff," he mumbled, never taking his eyes off the note.

Gabe's next stop would be the clinic to help Cash get Beau home. Before he took ten steps, Elijah Smith, the lead driver of the three wagons, intercepted him, holding out his hand.

"I've been looking for you, Sheriff. I want to thank you for saving us from those outlaws."

"Glad everyone's safe, Mr. Smith. How'd you run into those men?"

"We were camped west of Big Pine when they showed up last night. They seemed tired and hungry, so we shared what he had and let them bed down with us. While we packed up this morning, they drew their guns and threatened to kill everyone if we didn't do as they said."

"You made the right decision. Those men would've acted on their threats if you hadn't cooperated. What brings you to Splendor?"

"Me and my brother, Ebenezer, brought our families here. These wagons are full of our kin. I bought some property south of town, with plans to raise sheep and farm."

Gabe's brows knit together. "This is cattle country, Mr. Smith. Most ranchers around here don't take kindly to sheep ranching."

"That's what I've been told, but it's what we know. It's also why we bought land quite a ways south. We heard most of the big ranchers are west and north of here." Taking off his hat, he ran a hand through his thinning hair. "We need this opportunity, Sheriff. Other than what you see in the wagons, we have nothing left. When the war broke out, we thought we lived far enough north to miss the bloodshed. It didn't happen that way."

Gabe had heard similar stories over and over. In his mind, anyone willing to travel this far west deserved a chance at a new life.

"Splendor's a good town, with hardworking people. If you're church-going, you'll meet most of the ranchers on Sunday mornings. Might be a good place for you and your family to start meeting your neighbors."

"Thanks, Sheriff. We'll do just that. I'd better get back to my people so we can find a place to camp before dark."

"A mile south of here is a good spot, and it's near a creek. It should do well for you tonight. Best of luck to you." Gabe knew it would be a tough road for anyone in the sheep business. Several who'd tried to make it in Montana had been run off by neighboring ranchers who believed cattle and sheep couldn't mix. He hoped the local ranchers felt otherwise.

Nursing a beer, Gabe leaned against the bar, watching as Lena spoke with a gambler at a nearby table. As word spread about the gold strikes, more gamblers had made their way to Splendor, targeting miners and their newfound wealth.

He could hear bits of the conversation, his stomach tightening as Lena threw her head back, laughing at something the gambler said. They'd been together twice—once near the waterfall, then again at his house. The feeling of possession grew within him each time. He didn't like seeing her being friendly toward other men. Knowing she wasn't like the women who worked for her didn't decrease the sense of unease he felt at her relaxed manner with men such as the gambler.

"It's not easy, is it?" Nick came up beside him.

"What?"

"Watching her at work. Even when you know it won't go anywhere, it's not the same as if she were someone else."

Gabe turned toward him. "I'm not getting your meaning."

"Lena isn't your typical rancher's wife, or teacher, or nurse. She grew up in a saloon, around men such as the ones in here tonight. She knows nothing else, no other life." Nick sipped his whiskey, waiting for his meaning to sink in.

"Are you trying to warn me off?"

"Not necessarily. It's important you understand she's nothing like other women. Lena has seen and heard things most women are shielded from. I've protected her as much as possible, but still..."

At first, Gabe had struggled with the same thoughts, wondering how he'd become so attracted to a woman opposite of those he'd grown up around. That's why he'd kept his distance for so long, measuring her background against his growing feelings. It took months for him to accept a person couldn't help who they fell in love with, and he had no doubt love was what he felt for her.

"She doesn't share much with me." Gabe rested his arms on the bar as he stared into his empty glass.

Nick grabbed a nearby bottle, filling Gabe's glass, then his own.

"Lena is complicated. It may take her a long time to trust you enough to share her past."

"You mean her secrets." Gabe glanced at him, seeing Nick's brows raise a fraction before he tempered his expression.

"You say that as if the rest of us don't have them. I'm guessing your past isn't so easily shared, either."

Narrowing his gaze at the gilded mirror behind the bar, Gabe took a slow sip of his drink. "True, but if she asked, I'd answer." He took a minute to calm his increasing frustration. "They can't be that bad. Did she kill someone? Is she married? Those are secrets that matter."

Nick laughed at the questions. The thought of Lena hurting anyone or hiding a marriage was ridiculous. "Rest assured, it's neither of those. Some things are better left to the right time and place."

"You two seem to be enjoying yourselves."

Gabe turned around at Lena's smooth drawl, seeing her eyes sparkle in the light of the candelabra overhead.

Without thought, Gabe's arm shot out, his hand wrapping around her waist and pulling her close. "Not as enjoyable as with you here."

She shot an inquisitive look at Nick, her mouth tilting into a smile. "How much has he had to drink tonight?"

"Not enough for you to doubt my words," Gabe answered, letting his gaze wander over her face, settling on her eyes. He wanted to lower his mouth to hers, let everyone in the Dixie know who she belonged to. Instead, he dropped his arm and straightened. "It's been a long day. I'd better head home. Walk outside with me, Lena?"

She nodded, threading her arm through his. Stepping into the moonlight, the street seemed eerie after the violence, as if ghosts from those killed hours before already haunted the town. The South had been steeped in tradition and superstitions, especially for those from Louisiana. Neither seemed to matter in the territories.

Guiding her to the side of the building, Gabe faced her, settling his hands on her shoulders before lowering his mouth. She responded with an urgency that gripped him, digging her fingers into his arms as he deepened the kiss. Letting his arms slide down her back, he rested his hands on her hips, drawing her close, the heat of their contact becoming too intense to continue in the open.

"Come to me tonight, Lena," he whispered against her lips, his voice already thick with need.

She pulled back to look up at him. "I'll have to wait until Nick is asleep."

"I'll be waiting." He leaned down for one more kiss, then stepped away, hating the fact they were sneaking around. They had to talk about this...and soon.

Chapter Fifteen

Midnight passed with no sign of Lena. A few nights before, he'd asked her to come. She'd agreed, then decided against it when Nick's light still shown under his bedroom door long past midnight. Perhaps the same had happened tonight. The events of today cast a different light on it, however, and as he sat alone, a fire burning in the woodstove, he began to fear something or someone may have waylaid her.

Deciding he needed to look for her, he stood just as a knock on the door had him drawing it open. Lena stood in the darkness, the hood of her cloak doing little to hide her identity. Grabbing her hand, he pulled her through the opening, not letting her get more than two feet into the room before wrapping her in his arms.

Neither of them spoke as Gabe's mouth descended on hers, creating a trail of heat as he slid her dress over her shoulders and down her arms. His lips traced a path along her jaw to the sensitive skin below her ear, his hands moving under her skirt.

Lena reached between them, pulling out his shirt, her fingers loosening each button until it fell open, revealing a light dusting of crisp hair across his chest. Their frantic movements propelled them toward the bedroom, Gabe lifting her, setting her in the middle of the bed, then lowering himself beside her.

"It's almost impossible to keep my hands off you when you're at the Dixie," he breathed against her mouth, working her dress open as her soft moans filled the room.

"Please, Gabe. Don't wait any longer."

"We'll marry."

"No, Gabe, we won't."

"But you said—"

"I know what I said, and I do love you, but I won't marry you."

They'd spent hours making love, whispering their feelings for each other until both lay spent, wrapped in each other's arms. Gabe woke her before dawn. Her words of love and uninhibited response gave him the courage to broach the subject which had plagued him since their first time near the waterfall. Lena's answer stunned him.

"It makes no sense for us to sneak around, trying to hide how we feel. We love each other and I want everyone to know you belong to me and no one else. Marry me, Lena, then there'll be no doubt."

She cupped his face with her hands, pressing a passionate kiss to his lips. "The way we act when you're at the Dixie has made it quite obvious how we feel about each other. We don't have to marry for people to know."

"Their knowing doesn't make it any easier to be with each other. Dashing through the shadows, trying to keep your trips here a secret is ridiculous when we can marry, build a life together." Crossing his arms over his chest, his feet planted shoulder width apart, Gabe stared down at Lena as she laced her shoes and stood to grab her cloak. "We could have a family."

Her body stilled at his last comment, spoken almost in a whisper. They'd talked of how both liked children, envying Dax and Rachel. What she'd never mentioned was her fear of childbirth. Over the years, she'd witnessed many births by the women who worked in their saloons. Even though there were ways to reduce getting pregnant, none were close to reliable, and many babies died. Several of her friends never made it from their bed.

She let out a long breath, knowing there remained hardships from her past which Gabe knew nothing about. Each time she thought of opening up to him, telling him the truth, her fear of him walking away stopped her.

They'd met months before. Although neither had mentioned it until a few weeks ago, each felt an immediate and intense attraction to the other. Over time, they'd become friends, sharing small confidences and plans for the future. In their minds, making love had been an extension of their feelings. It made sense he wanted to marry. She simply hadn't expected it.

"We have time, Gabe. This isn't a decision we must make tonight, is it?" She couldn't quite control the tremble in her voice as her eyes met his. Reaching for him, she gripped his hands, hoping he'd give her the time she needed.

"How long, Lena?"

"How long?"

"How long do you need before you're ready to make a decision?"

She stared at his face, cold and devoid of expression. He was a proud, honorable man, and he loved her. Her insistence on keeping their love hidden went against all his beliefs and chafed his conscience. She knew he'd wait only so long before all the traits that attracted him to her would eat at him until he walked away.

"A month. Give me one month, then you'll have my answer."

He studied her, a look of unrestrained withdrawal coming over his face. "One month. But you'll still share my bed during that time."

She let out a sigh of relief and stepped forward, wrapping her arms around him. "Thank you," she choked out, unable to say more.

Kissing the top of her head, he stepped away, taking her cloak from her arms and wrapping it around her. "We'd better get you back before someone at Suzanne's misses you."

Their timing could not have been worse as they hurried across the silent street to the side door of the boardinghouse. As Gabe reached for the door, it flew open, an angry Nick standing on the other side.

"What the hell is going on here?" The heated intensity of his question had Lena leaning away and into the shelter of Gabe's arms. Nick's irate expression didn't change as he stepped aside. "Go upstairs, Lena. Gabe and I need to talk."

"It's not—"

"Don't even consider telling me it's not what it appears. And yes, I know you're an adult and can make your own decisions. But you're also family, and I take care of what's mine. Now, please, leave Gabe and me to talk."

Gabe tightened his arm around her, then let go. "Go on inside. We'll talk later."

Neither man spoke as Lena disappeared down the hall and up the staircase, glancing once over her shoulder at Gabe. When out of earshot, Nick's hard stare turned on Gabe.

"Don't go blaming Lena for this—"

Gabe stopped when Nick held up his hand. "We'll go to my office in the saloon so no one can hear us," he ground out, walking past Gabe without another word.

Shoving his office door open, he walked in and turned, stepping within inches of Gabe.

"You've taken her to bed."

"Yes." Gabe closed the door, hoping none of the girls upstairs heard Nick's words.

Nick paced away, running a hand through his hair before turning back to Gabe.

"You'll marry her." Nick took a step closer, face reddening as his hands balled at his sides, ready to slam a fist into Gabe's face at any moment.

"I asked her. She said no." Gabe didn't back down. If they were going to come to blows over Lena, so be it.

The anger seemed to bleed out of Nick as he absorbed the words. "She turned you down?" He didn't understand it. He knew she had strong feelings for Gabe, and from what he could see, there was no mistaking his love for her.

"She told me she had no interest in making it legal yet, saying her feelings for me won't change." Gabe backed away, lowering himself into a chair, his expression solemn. "She asked for time." He raised his gaze to Nick. "I don't understand it."

Nick's expression didn't change. It was obvious Lena hadn't shared certain aspects of her life. If Gabe knew of them, he might or he might not understand. You never knew how someone would react to another's secrets and Lena had chosen not to take the chance. From what he'd learned of Gabe,

Nick felt she misjudged him and his tolerance for accepting past actions. He needed to try and reason with her before she lost this chance for happiness.

Slumping into his chair, Nick leaned forward, resting his elbows on the desk. "She's been through a lot, and given her age at the time, made some decisions long ago I don't believe were in her best interests. But they were her decisions to make."

"I'm guessing you're unable to say what these decisions were."

"Unfortunately, Lena prizes her privacy above all else. The fact she didn't say there was no chance she'd marry you gives me hope. I've known her longer and am closer to her than anyone, except her friend, Isabella. I'll tell you this. If there wasn't any hope for the two of you, she would have said so. The fact she asked for time is a good sign." Nick stood, walked around the desk, and leaned his hip against it. "Do you love her?"

"Yes."

"Then I'd say to wait. I believe, given time, she'll make the right choice."

"Perhaps," Gabe answered, although there was little conviction in his voice. "I'll wait, but she'll have to choose at some point. She either loves me enough to build a life with me or she doesn't."

"And if she decides she doesn't?" Nick hoped it wouldn't come to that.

"I'll accept it and move on. Either way, it won't affect our friendship or business relationship. I plan to make my home in Splendor, with or without Lena."

"It's been two nights and he hasn't come in, Nick." Lena's heart sank every time her thoughts turned to the defeated look on Gabe's face when she'd asked for more time. The morning after Nick had caught her returning from Gabe's, he'd sat her down, asking questions about Gabe and what held her back from accepting his proposal. Nick already knew none of her answers would be simple, yet he listened without interrupting, letting her voice the emotions she'd been holding inside for years. Afterwards, he'd let it go with a warning that a man like Gabe wouldn't wait for long.

"It seems he's doing what you asked—giving you time." Nick stood beside her at the bar, the late afternoon sun filtering through the front windows. A few locals had wandered in, looking for ways to entertain themselves on a Friday afternoon. "It's early. He may still come in tonight."

Her chest tightened at the thought he stayed away because of her. Drumming her fingers on the bar, she shifted, keeping her eyes on the swinging doors.

"Neither Suzanne nor Fanny have seen him at the boardinghouse. He must be taking his meals elsewhere."

"If you recall, Gabe has a house with a kitchen." Nick's pointed gaze leveled on her.

Spearing him with a disgusted look, she turned toward the bar, gripping the edge with her hands before signaling Paul.

"What can I get you, Lena?" Paul wiped down the bar as he waited for her answer.

"She'll have a whiskey, same as me."

Lena spun around, a relieved smile greeting Gabe as he stopped inches away.

"Good evening, Gabe." She didn't reach out, waiting for him to make the first move. It didn't take long.

Stepping beside her, he wrapped an arm around her waist, pulling her close, then leaning down. "I've missed you."

His warm breath fanned against the sensitive skin below her ear, sending shivers through her body. She leaned closer, looking up. "I've missed you, too."

Grabbing their full glasses, he nodded toward a nearby table. "Do you have time to have a drink with me?"

"Always."

Gabe didn't smile as she thought he would, his face impassive as they walked to the table. Hoping she hadn't misread his comment about missing her, she sat down, rolling her glass between both hands.

"You haven't been in the last two nights."

He didn't look at her as his gaze wandered around the room, noting the activity at each table. "I had work to finish and needed time to myself."

The growing knot in her stomach began to burn at the same time her throat tightened. Taking a sip of whiskey, she let it flow down her throat, hoping it would calm the fear squeezing her heart.

"I wanted to let you know I'll be gone for a while."

Lena let his comment settle a moment, dread replacing hope. "To Big Pine?" She knew his reasons for going there in the past and hoped that wasn't the purpose for this trip.

He glanced at her, understanding why she asked. "I need to talk with Sheriff Sterling and order some supplies for the new hotel or I wouldn't be making the ride."

"Nothing more?" She hated the way her voice shook.

The corners of his mouth tilted up a little as his gaze raked over her, coming to rest on her eyes. "No, Lena. No other reason." Taking another swallow of whiskey, he leaned back. "Afterwards, I have some other business to take care of. I spoke to Nick about it this morning."

Her eyes widened. Nick hadn't said a word to her about seeing Gabe. Catching her lower lip between her teeth, she nodded. Lena pushed back from the table, knowing she had to get control of the emotions ripping through her.

"Will you leave tomorrow?"

"At first light." He didn't like the distressed look on her face, but he had some things to figure out and needed distance to do it.

"All right." Standing, she cast a wary look at him, debating her next question. "Should I come to your place tonight?"

His jaw tightened as he stood and faced her. "As much as I want you, given the way things are, I think it best we keep our distance, at least until you make a decision."

"The last we spoke, you still wanted me to share your bed. Have you changed your mind about us?"

He wanted to reach out, wrap his arms around her, and tell her not to worry, but he held back. "No. I just had time to think it through and believe it's better to stay away from each other until our future is settled. Assuming we have one."

"I see."

"If you need anything, Cash knows how to get a message to me." He leaned down, brushing his lips across her cheek. "I'd better go."

"Be safe, Gabe," was all she could get out before he walked out the doors.

"You should've told me he came to talk to you." Lena led the way into the dining room the following morning, finding a table in the corner. She had gotten little sleep the night before, wanting to throw off the covers, dress, and go to Gabe more than once. Each time, pride and common sense won out.

"I figured he'd tell you eventually. It's a pretty smart move on his part. He's handling some business in Big Pine while giving you what you want—time to make a decision without pressure from him."

"He isn't just going to Big Pine."

"I know. He told me he had other business to attend to." Gabe had said not to expect him back for at least a week, maybe longer, although he didn't share his plans. Nick tilted his head and shrugged. "Gabe's a grown man, Lena. He has no obligation to tell us his plans, the same as you don't need to confide in him. Everyone has their secrets, right?"

She squirmed in her chair, clasping her hands in her lap. "If he trusted me, he'd…" Her voice trailed off as she realized what she'd almost said.

"What?" he asked, his voice gentle.

Her lips twisted into a wry smile as so much became clear. "You believe I can trust him, don't you?"

"Yes, I do, and not only as a business partner. If he loves you, he'll understand your past. If he doesn't, then he's not the one for you."

She groaned, burying her face in her hands. "I've made a horrible mistake pushing him away, haven't I?"

"On the contrary. I think you and Gabe have made the right decision. If you're sure about how you feel, it won't change before he returns. You'll only be more certain of your choice." He reached across the table, squeezing her hand. "I'm not pushing you to tell him of your past, Lena. I know how closed you are about it. All I'm saying is I think you can trust him."

Big Pine

"I don't have to tell you how appreciative we are that you brought the money back, Gabe. Some men wouldn't have made the effort." Sheriff Sterling retied the last of the money bags and tossed it next to the others. He still couldn't quite believe the outlaws had kept all the stolen money in their saddlebags.

"It's part of the job, and I'm glad to do it. As I said, we dropped five of them. We found enough information on a couple to send a telegram to their

241

next of kin." Gabe thought again of Bobby, the youngest of the group, and wondered what would drive someone to join an outlaw gang. According to Beau, he knew the killing of the young man continued to haunt Cash. Looking into a man's eyes, then having to pull the trigger could take its toll on a man. "Did you ever get a good count of how many were in the gang?"

"Could've been more. We know there were five who robbed the bank here, the same number as tried to rob yours. In my mind, it's unlikely others are hiding out somewhere." He clasped Gabe on the shoulder. "I think you got them all. You want to come with me to the bank to turn this in?"

"You go ahead. I'm in need of a bath, food, and a bed. I have some more business to take care of before taking off."

Starting before dawn, it had taken Gabe all day to reach Big Pine. With the discovery of gold, the territorial capital had grown rapidly, now boasting a population of at least six times that of Splendor. The railroad planned a route through the town within the next couple years, which would mean more settlers. Many, Gabe believed, would make their way on to Splendor.

Getting an early start on building the hotel and accepting Nick's offer to partner in expanding the boardinghouse appeared to be smart decisions. It had taken a little persuasion, but Nick convinced

Suzanne to see the benefits of all of them working together. Tomorrow, Gabe would order supplies and make arrangements for men to haul the material to Splendor while he continued his journey.

Within an hour, he sat at a table in the most expensive restaurant in town, slicing into a steak cooked to perfection. He'd dressed for the occasion and couldn't mistake the looks of appreciation from several female patrons. The entire evening had been orchestrated in an attempt to pull his thoughts away from Lena and reexamine activities he'd enjoyed before the war. He understood her uncertainty about them. Perhaps he had moved too fast in asking her to marry. Their time apart would provide both with an opportunity to think through their feelings without the emotions when together. He'd ride back into Splendor with either a firm conviction she was the one or a certainty she wasn't.

"More wine, sir?"

Gabe glanced up and nodded, watching as the waiter poured red wine from a winery his Uncle James had introduced him to before the war. Great Western Winery had been started by a dear friend of his uncle's in the western part of New York. Gabe had smiled, not hesitating to order the wine when the waiter recommended it. Wine had never been his drink of choice. Tonight, however, was devoted to his past.

The sound of laughter across the room had him thinking of Dolly. He'd always been drawn to her uninhibited enjoyment of life, even as she struggled to make a living each day. Her injuries had healed and she'd returned to work, but that didn't erase the scars of the attack, both physical and mental. He'd ridden to the Devil Dancer mine the following day, looking for Pennington. The miners told him he and Carlyle had left the day before to check their claims to the north and south. They had no idea when the two would return. Gabe knew he'd have to find the man and warn him off, even if Dolly refused to press charges.

He picked up his glass, intending to return to his meal, when the maître d approached, followed by a woman he didn't recognize. Setting his glass down, he stood as they stopped by his table.

"I do apologize for the intrusion, sir, but Mrs. Iverson believes she recognizes you as an old friend."

Gabe stared into her face, his gaze moving to her eyes—green, the color of a bright emerald. His heart jolted at the memory.

"Caro," he breathed out, stepping forward and offering her a warm smile.

"Oh my. No one has called me that in years." Caroline Iverson set her hand on Gabe's arm. "Hello, Gabriel. I thought I recognized you, even after all these years."

Gabe nodded to the maître d, then offered her a chair.

"It's been…"

"Since before the war." Her laugh was rich, sensual, the same as he remembered when they knew each other in New York. She glanced at his plate. "Please, eat your meal."

"And you?"

"I've ordered. The waiter will bring it here, assuming it's all right."

"Of course it is." Gabe felt his chest constrict, recalling their youthful infatuation for each other. They'd never courted. He intended to start once he returned from the war. Then he received a letter from his mother telling him of Caroline's pending marriage. Gabe remembered thinking it had been for the best as the war had changed him in ways he couldn't have imagined before he left.

She adjusted her skirt, then squared her shoulders. "You've changed little since you left for the war. Older, maybe wiser, but still strikingly handsome."

He snorted out a laugh as the waiter set down her meal. "Older, yes. Wiser? I'm not so certain. I'll take the handsome part, though. A man can never receive enough compliments."

Caroline laughed, putting a hand over her mouth as others turned to stare. "Quite so, Gabriel."

Gabriel, he thought. No one, except family or close friends, ever called him by his given name. "And you, Caro, have grown into a stunning beauty."

She picked up her wine glass, tipping it toward him. "Well, here's to two older, perhaps wiser, and unapologetically handsome people sharing a meal in an inauspicious frontier town."

Gabe couldn't help his laughter as he touched her glass and sipped the wine. They ate in silence for several minutes, each lost in their own thoughts.

"Tell me what brings you to Big Pine." Gabe cut another slice of meat, slipping it into his mouth.

Her face clouded as she took another sip from her glass, then set it on the table. "It's a long story."

"I have time if you do." He sat back, crossing his arms.

"You already know I married David Iverson."

"Yes, Mother sent a letter to inform me." Gabe could still remember how he felt at the news—sorry for the loss of her affection, yet not as devastated as he would have thought. His feelings for her had always been conflicted, which was why he'd never made a claim on her. David had been a friend, a good man who'd chosen to stay out of the war.

Caro saw something pass over his face before Gabe concealed it. Swallowing, she continued, her voice dropping to almost a whisper. "You and I...well...we never courted and nothing had ever been formalized. When I didn't get an answer to my letters…"

Gabe leaned forward, reaching across the table to wrap his hand around hers, offering her whatever comfort he could. "It was my fault, Caro. I should've written, let you know my feelings. But the war changed everything. As the days passed, I couldn't find any trace of the person I was before, the one you knew. I may look the same, but inside, I'm not. I'm glad you married David. He's a good man." He let go, a hint of regret in his tone.

"He's dead." Her voice broke on the words. "Almost three years ago. Business required he travel to Europe." She glanced up. "I was pregnant and David insisted on going alone. He never returned."

"Cholera?" Gabe asked. The epidemic in Europe, Africa, and parts of North America continued, with word of the deaths spreading, even into the territories.

"Yes. I never saw him again."

"I'm so sorry, Caro."

"His parents had David's body returned, but it took months."

"And the baby?" Gabe asked, already seeing the answer by the pain in her eyes.

"I lost him, too." She looked up, trying to control her emotions, not wanting to embarrass herself in front of others in the restaurant. "Stillborn."

Gabe watched as her body began to tremble. "Come on. Let's take a walk."

He led her down the street at a slow pace, putting an arm around her and pulling her close as she shook with quiet sobs. He wondered if she had ever let herself grieve the deaths of both her husband and unborn child. From what he remembered of her, always strong and determined, it was doubtful.

"We'll go to my hotel. They have a small café where we can sit, have some coffee."

She leaned away, nodding. "I'm sorry, Gabriel. I didn't intend to cry all over you."

"Caro, never apologize for showing your feelings. I wish I had been there for you."

"No, no. You had your own life, and I needed to learn to live on my own." A bitter chuckle escaped her lips. "I feel as if I've done quite well—until tonight."

Leading her to a table, Gabe signaled for two coffees. "Are your parents still in New York?"

"They are. That's why I had to leave. Too many memories, people always asking how I was doing, and Mother pushing me to socialize, meet someone new." She took a deep breath. "It all became too much."

"You didn't make the trip out here alone, did you?" He couldn't hide the surprise in his tone. As independent as Caro had always been, he still couldn't see her traveling this far from home without an escort.

"Yes, I did." Straightening in her chair, she glared at Gabe, daring him to criticize her decision.

"And where are you headed? You do have a destination in mind, right?" Irritation flashed through him at the danger she'd already put herself in.

She picked up her cup, taking a sip, then reached for the sugar. Stirring, Caro took a breath, calming the tension she felt at being questioned.

"Caro?"

"No."

Placing his arms on the table and leaning forward, he speared her with a hard stare. "No?"

Clearing her throat, Caro moistened her lips, focusing her gaze on his. "No, I have no destination in mind, although I have heard San Francisco is interesting."

Unable to control himself, Gabe mumbled a curse, then signaled the waiter. "A whiskey and a sherry." Turning his attention back to Caro, he sat back and crossed his arms. "And just how do you expect to get to San Francisco?"

"I didn't say San Francisco was my final destination. I said I've heard it's interesting."

Pinching the bridge of his nose, he watched as she shifted in her chair. "Caro, are you meeting someone along the way, or are you traveling completely alone?"

"I already told you. I'm making this journey alone."

"And your parents let you leave?" From what he remembered, he couldn't believe they'd allow it.

"I left before they could stop me." Seeing Gabe's brows knit together, she clasped her hands, resting them on the table. "Listen, Gabriel. I'm a widow of means. I don't need anyone's permission to travel, and money is no problem. I'm glad we came across each other after all these years, but if all you're going to do is criticize my decisions, I believe we should say goodnight." She pushed back from the table, intending to leave.

He reached over and touched her arm. "Don't leave, Caro. Please."

"All right, but only if you act like the friend you used to be and not my guardian."

He chuckled, even though he found no humor in her situation. "I'm sorry if that's how I sound, but I know the dangers you face. To be blunt, I can't believe you've made it this far without incident."

"Up until this last part of my trip, I've traveled by train." Finishing her coffee, Caro set the cup down, then reached for her reticule. "I'm not certain what inspired me to come to Big Pine, except the conductor told me it's the territorial capital. When I asked, he arranged for me to continue by stage. I thought I'd stay a few days, then decide where to go next."

"Where are you staying?"

"Here, at the hotel."

"Good." Offering his arm, he escorted her up the stairs. "We'll meet for breakfast, then I'll show you the town. That is, if you'll allow me."

"Thank you, Gabriel. I would love to have you show me around." Stopping at her room, she looked up at him. "And I'd like to hear all about what you've been doing since coming west."

Chapter Sixteen

Stretched out on his bed, arms behind his head, Gabe stared at the ceiling, still unable to sleep hours after walking Caro to her room. He hadn't lied. She'd grown even more beautiful over the years. Rather than the tragedies making her bitter, she faced her future straight on, taking a journey few women of her background would consider.

What he couldn't understand was how his feelings for her had changed. They'd both made other choices—she falling in love with a successful, prominent businessman, and he shunning his social status and wealth to travel west. Yet, here they both were, years later, single with nothing holding them back from trying to reclaim what they'd started before the war.

Nothing except his love for Lena. Caro walking back into his life intensified, instead of diminished, his desire to marry Lena. Three hours before, he sat alone, debating the wisdom of his decision to ask her to be his wife. He no longer doubted his actions.

Of course, he had no reason to believe Caro wanted more than friendship. Closing his eyes, he draped an arm over them, a plan forming in his mind. If Caro wanted to find a new life, discover a world far removed from the one she'd left, he knew the perfect place.

Splendor

"Lena, come quick." Nick pounded on her door, knowing she'd returned to her room after breakfast to write a letter to Isabella. "Lena?"

"What in the world, Nick? I bet everyone in the place can hear you."

Ignoring her, he reached around her, picking up her coat and taking her arm. "You're not going to believe who just got off the stage."

She couldn't imagine anyone causing Nick to act this excited, except...

"They're here." She faltered at the stop of the stairs, her hand going to her throat.

"Yes. They just arrived."

Lena turned, intending to retreat back to her room, but Nick grabbed her arm. "Where are you going?"

"I'm not ready for this. I need more time..."

Turning her to face him, he settled his hands on each shoulder. "You are more than ready. It's been too long and now they've come to you."

She nodded. "How do I look?"

"Beautiful, as always. Now, let's not keep them waiting."

Lena spotted them the moment she stepped outside. Isabella spoke with Cash and Noah as the stage driver unloaded their bags. Jackson, clasping her hand in a tight grip, gazed up at the two tall men, his back to Lena.

Taking a steadying breath, she let Nick guide her to within a few feet.

"Isabella?"

She turned at Lena's voice, a broad smile lighting her face. "Lena!" Dropping Jackson's hand, Isabella ran to her with open arms. They clung together a few moments before pulling back. That's when Lena's gaze turned to the young boy standing alone, ramrod straight, hesitation on his face. Lena dropped to her knees and opened her arms wide.

"Mother!" Jackson closed the distance in seconds, clinging to Lena with every bit of strength he had. "Mother, Aunt Isabella told me you'd be here, but..." His words trailed off as a sob escaped.

"I'm here, darling, and we'll never be apart again."

Jackson's grip tightened, as if he never intended to let go. She knew how he felt.

"I missed you." His sobs quieted as he nestled his head against her neck.

"I've missed you, too. Oh, how I've missed you." Placing kisses on his forehead and cheeks, she pulled back to look at him. "You've grown so much. Isabella tells me you're the smartest one in your class."

"I believe I am, Mother." His solemn words cut through her. She'd missed so much, but no longer.

"Come on. It's time for you to say hello to Uncle Nick."

Cash and Noah stood several feet away, both stunned, their jaws open, listening to the exchange.

"Jesus," Cash mumbled, stopping himself before he finished. "Do you think Gabe has any idea?"

"None." Noah crossed his arms, unable to move his feet as the reality of what they'd heard became real.

Big Pine

"This is a lovely town, Gabe, and larger than I anticipated." Caro clung to his arm as they made their way around several blocks of stores, hotels, and homes.

"It's still growing. The gold mines are still producing and ranchers are moving in, taking as much land as they can afford to work."

They'd spent breakfast talking about his job as sheriff, surprising her with the news Noah Brandt had married. He didn't mention the pregnancy, honoring Noah's request that he and Abby make the announcement together.

When Caro asked if he'd met anyone, Gabe didn't hesitate telling her about Lena and his proposal of marriage. Instead of showing any disappointment, she'd grabbed his hand, offering sincere congratulations.

"When do you intend to ride back?"

"I have some business to finish here, then I'll go back. Why don't you come with me? You have no firm plans, no one expecting you, and I know Noah would be pleased to see you. And I'll introduce you to Lena." Gabe had intended to use Luke Pelletier's original cabin after leaving Big Pine. He, Dax, and Luke had business to discuss, and using the cabin would give him the extra distance from Lena they both needed. If Caro decided to accompany him to Splendor, he'd get her settled, then ride on to the Pelletier ranch.

Eyes widening, Caro pursed her lips. "After we parted last night, I'd made the decision to travel on to San Francisco. I hadn't considered going to Splendor."

"San Francisco will always be there. You may only have this one chance to pass through my town, see Noah, and meet the woman I hope to spend my life with."

The last got her attention. She'd like to see who'd captured Gabe's heart. If he'd responded to her letters, shown an inclination to return to her after the war, Caro would have waited. But he hadn't.

She'd fallen in love with David and never regretted her decision for an instant. Life now dictated she start over, seeking a new place to find peace, and perhaps love. Although she'd never felt oppressed in her marriage as some women did, the new sense of freedom allowed her choices never before available. Splendor could be one of those choices.

"All right, Gabriel. I'll accompany you to Splendor and meet your lady before traveling west."

"You won't regret it. Now, let's find a wagon and—"

"Oh no. I'd much prefer a horse."

Gabe had forgotten her skills as a horsewoman, besting most men when challenged to a race. An activity he felt quite certain never reached her parents' ears.

"Most women out here don't ride sidesaddle."

"I've ridden astride before." Her eyes filled with excitement.

"The supplies I'm ordering will be delivered by wagon. We'll arrange to have your trunks included. I need two days to finish my business before heading back. Will that suit?"

"Yes." Caro gripped his arm and squeezed. "I'm so glad you made the offer."

Gabe smirked. "I hope you feel that same way after being in the saddle for a full day."

Rance Stillwell sat across the desk from Amos Henderson, staring into the older man's eyes.

"It's a fair offer, Henderson." Before their meeting, he'd looked around the Wild Rose, surprised at the amount Carlyle and Pennington offered for what he considered a dump, especially compared to the Dixie. "You'll never get as much from anyone else." Stillwell crossed his arms and leaned back in his chair, making certain the butts of his twin Colt revolvers were in plain sight.

Never one to be intimidated, Amos glanced at the guns. He had one other offer. Neither party knew about the other, and for now, he intended to keep it that way. There would be more to his decision than the amount of the offer.

"I understand them wanting a decision right away, but I need more time."

"How much time?" Stillwell's face didn't change expression, other than hardening an almost imperceptible amount.

"A week, maybe two. I've got a lot to think about." Amos rested his arms on the table, clasping his hands together.

"I'm afraid that won't work. My bosses want a decision when I return to the mine, and I'm not waiting around two weeks." Stillwell stood, stone cold eyes locking with Amos'. "I'll give you three days. Let me give you some advice. Take their offer, Henderson. Life will be much easier for you and your women if you do."

Amos pushed from his desk and stood, his nostrils flaring at the unmistakable threat. "You'll have my decision when I'm damn good and ready to give it to you. Now get out."

"I'll leave for now. Like I said before, I'll return in three days and expect you'll give me the decision my bosses want."

The smirk on Stillwell's face almost had Amos rounding the desk. Instead, he watched the man's retreating back as he left the office, closing the door with a firm click. He'd been hesitant to accept either offer, taking his time. It appeared his time was up.

"Tell me again how old you are, Jackson." Suzanne sat at the table in the kitchen, staring at the young boy sitting across from her, drinking hot cocoa. Fanny glanced over her shoulder from her spot in front of the stove.

"Six, but Aunt Isabella says I act more like twenty." His serious expression made both her and Fanny smile. He had clear blue eyes and dark hair, the same as his mother. *The fair complexion must come from his father*, she decided, wondering about the man.

"Tell me what you like to do?"

"Uncle Arnott used to take me fishing and riding." The sadness in his voice at the death of Isabella's husband pained Suzanne. Isabella hadn't mentioned it to Lena until arriving in Splendor. She'd made the decision within days of Arnott's death, packing up what they needed and taking the train west. Their servants would keep the house going until she returned to her life in Philadelphia.

"With winter coming, it's a little cold for fishing, but I'm certain your Uncle Nick would still take you. And there are plenty of horses available for a skilled horseman such as yourself."

Jackson beamed at Suzanne's praise, then returned his concentration to the half-full cup.

"There you are." Lena took a seat next to her son. "Aunt Isabella is a little tired from the journey. She's taking a nap in my room. If it's all right with you, Suzanne, I thought she and I could share my bed, and Jackson could stay with Nick until we find accommodations." The whole town knew rooms were at a premium and every house had been taken.

"Of course I don't mind. It may be a while until a place opens up in town. I hear people are taking houses as fast as they're built."

"Why don't you ask Luke and Ginny Pelletier?" Fanny asked. "They have that big house with lots of room. It's not too far from town, and Mary is close to Jackson's age."

"That's a wonderful idea. Would you like to take a ride to see some friends today, Jackson? They have a large ranch with lots of horses and cattle."

A grin split his face as he nodded at his mother.

"Good. I'll go speak with Mr. Brandt right now. Would you like to come along?" Jackson jumped out of his chair as Lena stood. "Will you let Isabella know where we've gone?"

"Of course," Suzanne answered. "And don't worry about beds here. We'll figure it out."

Willie Carlyle studied the map of their claims. The amount of ore the men hauled out exceeded his expectations, yet it could play out at any time. There were no guarantees on the longevity of a vein. He and Thomas had groups of men panning the streams, seeking placer deposits that could turn into lucrative mines. He thought the flow of men wandering into their camp seeking work would slow, but if anything, the number increased each day.

"How many have you turned away today?" Tommy slipped a slim cheroot from his pocket and lit it as he watched the men at work.

"Not many. Three or four. I send them on to Splendor where there's some building going on."

"Heard some news." Tommy blew smoke into the air, watching it curl and spread as it disappeared.

"What did you hear?" Willie pushed the papers away and stood, pacing to within a few feet of Tommy.

"A woman and child arrived on the stage." Tommy crushed the cheroot under his boot.

"And?"

"The boy ran up to your lady friend, Magdalena Campanel, and called her mother."

Willie's eyes widened, his expression unreadable as he absorbed each word. He'd known about the boy from the time Lena gave birth to him. He also knew Jackson was his son, making certain Lena was aware of this knowledge. It never occurred to him to make an offer of marriage any more than he thought of providing money for the boy's support. If Lena had been stupid enough to keep the child, he figured it became her responsibility to feed and clothe him.

"Jackson."

Willie turned a bewildered look to Tommy.

"The boy's name is Jackson, according to one of our men who saw the pair arrive. They're staying at the boardinghouse."

Willie had thought about Lena a lot since learning she and Nick owned the Dixie. From the first time he saw her in New Orleans, he knew he had to have her. The timing had coincided with easy access to their safe and her jewelry, but he'd taken her anyway, knowing he'd be gone by the time she awoke the following morning. He'd corresponded with her over the years, just to make certain she knew he had easy access to her and the boy whenever he wanted. Twice, he'd watched from a distance as she read one of his letters, her body shaking as fear flashed across her face. His elation at her distress fueled his desire to continue the subtle torture. The letters to her continued until he'd become otherwise occupied in San Francisco, losing track of both Lena and Nick.

Although he wouldn't breathe a word to Tommy, the appearance of the boy meant it could all begin again. The time had come for him to marry and settle down. A sleepy frontier town such as Splendor seemed the perfect place. A marriage would produce the appearance of propriety, while his wealth would afford him the means to travel, take a mistress when he wanted, yet still have a strong hand in the growth of the town. Power and respect were what he craved, and marriage to a woman who already had roots in Splendor would help him achieve those goals. If needed, he'd use the boy as leverage.

"I believe it's time I made a trip to town and take a look at the boy myself, perhaps renew my friendship with Miss Campanel."

Tommy hesitated, not liking the almost feral look on Willie's face. "As I recall, the last time you tried to renew your friendship with the woman, the deputy intervened on her behalf. From her response, I don't believe Miss Campanel has any intention of renewing anything."

"Trust me. She can be persuaded with the right kind of encouragement." Which was what Willie planned to provide.

"It would be wonderful to have you, your friend, and Jackson stay here. We have lots of room, and Mary would love someone to play with. Jackson can go with her to school, if that's what you want." Ginny Pelletier had returned from a day at Dax and Rachel's house to find Lena and Jackson waiting on the front porch.

As Jackson and Mary ran into the barn to check on a new calf, Lena explained how Isabella and Jackson arrived in Splendor, and their need for a place to stay.

"I know it will come as a shock to most that Jackson is my son, but it's time he lived with me and not Isabella."

"Of course he should be with you. No matter how wonderful Isabella has been, no one can take the place of a child's mother." Ginny's brows drew together as she pondered what she wanted to say. "You don't need to tell me or anyone why Jackson hasn't been with you. I'm sure you have good reasons for making that decision. Remember, Lena, you have friends in Splendor. If you need anything or just want to talk, Rachel and I are here for you."

Lena had never lived in a town like Splendor. She had never been in a place where people accepted each other without judgement, where they reached out to help their neighbors without expectations of something in return. Swiping at tears pooling in her eyes, she took a relieved breath.

"Thank you, Ginny. You don't know how much your friendship means to me."

Big Pine

"Are you comfortable, Caro?" Gabe swung up on Blackheart, his gaze moving over her to make certain nothing looked amiss.

"Yes, quite comfortable."

"If the weather holds steady, we should make it to Splendor by tonight."

"And if it doesn't?" She looked up into a sky sprinkled with menacing clouds, a huge thunderhead forming in the east.

"We'll find a place to bed down. Other than weather and Indians, we should have an easy trip."

"Indians," she gasped. "Is that truly a possibility?"

"I told you before, anything can happen out here." During the last few months, they'd had a few incidences with one local tribe, but no one had been killed. Before that, a group of renegades had haunted the trail between Big Pine and Splendor, making travel more treacherous. Gabe heard they'd moved north.

Placing a hand to her stomach, she nodded. "Well, I'm not changing my mind. Let's go."

Two hours into the ride, the clouds broke loose, pummeling them with rain. He'd been watching for it, steering them close to the shelter of a stand of cedars. They weren't the best cover, but it was better than being caught in the open.

"It seems to be passing quickly."

"There's still the mass of black clouds moving in from the east." Caro slipped on the duster Gabe had tied behind her saddle. Heavy and warm, it kept the chill away, even if the rain did soak through.

"After this one moves on, we'll go as far as we can, then find shelter for the night. There's a place several miles ahead with a large rock formation and trees. If we have to, we'll bed down there."

"While we're waiting, tell me more about Splendor and why you stayed." She pulled the duster tight as she leaned against the trunk of a tree.

"I hadn't planned to stay. After Noah and I arrived the first time, he stayed and started his business while I moved on. I received word they needed help, so I rode back, again not intending to stay. They'd lost their sheriff months before. All efforts to find a replacement had failed, so I took the job on a temporary basis."

"How long is temporary?"

He let out a short chuckle. "Longer than I'd first thought. Now that I'm partnering in the hotel, I plan to stay."

"Even if you don't marry?" Caro remembered how women had flocked to Gabe in their youth. He'd always seemed oblivious to their attentions until he'd met her. Even then, they never truly courted, so in her mind, his interest had never been too serious. To her knowledge, no other woman, besides Lena, had gotten to him in such a deep way.

"Honestly, I don't know."

Within minutes, the rain ceased and they were back on the trail, riding at a faster pace than when they'd started. Caro's question about whether he'd stay in Splendor if Lena refused his proposal plagued him. He wanted her, but it didn't change the fact he knew she held secrets. Ones she felt would impact his feelings enough for him to change his mind. Whatever they were, he doubted they would be as significant as she believed. The fact she didn't trust him enough to be honest bothered him a great deal. He couldn't abide falsehoods and secrets.

The longer they rode, the stronger his belief to get Caro settled, then continue to the Pelletier ranch and finish the last part of his time away. Lena needed to decide whether she trusted him or not. If she didn't, he knew they'd never have a future.

Chapter Seventeen

"What will you tell him when he returns?" Isabella asked as she and Lena sat on the front porch of Luke and Ginny's home, sipping tea, watching Mary and Jackson play. Hank and Bernice had taken the wagon into town earlier, and Ginny had left to help with Patrick, leaving them to settle in.

"The truth, which is what I should have done before he left. He deserves to know about Jackson and why you've been raising him."

"Keeping him safe, you mean." Isabella set down her cup and took Lena's hand. "I wish you'd told me before about Willie being in Splendor. I never would've brought Jackson here if I knew he might still be in danger. Arnott dying came as such a shock, I suppose I wasn't thinking too clearly when I made the decision." She sat back, resting her hands in her lap. "The doctor told me to prepare myself. I always knew he had a poor heart, and at twenty-five years older than me, we both thought he'd likely pass before I did. Too bad knowing didn't make his death any easier."

Lena's heart twisted at the pain on Isabella's face. "You made the right choice. It's time Jackson lived with me."

"And Willie?"

"He'd be foolish to try anything here. Unlike in the other towns we've lived, Nick and I have made friends here, people who will help us if he tries his shenanigans. Then there's Gabe."

"I do suppose marrying the sheriff does have its advantages."

"If he still wants me once I tell him about Jackson and Willie." She stood, moving to the railing on the porch to get a better view of the two riders approaching. Fear pooled in the pit of her stomach as she raced down the steps toward Jackson and Mary. "Go inside, both of you. Now." Both children noted her stern voice and moved at once, running to do as she asked.

"What is it, Lena?" Isabella closed the door firmly behind the children, telling them to stay inside, then moved next to Lena at the edge of the porch.

"It's Willie and his partner, Thomas Pennington." Her voice shook as she worked to keep her panic under control.

Isabella's hand flew to her throat. "How did he find us?"

"It doesn't matter. He's here now. It's time I dealt with him and put an end to his intimidation and threats." Crossing her arms, Lena planted her feet and straightened her spine. She would not let Willie bully her anymore. Keeping silent as the two men reined up their horses, she glanced behind her to see two small faces staring out the window.

"Good morning, ladies." Willie tipped his hat, intending to dismount.

"Don't even consider staying, Willie. You and your friend aren't welcome here."

"That's not too hospitable of you given how close we used to be." Willie's sneer caused her to take a step back in disgust.

"Your memory seems to be quite different than mine." A chill ripped through her at the way his gaze raked over her, making her feel dirty and vulnerable. Lifting her chin, she fought her growing unease.

"I can't understand the hatred you have for me when we share something important to both of us." He leaned forward, his penetrating stare leaving no doubt of his meaning.

"We share nothing. Don't for a minute believe we do." Lena glanced past the barn to the bunkhouse to see Luke's foreman, Dirk Masters, walking toward them, shotgun in hand.

"Miss Campanel." He nodded before stepping in front of Willie's horse. "Can I help you gentlemen?"

Willie straightened in the saddle, his hand moving to the butt of his gun.

"I wouldn't do that, mister." Dirk raised the shotgun enough to signal his intentions. "These men bothering you, Miss Campanel?"

"As a matter of fact, Mr. Masters, I've asked them to leave."

Willie brought his hand back up to rest on the saddle horn, then turned toward Tommy. "Appears it's time we leave." Shifting, he fixed his gaze on Lena. "This isn't over. I want what's mine and I'll do what's necessary to get it."

"There's nothing for you here, Willie. Not now, not ever. Go back to your mines, make your money, and leave us alone."

"I'll do as you ask, but don't think this is over."

Dirk didn't lower the shotgun until the men were a good distance away. Turning toward the women, he walked up the steps, noticing Lena's body beginning to shake.

"You all right, Miss Campanel?" He leaned the gun against the post.

"Yes, I'll be fine. Thank you for coming when you did." She continued to watch as Willie and Tommy disappeared around a bend.

"Good thing I was still around. It didn't take much for me to see you didn't want him here. Who are they?"

"Willie Carlyle and Thomas Pennington, owners of the Devil Dancer mine." Lena clasped her hands on the porch rail, letting the last waves of panic pass through her body.

"What does he want with you?" Dirk removed his hat, holding the brim with both hands.

"We have a history...and it's not a good one."

"Forget about her, Willie. She and the boy will cause you nothing but trouble. Who are they to you, anyway?"

Willie sat at a table in the Rose, using whiskey to stall his swelling anger. "You already know my intentions with the woman. The boy? He's my son."

"What the hell are you talking about? You've never said a word about a son."

"There's been no reason to talk about him until now." Pouring another glass, he rested his arms on the table. "If these mines keep going, we'll be the wealthiest citizens in this town, able to do whatever we want."

"What does that have to do with the woman and boy?" Tommy didn't know if the drink or his anger produced such unreasonable thoughts.

"After the Pelletier women and Suzanne Briar, Lena is the most powerful woman in the town. Marrying her would put me right at the top with the men who stand to run it."

Tommy sipped his drink, not understanding his logic or the sick gleam in Willie's eyes. "How do you figure marrying a saloon girl helps you? Seems to me the town would look down on any man who married a woman of her background."

"That's where you're wrong. From what I've learned, the town sees her as a successful woman, even if not all of them approve of her business. And Nick's made it clear her job isn't the same as the other girls. With the arrival of the boy, I can do the right thing."

"And what's that?"

"Marry her. She knows I'll spread word he's my son. Lena won't want the stigma of being an unwed mother. She'll marry me to protect the boy and her reputation."

"Make her an honest woman in the eyes of the town," Tommy mumbled, staring across the room at Dolly. He'd enjoyed her company a couple weeks before, even though she had to be persuaded to do what he asked. Unfortunately, he hadn't been able to see her again. He needed to rectify that, and soon.

"Do you see a problem with that?" Willie's voice rose

Tommy looked at him. "Yes. I don't understand how it helps you."

"I've decided to make Splendor my home. It would be unseemly to have my ex-lover and bastard son roaming about, causing talk."

"You'll blackmail her?"

"Blackmail is a strong word. I believe with the proper persuasion, she'll make the right decision. I've decided to stay in town a few more days. She has to return from the Pelletier's at some point. When she does, I'm certain Lena will make time to speak with me."

"We'll need to bed down here tonight. There isn't any chance we'll outrun the storm following us." Gabe slid from his horse, then helped Caro from hers. It had been a long day in the saddle, with three extra stops due to weather. He knew she must be sore and tired.

"What can I do?" Slipping out of her duster, she shook it out, then hung it on a branch to dry out.

"Help me gather wood. I'll start a fire while you lay out the bedrolls."

The wind kicked up a little as Gabe lit the leaves and sticks. One at a time, he laid larger branches on top. Within a short time, he had a passable fire to keep them from getting too chilled. At least the rain held up until he'd erected a wedge tent where they could sit and eat their meal. Caro pulled a short coat from her saddlebag, pulled it on, then slipped the duster over it. She'd yet to utter one word of complaint about their journey.

"This isn't so bad." Caro took a bite of the hard biscuit, then held it up in the air to inspect it. "Too bad we have no jam." After taking a sip of water, she bit into the dried beef Gabe had given her. "Where do we sleep?"

Gabe looked at the walls of the tent he'd used during the war. "This is the only shelter I brought. We can share it or I can sleep outside."

"Don't be ridiculous. Of course we'll share the tent." Her eyes twinkled as she took another sip of water. "I doubt your fiancée would prefer you come back ill."

Gabe snorted at the reference to Lena already accepting his proposal. "The marriage part is still unsettled between us, but I'll definitely accept the offer to share the tent."

Within an hour, the wind roared, pelting the tent with rain and hail. Gabe could hear Caro pulling her clothing and blankets tight. Glancing over, he could see her body shake as the chill penetrated the layers. Throwing off his blanket and lifting hers, he moved to her, pulling Caro's back against his chest, then covering them again with the blankets.

Lowering his head, he spoke into her ear. "I hope I can trust you not to compromise me."

"I wouldn't even consider it, Gabriel," she replied, her voice shuddering from the cold.

Chuckling, he relaxed. Within minutes, they both drifted off to sleep.

"Do I *have* to go to school with Mary, Mother?" Looking miserable, Jackson picked at his breakfast of eggs and bacon.

"It would be good for you to meet more children since you'll be staying in Splendor with me." She understood his concern. Nick had been the one to escort her to school in New Orleans because she'd been too frightened to go alone—although for different reasons than Jackson. "Mary knows all the children and will make certain you meet the others."

He took an exaggerated breath, letting it out at a slow rate. "All right. But I want them to call me Jack and not Jackson."

Lena glanced at Isabella and Ginny, who both hid their amused expressions.

"And why is that, sweetheart?"

"The boys at my last school teased me, saying I was named after a Confederate general." He lowered his eyes to his almost full plate.

"I see." Lena could understand how children raised in a Union city would make that conclusion, although it wasn't true. "You were named after a good friend of Uncle Nick's and mine, not General Jackson. However, I can see the confusion. If that's what you want, we will all start calling you Jack."

His eyes lit up. "Yes! That would be wonderful, Mother." He attacked the rest of his breakfast with a new eagerness.

"Mary, do you understand what Jackson...Jack is asking of you?" Ginny asked, glancing at her sister.

"Yes. He doesn't like Jackson. I don't, either. From now on, I'll call him Jack, and I'll tell everybody else his name is Jack." Finishing her hotcake, she slid from the table.

"Mary?" Ginny questioned, raising her eyebrows.

"Oh, sorry." She jumped back on her chair. "May I be excused now, please?"

"Me, too?" Jack added.

"Yes, you are both excused. We'll leave for school in a few minutes," Ginny answered, then stood.

"I'll take them today, Ginny. I'd like to speak with Miss Murton about our circumstances." Neither Ginny nor Isabella had to question her concern. Children could be quite harsh to others whose mother had never married. "May I borrow a wagon?"

"It's already outside. One of the men always gets it ready each morning that Mary has school." Ginny sighed. "Luke has told me more than once that Mary is quite capable of riding to school on her horse, but I'm just not ready for that. Margaret, Selina, and Samuel all ride horses from Rachel and Dax's ranch, but Mary would need to ride alone until she met them on the main trail." She glanced at Isabella. "The men found a group of orphans in the hills almost a year ago. Margaret, Selina, and Samuel are the youngest and still go to school. Lydia is of marrying age and helps Rachel with the chores. The oldest boy, Billy, lives with some widowed ranchers and works as a ranch hand. I'm sure you'll meet them while you're here."

"Sounds as if they have a full house." Isabella found she struggled as much with losing Jackson as she did with her husband's death. "I'd love to meet them before I leave."

"Since there's no reason you must hurry back to Philadelphia, you have lots of time to visit." Lena wanted to find a way to encourage Isabella to stay. All her friends back home were much older, having little in common with her friend. Quiet and shy, Lena feared Isabella would fall into a life of a lonely widow, memories of Arnott and Jackson all she had to look forward to each day.

"True, I have time." Isabella pushed from the table. "I'll check on Jackson, make certain he's ready to leave when you are." She stopped, then turned toward Lena. "Unless you want to get him."

"No, you go ahead. That will give me time to gather my belongings." Lena's heart squeezed, knowing how Isabella felt. She struggled with the same pain each time she left her son behind. If she could just convince Isabella to stay.

"Thank you, Miss Murton. I knew you would understand." Lena kept her eyes on Jack as Mary introduced him to the other children.

"I'll do my part. Splendor is a good town, but not all families will accept your situation. Some children will taunt Jack once news gets out. And it will."

"You're right. All I can do is help Jack adjust and handle problems as they arise." Lena smiled when Mary grabbed Jack's hand, drawing him toward a desk in the center. "We are staying at Luke Pelletier's house for a while, although I'll continue working. If you need to speak with me, please send word to either place. I'd better say goodbye to Jack."

Sarah placed a restraining hand on her arm. "My suggestion is to leave, let him continue as he is without interruption. Of course, if you'd rather—"

"No, I'll take your suggestion. I'll be by after school. Thank you again, Miss Murton."

"Please, call me Sarah."

Lena nodded, grateful this part of the day had gone so well. The next portion might not. She had to find Nick, tell him about Willie's visit, and figure out how to handle any further threats. She cringed thinking of how Nick would react to what he'd consider intimidation. No matter what, she wouldn't let Jack go. They'd waited a long time to be a family, bowing to Willie's threats in the past. Those days were over. Never again would she allow him to dictate how she and Jack lived, keeping her away from her son through fear of what Willie would do.

"Good morning, Suzanne. Is Nick still here?"

"No, he left early. He mentioned stopping by the saloon, then meeting some men at the site of the new hotel. From what I can see, they've made quite a bit of progress already. Do you want breakfast or coffee?"

"No, thank you. I need to find Nick right away." Lena didn't wait for Suzanne to respond. Hurrying down the boardwalk, she didn't pay attention to the man who came up beside her, grabbing her arm.

"What are you in such a hurry about?"

Lena stiffened and yanked her arm away at the sound of Willie's voice. "I told you to stay away from me and I meant it." Ignoring him, she turned and continued toward the other end of town.

"I think it best you take a few minutes to speak with me, Lena. Otherwise, I will be forced to make decisions that might prove quite embarrassing to you."

A cold chill ripped through her as she spun around, facing him. "Don't threaten me, Willie. I've had quite enough of your bullying. You are not a factor in Jackson's life and never will be, no matter what you believe."

Approaching in measured steps, Willie stopped in front of her. "I'll be in town until tomorrow, then I'll need to ride back to the mine. If you know what is good for you and Jackson, you'll agree to meet with me and discuss our future." He spoke in a hard, unyielding tone, the menace in his voice clear.

"We have no future."

"I believe you'll reconsider once you hear my plans. Shall we say breakfast tomorrow at the boardinghouse?" His smirk made her cringe.

"No." She turned her back to him, continuing to walk.

"Think carefully about your decision. If you don't meet me, you will regret it."

The knot in her stomach turned into a ball of ice, but she refused to acknowledge his last comment. Forcing her shoulders back, she continued toward the site of the new hotel, telling herself nothing he said would change any of her decisions. She moved from one end of the boardwalk to the other, oblivious to the morning activities of the town, her mind clouded. Talking with Nick would help. His sound counsel had pulled her out of more than one bad situation. She had no reason to believe he wouldn't come through again.

Stepping off the end of the wooden walkway, her eyes grew wide at the sight before her. Suzanne had been right. They'd made considerable progress in the last few days.

"Lena, over here." Nick stood near the back of the site, waving, a grin splitting his face.

Picking her way between piles of dirt and open trenches, she marveled at the amount of work the few men had accomplished. The foundation had already been laid, and they'd begun the framing.

"What do you think?" Nick asked as he scanned the site.

"Suzanne told me you'd made a lot of progress and she was right."

"Gabe found hardworking men who have experience constructing buildings. It's made the difference in how far they've gotten." He studied her, seeing a worried expression he didn't expect. His smile faded. "What's wrong?"

"Do you have time to talk with me?"

"Of course. Let's go to the Dixie."

They walked in silence. Getting to his office, he held the door open for her. "What's worrying you?"

Clasping her hands together, she stared out the window. Her heart had been pounding in a painful rhythm since her encounter with Willie. No matter how she told herself all would be well, the tightness in her stomach said otherwise.

"It's Willie. He knows Jackson is here."

Chapter Eighteen

"Another two hours and we'll be in Splendor." Gabe reined up alongside Caro, noting the weariness on her face. "We'll get you settled in my house so you can rest and freshen up, then I'll take you to supper."

"Is there any chance you have a tub?"

He smiled, knowing she had no idea what to expect. "I do, and I'll bet I can get some hot water into it also."

Flashing him a grateful look, she shifted once more in the saddle, trying to relieve her stiff back and aching shoulders. She knew another part of her body would hurt once she dismounted, but it was too numb to worry about now.

They'd made good time. The sun still shown high in the sky, basking them in warmth, even though the wind whipped around and the temperature had dropped from the day before. Fall had moved in fast, and Gabe knew they'd be buried in snow within weeks—a fact he hadn't thought to mention to Caro.

"How long before the wagon with the supplies arrives?" Caro knew she could go perhaps two or three days without her belongings.

"There will be two wagons. The drivers planned to start today. If they don't encounter any delays, they should arrive within two days."

"Tell me more about your job, Gabriel. Do you have deputies?" She'd grown tired of living with her own thoughts and memories of David. No matter how much she'd loved him, thoughts of the past often weighed on her.

"I have two—Cash Coulter and Beau Davis."

"Southern names," she commented without condemnation. As a northerner, she often thought of those from the south who'd suffered so much more than she or her friends.

"Yes. Both fought for the Confederacy. Splendor is full of men who fought on both sides. Even our doctor and his nurse worked in Union field hospitals." He thought of Doc Worthington and his niece, Rachel Pelletier. They'd patched up and cured more people than Gabe could count. Since Patrick Pelletier's birth, Rachel had to trim back her work at the clinic. He knew Doc would need to start looking for another nurse soon.

"Many people were displaced due to the war. It must be hard to start over."

"It takes strong men and women to leave what they know and move west." Gabe thought of the sheep farmers who'd come to town before he left. He feared they were facing hard times.

"Does that include you and Noah?" Caro never thought of either man as adventurous.

"Yes and no. After the war, neither of us were ready to resume our lives in New York. Riding west seemed like the lesser of two evils," he joked. "I haven't decided if the decision indicated we were strong or naïve."

"From what you've told me, I would say strong. You may not have known what you faced, but you went forward, not dwelling on the obstacles. It takes courage to walk away from a family such as yours to seek a new life."

Gabe wondered if Caro realized she spoke as much about herself as about Noah and him. Wealth and privilege hadn't deterred her from leaving the comforts of home and striking out on her own. He admired her a great deal.

Nick cursed as he listened about Lena's two encounters with Willie. "I won't let him harm you or Jack. Don't let Willie make you believe otherwise."

"He thinks what he has to tell me will change my mind about keeping Jack away from him."

"Carlyle is a liar and a thief. What could he say that would make a difference?" Nick paced to the window. The storm of last night had passed, leaving the street thick with mud.

"I don't know. Now that Jack is here with me, the danger seems more real."

Nick turned from the window, crossing his arms. "You could send him away with Isabella again. Willie never bothered them when you were separated from Jack, even though he knew where to find him."

"No." Her eyes sparked and voice hardened at the suggestion. "I've made up my mind. I'll never let Jack go again."

"You think it might be wise to hear him out?"

"Yes. At least I'll know what he plans."

"Then I'll go with you." Nick didn't want Lena alone with Willie, even if their meeting took place in a crowded restaurant.

"I don't think he'll talk in front of you."

"He will if we give him no choice." Lowering himself back into his chair, he leaned forward, resting his arms on the desk. "The meeting is for tomorrow at breakfast. I'll either sit with you or at a table nearby, but I won't let you be in the same room with Willie without being there."

No one except Nick and Isabella knew of the letters she'd received from him over the years. He'd been tracking her, knew where she lived, knew about Jackson, and knew about the businesses she and Nick owned. If she'd done what she wanted, what was best for her, she would've ignored the threat and kept her son close. But she wasn't willing to risk Jackson. It had been clear he would've used her love for Jackson against her and she'd never allow Willie to do that. Separating herself from the son she loved seemed the only alternative to keep him safe. Even though he disagreed, Nick had always supported her decisions and been willing to protect her from Willie. His suggestion of being close during her meeting with Willie made sense and gave her comfort. He'd always been there for her.

"It's charming, Gabe." Caro rode next to him as they entered Splendor, the church on a small knoll to her left. "What are they building?"

"That is the hotel I told you about." Gabe noted how much progress they'd made in the few days he'd been gone. He'd reined up next to it.

"The one you and your two partners are building, correct?"

"That's right. Hold on a minute. I need to speak with one of the men." He headed straight toward Bull, who stood at the back of the site, speaking with the other men. "I didn't expect to see you here."

Bull looked up, a smile spreading across his face. "Dax said it would be all right if I rode in early, see how your boys here are doing. Nick said you'd be gone a while."

"I planned to. Ran into an old friend in Big Pine and convinced her to visit Splendor." Gabe nodded toward Caro.

Bull's eyes widened when he saw the beautiful woman astride the horse. "You say she's an old friend?"

"Caro, Noah, and I grew up together. Let me introduce you."

Caro pulled her bonnet low and shielded her eyes, trying to get a good look at the man with Gabe.

"Carolyn, I'd like you to meet a friend of mine, Bull Mason. Bull, this is Mrs. Caroline Iverson." Gabe lifted his arms and helped her to the ground.

As they exchanged greetings, Noah came out of the bank, spotting them across the main street.

"Caro!" Taking long strides, he took her in his arms and swung her around, both laughing as he set her down. "What are you doing here?"

"It's a long story. How much time do you have?" Her gaze wandered over Noah. He'd always been tall, but he'd filled out, his face that of a mature man.

"Caro will be staying at my house for a spell. Why don't we all meet at Suzanne's for supper so you two can visit?"

"Sounds fine. I'll bring my wife, Caro. I know you'll love Abby. Everybody does. Here. Let me help with the horses." Noah grabbed the reins, walking toward the livery.

"Bull, you're welcome to join us. I'd like to hear your thoughts on the progress so far." Gabe nodded toward the construction.

"My pleasure, Gabe. I'll see you tonight."

Hearing the loud voices outside the saloon, Lena walked to the front window, her breath catching at the site of Gabe. She almost ran outside, then stood rooted in place when she saw his hand settle on the back of a woman she'd never seen. He didn't even spare a glance at the Dixie as he strolled past, his head bowed, listening to something the woman said.

She wrapped her arms around her waist, pain and irritation boiling within her at how naïve she'd been to think he went to Big Pine just for business. Waiting until they disappeared toward Noah's livery, she made her way to the bar.

"Something I can get you, Lena?" Paul asked, tossing the bar rag onto a shelf.

"Coffee would be wonderful," she mumbled.

"Would you like some company? I'm so bored, I may lose my mind." Deborah leaned against the bar, facing the doors. "How about some coffee, Paul? And sugar."

"Sure thing, Deborah."

"Saw your man ride into town with another woman." Deborah had never been one to mince words.

Lena bit her lower lip. Even though she enjoyed her company, sharing confidences with Deborah wasn't a good idea. Whatever she said would spread through the Dixie in no time, eventually reaching Nick. Seeing Gabe with another woman didn't call for Nick's sage advice. Whatever happened would be Lena's doing without guidance from him.

"Yes, I saw him."

"Do you know her?" Deborah held her cup up, waiting for Lena to respond.

"I'm certain he'll introduce me when he has time to stop by." She told herself he still loved her and would have a good explanation. Gabe wouldn't flaunt another woman in front of her—at least she hoped he wouldn't. In her life, she'd seen it all. A truth she'd learned the hard way about men was that you could never be certain of their sincerity. Most of them always seemed to have an angle, one a woman didn't find out about until it was too late.

"She looked fresh off the boat, if you know what I mean." Deborah turned and rested her arms on the bar. "You got more coffee, Paul?"

"Hold on. I'll get it for you."

"Anyway, she doesn't look like a woman from Big Pine. More East Coast, same as Rachel Pelletier." Deborah added a small amount of sugar to the coffee and stirred it absently, waiting for Lena to respond. When she didn't, Deborah continued, trying to fill the quiet. "Isn't Gabe from back east somewhere? Boston, Philadelphia—"

"New York."

"Now I remember. He told me that he and Noah grew up together in New York. Maybe she's a woman he knew from back home." She drained the last of the coffee. "Guess I'd best get upstairs and get ready. It won't be long before the men start asking for something stronger than whiskey." She winked at Lena, then walked up the stairs, holding her long skirt up so she wouldn't trip.

Glad to see her leave, Lena let out a breath, staring at her now cold coffee. With the arrival of Jackson, and the woman he brought back with him from Big Pine, she and Gabe had a lot to talk about. She thought of their time together, wondering if what they had could last a lifetime. She doubted it. Why would any man, especially one as well-bred as Gabe, want a woman who not only made her living running saloons, but had a child outside of marriage? Perhaps he'd realized he didn't need to settle for a woman of her background.

Lena placed two fingers on each temple, rubbing to ease the headache which had crept up on her. Getting Jackson settled in a new town, without feeling the stigma of being seen as a bastard, and dealing with Willie's threats would take all her energy. Both of those fights had to be won. She didn't need one more battle, and keeping Gabe might turn into one if the woman she saw with him was more than a friend.

Pushing her cup across the bar, she straightened, deciding she had to focus all her energy on fighting Willie and keeping Jackson safe. She loved Gabe. It would break her heart if he turned away. But if his attentions now belonged to another, she'd accept it as graciously as possible, no matter how much it would hurt.

Getting Caro settled in his house and arranging to bunk down at Cash and Beau's didn't take long. Beau had done as the doctor asked, stopping by each day for a clean bandage. He'd pinned on his badge and resumed his duties that morning, becoming too irritable to stay in the house any longer. Afterwards, Gabe sought out Noah, explaining about David Iverson's death and Caro's decision to start a new life.

While Caro rested, Gabe would find Lena, ask her to join them at supper, and tell her he'd be leaving the following morning to finish his trip. Entering the Dixie, he saw her at the bar, her back to him, appearing to be lost in thought. He covered the distance between them in a few steps, settling his hands on her hips. Startled, she looked up, seeing his reflection in the mirror behind the bar.

"Gabe..." she breathed out, turning in his arms, her hands lacing behind his neck.

He looked her up and down, his grim expression fixing on her face, as if he didn't know what to say. Making no move to kiss her, he continued to stare, his jaw tightening.

"I saw you had returned," she said as a way to break the silence.

"I brought someone back with me." He let his arms drop and moved to stand beside her.

"Who is she?"

Gabe realized Lena had seen him with Caro. He could only imagine what she thought.

"Caroline Iverson. I've known her since we were young. Our homes were a block apart."

So she came from wealth, Lena thought, although she'd already suspected it.

"She'll be staying at my place until she decides what to do next." He signaled Paul for a whiskey, not noticing the acute distress on Lena's face. "She had traveled to Big Pine, spotting me while at supper in the same restaurant. We haven't seen each other in years." He sipped the whiskey, still oblivious to what his words were doing to Lena. "We're having supper at Suzanne's with Noah, Abby, and Bull. I'd like you to join us, meet her. Nick, too, if he can spare the time."

Lena could barely draw a breath, her chest heavy, her mind fogged in confusion. If this was his way of breaking it off between them, she didn't want to hear another word. And she'd be damned if she'd spend a night making small talk with his new woman across the supper table.

"I don't think so, Gabe." She swallowed the lump in her throat, trying to control the edge to her voice.

"Sounds as if you already have a full table. I'll stay here while Nick joins you. I'm sure you and he have much to talk about with the progress of the hotel. He mentioned you picked some very good men with strong skills." She rambled on, unable to control the flow of words, her mind wrestling with the reality he'd found someone else. If he hadn't, his welcome would have been sweeter. Instead, it felt as if a wide chasm separated them, extinguishing the love she thought they had when he left.

"You can't take half an hour to eat supper and meet her? Caro is anxious to get to know you."

She could feel her eyes fill, forcing her to turn away before a tear broke loose to run down her cheek. "Another time, Gabe."

His jaw worked as he stared at her, confused at her response. Gabe wondered if she'd already made up her mind to refuse his proposal. Deciding not to ask, he gripped his glass tight.

"You'll know where I am if you change your mind." His hard words preceded the glass tipping up as he emptied it, the whiskey burning a path down his throat.

Chapter Nineteen

"I'm sorry your lady won't be joining us. I so wanted to meet her." Caro lowered herself into the chair Gabe held out for her at the table closest to the front entry.

"She may still come by for a few minutes. If not, I'll introduce you to her tomorrow." He'd just sat down when Noah, Abby, and Bull walked in.

Abby glanced around. "Where's Lena?"

"She'll be along in a little bit," Nick said as he walked up behind Bull. "An urgent matter with one of the girls must be dealt with." He nodded at everyone, his gaze settling on the woman next to Gabe.

"Nick, this is Caroline Iverson, an old friend of Noah's and mine. Caro, Nick Barnett. He and Lena own the Dixie saloon." Gabe glanced at the door, hoping to see Lena walk in.

"It's a pleasure, Miss Iverson." Nick took her hand, placing a kiss on her knuckles.

"It's Mrs. Iverson, Mr. Barnett, and it's good to meet you."

"Please call me Nick. Mr. Barnett makes me feel old." He smiled, showing his southern charm. "Did your husband not join you?" He took a seat across from her, leaving an empty chair between Gabe and him.

Caro shot a quick look at Gabe. "My husband passed away a few years ago. It took me a while to make the decision to move on, seek a new life."

"I'm truly sorry. If it's any consolation, Splendor is a wonderful town for new beginnings." Nick's gaze settled on Suzanne moving toward them. His chest tightened, as it did each time he saw her. The more time he spent around her, the more intrigued he became. He needed to find a way to break through her defenses, but not now. With the new partnership formed to expand the boardinghouse, he had plenty of time.

"That's what Gabriel has been saying. He encouraged me to change my plans of traveling to San Francisco." She glanced at Noah. "Of course, once I learned Noah lived here, I didn't want to miss the chance to see him after such a long time."

"Your arrival is perfect, Caro. As soon as Lena arrives, Abby and I have some news to share." Noah took Abby's hand and rested it on his thigh.

"It looks as if she's here." Nick watched as Lena came through the door, removing her coat and draping it over her arm. Cursing under his breath, he sent her a scathing look. They'd had a fierce argument about her ignoring Gabe's invitation. In the end, she'd agreed to at least make an appearance. Seeing her now, he wished he hadn't pushed so hard.

"I hope I'm not too late." Lena stopped behind Gabe's chair, ignoring the venomous look on Nick's face.

No one spoke as they took in the dress she'd chosen. Discarding her usual clothing with full-length sleeves and conservative neckline, she wore a bright green dress of silk, cut low in the front, with capped sleeves and black lace, a black shawl draped over her back and arms. The dress hugged every curve, leaving little to the imagination. The deep red lipstick and rouge replaced the minimal makeup she'd always preferred.

"Um...that's quite a pretty color on you, Lena." Abby's gaze shifted between Lena, Nick, and Gabe, knowing Gabe hadn't turned to see her attire.

"Why, thank you. It's a dress I've been wanting to wear for some time."

Gabe's eyes narrowed as he shifted in his seat, and for the first time, saw what everyone else already had.

"What the hell?" He shot from his chair, taking her by the arm. The muscles in his jaw tightened and his eyes flared as he took in her outfit. He'd never seen her dress as one of the girls in the saloon, and he sure as hell didn't like others to see her like this. "Do you want to tell me what you think you're doing dressed like that?" His low, controlled, deep drawl should have been a warning of the inner turmoil about to explode.

Her eyes widened as if in surprise. "You don't like my dress, Gabe? I borrowed it from Deborah. She mentioned it is a customer favorite." Smoothing the skirt with her hands, she looked up, resting her gaze on Caroline. "Are you going to introduce me to your new lady, Gabe, or should I do it myself?"

Tightening his grip on her arm, he turned her toward the stairs. "Go ahead without us. Lena and I need to talk," he called over his shoulder as he guided her out and up the stairs to her room. "Key." He held out his hand.

Lena crossed her arms, refusing to do as he asked.

"Fine." One strong kick and the door broke loose, flying open and slamming against the wall. "Inside." When she didn't budge, he applied just enough pressure to get her moving, then kicked the door closed behind them. Dropping his hand, he crossed his arms, his eyes blazing as he assessed her clothing. "What's going on, Lena?" His voice hardened in a way she'd never heard.

She wrapped her arms around her waist as if a powerful chill had blown through the room. "I thought you would like it," she lied, knowing Gabe would hate the dress and what it implied.

"I don't. Take it off." His tone was cool, disapproving.

"No."

His face reddened and before she could react, he grabbed her shoulders and turned her around, popping the buttons as he tore the back open. "I said to take it off." He turned, opening the doors of her wardrobe, pulling a dress from the hanger. "This is one of *my* favorites," he growled, tossing it at her. A shimmering shade of lavender with a scooped neck and long sleeves, he'd always thought she looked like a queen when she wore it. He knew once on, it would fall to the floor, covering up legs he wanted no man but himself to see.

When she didn't move, he took a step closer, hands on his hips. "Do you want me to dress you?"

She knew his threat was real. So far, his anger had only extended to ripping her dress. She knew he'd never strike her, but the thought of defying him further held no appeal.

"Fine. I'll be down in a few minutes." She turned, pushing on the fabric of the dress and letting it drift to the ground. Casting a look over her shoulder, she frowned. "You don't need to stay."

"True, but I'm going to anyway." He leaned against the nearby wall, arms crossed, watching her every movement. Once she'd slid into the lavender dress, he stepped forward, pushing her hands aside as he fastened the tiny buttons in the front. "Why, Lena?" His voice had softened, but his eyes still held a trace of anger...and something else. Betrayal, perhaps?

"I wanted to make an impression on your new lady." Her voice shook as his fingers skimmed her sensitive skin while he finished closing her dress.

"That's the second time you've called her my new lady and I want to know why."

Biting her lower lip, she backed up, her legs hitting the edge of the bed. She could feel her face heat at his intense stare and wished she could disappear.

"Your manner when you spoke of her earlier. You talked as if you'd found someone special, important." She took a shaky breath, not letting her eyes meet his. "You didn't kiss me or do anything to make me believe you still cared. I thought..."

Gabe took in the misery on her face and felt a pang of guilt. What she said was true. He had avoided mentioning how much he'd missed her, hadn't drawn her in for a kiss, hadn't done anything to contradict her suspicions. He'd seen her reaction at the saloon when he spoke of Caro and knew how she'd misinterpreted his feelings about her. Yet he never once tried to explain they were just friends.

Spearing a hand through his hair, he let his arm drop to his side, taking a cautious step closer. "I'm sorry if I gave you the wrong impression about Caro. She's an old friend, nothing more. If I ever did have feelings for her, they're long gone. You're the only woman I want, Lena. Just you." He sat down on the bed, reaching for her hand. "I love you and want to marry you, but I know you aren't ready to make that decision. I'll be as patient as I can, but you need to understand this isn't easy for me."

She sat down next to him, looking at their joined hands. "I'm sorry if I embarrassed you. It wasn't my intent."

"Don't lie. You're not good at it." His mouth lifted a little at the corners.

"You're right. It *was* my intent to show you how much you'd hurt me."

He brought her hand to his lips, kissing the inside of her wrist, feeling her shiver. "Do you think they'd miss us if we stayed up here a little longer?"

"Yes," she laughed, pulling her hand away. "We'll go down and I'll apologize to everyone. Then can we start again, all right?"

He wrapped his arms around her, lowering his mouth to hers for a deep, searing kiss before pulling back. "Yes, we can start again."

Escorting her down the stairs, they'd just entered the dining room when the front doors flew open, a young boy and woman he'd never seen entering.

"Mother! Guess what Aunt Isabella bought for me!"

The world seemed to tilt as Gabe stared at the boy, whose bright smile flashed at Lena. He hadn't heard wrong. The boy had called her mother and she hadn't denied it. Moving his gaze to Lena, all he could feel was a keen sense of betrayal that she hadn't shared the fact she had a child.

The instant his eyes met hers, Lena knew she'd made a terrible mistake in hiding Jackson from him.

"Mother, did you hear me?" Jack stood in front of her, looking up, a hint of confusion on his face. She knelt in front of him.

"Yes, I did hear you, sweetheart. What did Aunt Isabella buy you?"

From behind his back, he pulled out a child's cowboy hat. "Isn't it wonderful?"

Sending him a smile she didn't feel, she reached out and touched the brim. "Yes, Jack, it is..." Lena sensed movement behind her, then heard the quiet closing of the door as Gabe walked out.

"Was that Gabe?" Isabella put a hand on Lena's shoulder as she began to stand.

"Yes."

"Go after him. I'll stay here with Jack."

Without hesitation, Lena dashed outside, spotting his long strides as he walked up the steps to the Wild Rose. Running after him, she called his name. Stopping, he didn't turn around.

"Gabe, let me explain." She placed a hand on his arm, which he shook off.

"Not now, Lena." He took another step.

"Wait. Please." Her voice was strained as she pleaded for him to listen.

Turning, he schooled his face, not letting it show any of the turmoil he felt inside. The betrayal at her keeping such a secret almost brought him to his knees. He'd bared himself to her, opened up more to her than anyone, except Noah, and she'd repaid him with nothing but lies. He was done with her games.

"I'm going inside for a drink. You won't be welcome at my table." His eyes bored into hers another moment before he turned to leave her standing alone.

"I'll go speak with him." Noah sat down next to Lena, seeing the broken expression on her face. "He may listen to me."

She'd walked back to the boardinghouse in a daze, taking a seat in the parlor, still unable to accept what his actions implied. "I've hurt him, Noah. He might never understand."

"Maybe not, but he should hear the explanation."

"I planned to tell him as soon as he returned. His arrival with Caroline took me by surprise." She gripped her hands in her lap, unable to control the tears streaming down her face. Looking around, she cast her gaze at Noah. "Where are Isabella and Jack?"

"She and Abby took him to your room. Nick told me you can find him at the Dixie. Why don't you go on upstairs? I believe I'll go have a drink at the Rose." Noah stood, reaching out his hand to help her up. "Would you let Abby know where I am?"

Her red-rimmed eyes looked up at him. "Yes, of course." She took the stairs at a slow gait, defeat evident in each step.

As Noah crossed the street and entered the Rose, he thought of what he'd say, how he'd get Gabe to listen. From experience, he knew Gabe might need a few days to calm down, wrestle with his own demons until he was able to listen to reason. Noah could plant the seed, though.

"The table's full," Gabe mumbled as Noah pulled out a chair, ignoring the attitude.

"Looks depressingly empty to me." He noted the already open bottle of whiskey and turned toward Al. "Another glass." Noah might not be able to stop Gabe's destructive actions, but at least he could slow it down.

They sat in silence for a long time, Gabe staring nowhere in particular, Noah keeping watch on his friend. He'd never seen Gabe so conflicted by a woman before. Any other time or any other person, Gabe would go out of his way to listen to the story, hear the explanation, commenting if asked. Pain from betrayal is a powerful emotion, one no man wanted to face.

"Is he all right, Noah?" Dolly stood beside him, her gaze fixed on Gabe.

"I can't say he is."

"Anything I can do?"

"I think he just needs time."

"And more whiskey." Gabe raised his glass, jostling it to emphasize the dry interior.

Noah picked up the bottle and filled Gabe's glass.

Tossing it back in one swallow, his gaze locked on Dolly. "How about you and I go upstairs? It's been a long time." He started to stand, Noah's firm hand on his shoulder pushing him back down.

"I don't believe you want to do that, no matter how tempting." Noah winked, nodding at Dolly, who took the hint and left to check on another table.

"How the hell do you know what I want?"

"Well, now, I may not know exactly what you want, but I do know what you don't want, and that's to ruin any chance you still have with Lena." Noah stood, turning the chair around and straddling it, his arms resting on the back. "Don't you think you should at least hear her explanation? She might have a damn good reason why she didn't tell you about Jack."

Gabe's gaze snapped to Noah. "You already knew about the boy?"

"I found out when Isabella and Jack got off the stage while you were in Big Pine. No one knew until that day. To tell you the truth, I don't believe Lena knew they were coming."

"It doesn't matter if she knew it or not. She had plenty of time to tell me about her son. She chose to keep him a secret." He poured and downed another whiskey, his vision beginning to cloud. "I'm leaving tomorrow morning and don't plan to be back for a while."

"Where are you headed?"

"To see Dax and Luke, then I'll be staying in Luke's old place. Come for me only if it's an emergency." He pinned Noah with a cold stare. "And I mean life or death. Besides the Pelletiers, you, Cash, and Beau are the only people who know where I'll be. Don't tell anyone else. You understand?" Gabe pushed up, his wobbly legs making it hard to stand without help.

"You need any help with him, Noah?" Al called from the bar.

"No, I have him." He wrapped one of Gabe's arms around his neck and braced an arm around his waist, steadying him.

"I can stand," Gabe protested as they walked toward the back door.

"Sure you can," Noah said, his voice heavy with sarcasm.

Cash and Beau's house stood half a block away. Both deputies were gone, probably still checking the town before calling it a night. He lowered Gabe to a pallet they'd set up in the front room, then pushed him onto his back.

Noah stared down at him, hoping Gabe would find a way to work through the problems with Lena. He wanted him to find the same happiness he had with Abby. The thought reminded him that he and Abby still hadn't been able to share their news. He guessed it would have to wait a little longer.

"I always knew you were a smart woman, Lena." Willie's feral smile had her stomach churning. Nick sat two tables away. Not close enough to hear their conversation, but ready to intervene if needed. "Although I *did* believe you were brave enough to have breakfast with me without the need of a bodyguard." He nodded toward Nick.

She raised her chin, refusing to be intimidated. "We always have breakfast about this time. There's nothing unusual about him being here. Now, what do you want?"

"Direct. That's one quality of yours I always admired." He cut into his ham and took a bite, chewing slowly, letting her wait.

Lena had no appetite. The combination of Gabe's departure the night before and Willie's presence at breakfast killed any hunger she might have felt.

"I believe it best we marry." Willie spoke without explanation, startling her.

She laughed at his bold statement. "You must be mad. What makes you believe I'd even consider marrying you?"

"I'm only thinking of what's best for you and my son. Think of how people will react when they learn of Jackson's bastard status. Children can be so hard on each other. And adults, well...their opinion can destroy you and anyone associated with you." He took another bite of ham, his eyes dancing in amusement, watching her face go ashen.

He didn't make veiled threats. "The people in Splendor will understand. Once they get to know you, my reasons for keeping you out of our lives will become clear."

"You are still as naïve as ever, giving credit to people who don't deserve it. When the word is out, you'll see how many stand beside you. I'm afraid it won't be as many as you expect." He sipped the still steaming coffee, then set the cup aside. "It would be a shame for you and your partners to spend thousands of dollars building a hotel only to lose it all to a scandal."

Her stomach churned. She knew he might be right. There would be some who would stand by her—the Pelletiers, Noah, Abby, Suzanne, some of the other merchants—but would it be enough to prove Willie wrong? Would most shun her and Jack, making their lives miserable, dragging Nick, and possibly Gabe, down with them?

As much as she loathed Willie, she loved the son their union produced and would do anything to protect him from needless scandal. The thought of marrying Willie made her physically ill, yet his threats held a real fear for her.

Finishing his meal, he set the napkin beside his plate and leaned toward her. "I can see you don't quite see the gravity of the situation you are in. Let me assure you, my threats are real. But I am a reasonable man. I'll give you three days to consider my offer of marriage. Three days, Lena, and not a minute more. If you do not see your way clear to marry me, I will make good on my threats." Standing, he glared down at her. "And don't think you can disappear. If you take Jackson, I *will* find you, and my terms won't be as generous the second time."

Clutching her hands so tight the knuckles appeared white, she watched his retreating back. She knew he meant every word. What bothered her the most was the almost maniacal look in his eyes as he spoke. As opposed to the way he'd presented himself as a younger man, she now saw past the charm to the menace he'd become.

He'd make her life and Jackson's a living hell if she didn't bend to his will. A decision to marry might mean alienating Nick, as well as the loss of any relationship with Gabe. She might be on her own if she took such a drastic step.

"Are you all right?"

She heard the scraping of a chair across the wooden floor, her clouded mind noticing Nick taking a seat beside her. Unable to meet his gaze, she continued to stare into her lap.

"What did he say?"

"He...uh..." Her voice broke as she tried to choke out a response.

Grabbing her untouched cup of coffee, Nick held it out her. "Drink this."

Taking the cup in both hands, she took a sip, the liquid tasting bitter in her mouth.

"Is that better?" Nick leaned forward, anger building at seeing her so upset.

She didn't respond right away, her hands trembling as she set the cup on the table.

"He insists I marry him—"

"Not in this life or any other, Lena."

She'd never heard his voice sound so hardened and ruthless.

Looking around, the faces of several people she knew came into focus, all glancing up from their meals to see what had Nick so agitated.

"We can't talk here. Let's go to the Dixie." She stood, nodding at a few people as she passed their tables. Taking a breath, she steeled herself for the unavoidable discussion.

Chapter Twenty

Reaching across the desk, Gabe shook Dax's hand, then turned to shake Luke's.

"Thank you both. I'm looking forward to the day my home sits atop the hill with a view of the waterfall." A smile that didn't quite reach his eyes twisted the corners of his mouth. He'd started the negotiations with the Pelletiers when he'd felt certain Lena would be joining him. Now their future seemed anything but certain.

"We're glad to put the land to good use. The property is too far removed from our ranch and we've expanded so far north and east, we have more than we'll ever need for generations." Dax walked around the desk, leaning against the edge. "Of course, that doesn't mean we won't be acquiring more. When will you start building?"

"I'm afraid it will have to wait until spring. All the men available are being used at the new hotel site, expanding the boardinghouse, and finishing Noah's houses."

"Sounds as if you'll be building your home about the time Noah and Abby start theirs on the hill east of town." Luke opened a bottle of whiskey, filling three glasses. "She wanted it done by Christmas. Instead, they decided to build houses for those who had no other shelter this winter. I hear every one of them is already taken."

"Noah is finishing the last two now and already has them sold. I suppose we'll be utilizing the same workmen come spring." Gabe accepted the glass Luke handed him. "And assuming it's all right with the two of you, I'd like to use Bull again to check my plans."

"No problem." Dax took a glass from Luke.

"Here's to your new home and future in Splendor. We all hope you'll continue as our sheriff for a long time." Luke lifted his glass in the air.

"I do plan a future in Splendor," Gabe chuckled. "I'm not ready to commit to how long I'll stay on as sheriff, though."

"At least you'll be here, whether it's as sheriff or not. Are you still planning to stay at my old place for a few days?" Luke set his empty glass aside, leaning forward and resting his arms on his knees.

"If the offer is still open."

"Anytime," Luke responded. "You'll need some supplies, which I've already packed and loaded into a wagon."

"You didn't have to—"

Luke held up his hand. "It wasn't any problem. We had the supplies and I knew what you'd need, at least for a week. If you stay longer, come back here rather than ride into town. Unless there's someone you'd like to see..." Luke shot him a knowing look.

Gabe should've known they would have heard about him and Lena. He suspected most everyone in town already figured they were together. If he could just find a way to reconcile what she'd kept from him with his love for her. He had no desire to form a union with a woman he couldn't trust. A marriage built on secrets would never work.

"No." He rose, grabbed the bottle, and poured a glass. "I suppose you're both aware of Jackson." When both nodded, he shook his head, then downed the whiskey. "I found out yesterday. By accident."

"You'd just gotten back to town. Perhaps she hadn't had a chance to explain," Luke offered.

"She'd mentioned Jackson to me several times before I left for Big Pine. Not once did she indicate he was her son, leaving me to believe he belonged to Isabella. Now I must decide what to do next."

Luke walked up next to him, clasping him on the shoulder. "I always found putting a fishing pole in Wildfire Creek to be quite conducive to thinking through troubles. Two are still at the cabin. Give it a try. You might be amazed at how much your head clears when watching fish swim right by your hook. Come on. I'll take you to the wagon."

"Suzanne asked me to come and get Lena. Is she here?" Fanny had run from the boardinghouse to the

Dixie when Jack burst into the kitchen, blood dripping from his nose, one eye swollen shut.

"Upstairs. I'll get her." Paul tossed the rag down and dashed up the stairs, returning moments later with Lena.

"What is it, Fanny?"

"You need to come quick. Jack's been hurt."

"I'll let Nick know," Paul called after Lena as she ran out the door.

"Bring the doctor," Lena yelled over her shoulder to Fanny as she passed the clinic. "Suzanne?" she called, slamming the front door open, thankful the restaurant was empty.

"In the kitchen." She glanced up from tending to Jack as Lena hurried toward them, her face ashen, eyes full of worry.

Kneeling next to him, she looked into his face, seeing the remnants of blood, a split and swollen lip, swollen eye, and color spreading onto his cheek.

"What happened, Jack?" She kept her voice low, trying not to show her apprehension.

Looking down at his lap, he shook his head. "Nothing."

"I can see it must have been something, unless you did this to yourself. Did you?"

He glanced at her, then quickly looked away. "No."

"Then who did?"

Jack winced as Suzanne dabbed a small amount of whiskey on his split lip. "No one."

"What do we have here?" All three glanced at the door as Doc Worthington walked in, already looking Jack over. "It appears you've been in an altercation, young man."

"Yes, sir." Jack's voice dropped to a whisper.

"Let's take a look."

Lena, Suzanne, and Fanny stood several feet away, giving the doctor space, although their eyes missed nothing. After checking the injuries, Doc stood. "No broken bones, but you'll have swelling and pain on your face. How did this happen, Jack?"

He pursed his lips, again refusing to explain. When his gaze caught sight of Nick striding into the room, a hard expression on his uncle's face, his confidence slipped.

"Come on, Jack. Let's head outside and get some air." Nick held out his hand before the two disappeared out the back door.

The women moved to the window over the sink, seeing them walk at a slow pace toward the creek, then head north along the water's edge.

"Well, if anyone can get Jack to talk, it's Nick. Guess all I can do is wait." Lena clasped her hands.

"He was in a fight," Suzanne said with conviction.

"Did he tell you that?"

"I think he started to before you came in, then stopped. He's embarrassed and probably angry. I know I'd be if I were jumped by other boys." With a disgusted snort, Suzanne tossed the soiled apron she'd been wearing aside. "You're right, though. Nick will get the whole story, then you'll know what to do." Without asking, Suzanne poured coffee for each of them, taking down a cup for Nick to have when he came back inside. "So, now, tell us what you're going to do about Gabe."

"Three boys cornered Jack after school and pushed him around. He shoved back, and one of the boys punched him. When he held his ground, another hit him, then a third." Nick paced back and forth in the kitchen, having sent Jack upstairs to Lena's room.

A deep red crept up Lena's face as Nick spoke, rage swelling at what the boys had done. When she started to stand, Nick placed a hand on her shoulder and pushed her back down.

Suzanne and Fanny leaned against the counter, arms crossed, cold fury on their faces.

"Why would they do such a thing?" Lena asked, her heart breaking, remembering how Jack looked when she first saw him.

"Apparently, the boys called him names."

Lena's eyes blazed at what she suspected. "What did they call him?"

Nick knelt in front of her, taking her hands. "It's not important what they said. It's the fact they intimidated and beat him."

"What. Did. They. Call. Him?"

"A bastard." Nick cleared his throat. "They said his mother was a whore."

Lena stilled, her face turning ashen. Staring ahead, she spotted a picture Suzanne had hung when she first built the boardinghouse. It showed her, her husband, and their daughter. The girl couldn't have been much older than Jack when it was taken. Suzanne had lost both in a severe snowstorm years before. The image made her think of Jack and how she'd do whatever was needed to protect her son.

Lena felt her resolve crumble as her gaze moved across the figures in the framed image. The girl had a broad smile, while Suzanne and her husband showed more stoic faces. Even so, you could see Suzanne's eyes sparkle. A braver woman Lena had never met. She didn't know if she could suffer such loss and move on the way her friend had. She knew she couldn't lose Jack, or see him suffer at the hands of ignorant children and adults.

Pushing herself up, she felt her body tremble as anger and resentment took control. "I need to go up and see Jack."

Nick cursed under his breath when he saw her shoulders sag as she moved toward the stairs. "I'll tell Cash and Beau. They need to know what happened."

She didn't answer, nodding once, then continuing to the second floor.

Darkness engulfed the street with no sign of Lena at the Dixie. Nick had taken Jack to Luke and Ginny's so he could stay with Isabella. He'd tried to encourage Lena to leave town, but nothing he said persuaded her to move from a chair she'd placed by the window with a clear view of the school.

She'd given Jack a hug, told him he wouldn't be going to the school for the next few days, then looked at Nick. His jaw clenched at the utter despondency on her face. He knew what she wrestled with, promising himself to find a way to dissuade her from doing what she believed best for Jack. In his mind, surrendering to Willie's ridiculous demand would result in a lifetime of fear and pain, for both her and Jack.

"I'm going to look for Lena. I shouldn't be gone long," he told Paul, glancing once more at the customers, noting nothing that would prevent him from leaving. Some nights he couldn't leave, having too many drunken cowboys and miners to keep watch over. Tonight was quiet.

Taking the steps two at a time to Lena's room, he knocked. "Lena, it's Nick. Open the door."

He heard the lock click before the door opened. Lena's resolute gaze sent waves of concern through him, hoping she hadn't come to the decision he expected.

"We need to talk before you make any decision about Willie." He walked to the window before turning toward her.

Closing the door, she leaned her back against it, arms crossed. "I know what I have to do, Nick. Please, don't try to stop me."

"The man is a thief and who knows what else. You can't put yourself or Jack in jeopardy by marrying him."

"You saw Jack. It won't get better, especially if Willie makes good on his threats. It won't be just the children who taunt him. It will be adults." Her eyes began to water. Blinking several times, she ignored them, focusing on what she had to do.

"You don't know that. There are a lot of fine people in Splendor. The ones who matter will stand beside you and make sure their children do the same." He paced toward her, taking her hands in his. "We'll speak to Miss Murton."

Pulling her hands free, she shifted away. "No. This is a decision I must make to protect Jack."

"It doesn't have to be Willie. If you're so determined to do this, why not accept Gabe's offer of marriage?"

Pressing fingers against her temples, she let out a shaky breath. "He's gone and wants no part of us," she sighed. "I should have told him about Jack in the beginning. I just...I didn't want to lose him."

"I don't believe for a minute that Gabe has changed his mind. He loves you, but he's a proud man. Yes, you should've confided in him, trusted he'd accept your past, but you didn't. Your decision can't be changed now, but you can go to him, explain, and ask him to forgive you. What you can't do is marry Willie. Hell, Lena. Do you think I'd stand by and let you throw your life away for a man like him?"

Her lips twisted into a grim smile. "It's doubtful."

"Not just doubtful. If need be, I'd lock you away until you came to your senses. Let me send someone for Gabe. If my guess is correct, he'll honor his offer to marry you."

"I don't want Gabe to marry me out of a sense of obligation. If he can't accept Jack or let me explain my reasons for hiding his identity, I won't marry him."

"Yet you'll marry a man you despise to gain respectability?" Nick asked, frustration seething within him as his voice rose, his hands clenching at his sides. "That's absurd, Lena. You're a better person than that. The strong, resilient woman I know wouldn't even *consider* letting a man like Willie coerce her into a decision she'd later regret."

In all their years together, it had been rare that Nick's anger had been turned toward her, yet she felt the sting of his words as if he'd slapped her.

The man she loved as a brother, respected more than anyone she'd ever known, had always wanted the best for her. He'd gone without, not allowing himself to fall in love or build a family because of the obligation he felt toward her. Even though her past and future remained grounded in being a saloon owner, she was proud of the opportunities Nick had given her. She was proud of him.

All she had achieved was due to Nick. Without him, she would've ended up like Deborah and the other girls, making a living on her back. She owed Nick everything.

Taking a seat on the bed, she covered her face with her hands.

"Give it more time. Talk to Gabe. You might be surprised at what he'll say," he encouraged.

Dropping her hands, her red-rimmed eyes gazed up at Nick as she shook her head. "No. I'll not marry Gabe if he has doubts about me. He's too good a man to feel forced into a marriage out of a sense of duty. I'd rather leave Splendor, settle in a place where no one knows us. I'll tell people Jack's father died during the war." Her pleading eyes searched his. "There's no reason they wouldn't believe me."

"And what will you do if Willie finds you? He's a man who hungers for control above all else. He'll look for you, and once found, drag both you and Jack back here, if only to make a point. He will not let you go, Lena." Nick didn't voice his concerns about Willie's mental state. For the longest time, he'd thought the man wasn't right in the head, but he had no other proof beyond a gut feeling. God help him, if Lena decided to marry him, Nick knew he'd find a way to kill Willie and make his body disappear.

"And what do I do if I refuse Willie and Gabe doesn't want us? I can handle the scorn, but Jack? He won't understand, and he'll take the worst of it. A bad decision I made years ago will cause him to suffer, and there will be nothing I can do to stop it." Her eyes gleamed with tears as her voice broke.

Grasping her shoulders, he knelt before her, his voice low, controlled. "If you had not made that decision, you wouldn't have Jack. Tell me you'd give him up if you could go back and change what happened."

Shaking her head, she swiped at the tears streaming down her face. "I can't."

"Of course not. Tell Willie no. Explain everything to Gabe and give him a chance to trust you. If he still walks away and you're determined to marry for Jack's sake, I'll be your husband."

She shot a shocked look at Nick. "I would never let you do that. You've given up enough for Jack and me, and I will not have you sacrificing yourself any further. Besides, you're like a brother." She offered him a weak smile. "No matter how handsome you are, how much you're worth, or what a wonderful man you are, I could never, *ever* share a bed with you."

Nick's head tilted back as he roared with laughter. "Well spoken, Lena. And I feel the same." His expression became serious. "But I'd do it for you."

She touched his cheek, warmed by the offer. "I know you would."

Pushing himself up, he stood over her. "Give it a few more days. You can keep Jack home another day or two, then send him back. One of us will meet him after school each day to thwart further attacks by these bullies, at least until I can teach him how to defend himself."

"Don't you mean teach them a lesson?"

"Well, yes. I can't have my nephew be seen as weak, can I?" He reached out his hand, helping her stand. "Now get dressed. I'll escort you to the Dixie." His finger lifted her chin. "We will resolve this, Lena. And we'll do it without you accepting that madman's offer of marriage."

Chapter Twenty-One

Cash spotted Blackheart in a small corral near the barn. Knocking on the door, then shouting as he walked around Luke's old cabin yielded no sign of Gabe. Taking off his hat, he slapped it against his thigh to get rid of the rain, which had pelleted him on and off during the ride from Splendor. Adjusting his duster, Cash saw the trail behind the house. On a hunch, he followed it toward the sound of water not far away.

"I thought you might be out here." Cash stopped at the edge of Wildfire Creek, watching as Gabe reeled in a fish that appeared to be about as long as his forearm.

Gabe nodded at the intrusion, not taking his gaze off the catch he hoped to have for supper. If he landed this one, he'd have three trout, plenty enough to offer Cash a decent meal. Making the last few turns of the reel, he hauled the fish to shore, admiring the size and color.

"I haven't eaten all day. You'll stay for supper so you can tell me what brought you all the way out here." Securing the fish to his stringer, he grabbed the pole, making his way to Cash. "Hope this isn't some type of emergency."

Cash hated to intrude on Gabe's time away, and he wouldn't if the three matters he had to discuss weren't so urgent. He knew how to handle the one situation, but the other called for Gabe and no one else.

"I can stay, but you're not going to like any of the news I've brought."

Gabe retraced the trail to the cabin. Almost three days of doing whatever he wanted, which included a good deal of fishing—with little success until today—had been what he needed. Taking a few minutes to clean and prepare the fish while Cash got a pan hot on the stove, Gabe's concern grew. He knew it must be urgent to bring him all the way from town, especially knowing he'd have to make the ride back in the dark.

Setting a plate of fried fish, biscuits, and a jar of peaches Rachel had given him on the table, they sat down.

"All right. What's so urgent?" Gabe peeled the tender white meat from the bones, placing a forkful in his mouth, enjoying the delicate flavor.

"I've got Tommy Pennington in jail, and he'll stay there."

Pennington should've been arrested after his first attack on Dolly weeks before. She'd refused to press charges, saying it was more her fault than his. Gabe knew her words were a lie and suspected it had more to do with losing the much needed income.

"What are the charges?"

Cash swallowed, then took a sip of coffee. "He beat Dolly again. Bad. Al found her and called Beau and me. I'll spare you the details, but Doc won't let her leave the clinic."

Gabe stopped chewing, choking down his mouthful of fish as anger boiled through him. "Will she press charges this time?"

"Al told her if she didn't, he would. He found her when she refused to come down for breakfast or lunch. He told Amos, who said he'd fire her if she didn't speak up against Pennington."

"Finally," Gabe ground out. "These gals need to come to us when they've been abused. Not hide in their rooms in fear."

"I hate to say it, but I understand why they don't. A lot of bosses aren't like Amos or Nick. They'll side with the customer, assume it's the woman's fault, and dock their pay or even fire them. It's good all the gals at the Rose know what happened and saw how Amos and Al handled it. Maybe they'll speak up sooner next time."

"We don't want a next time, but I agree. How long will she be laid up?" Gabe stood, grabbing the coffee pot and filling their cups.

"At least three weeks, maybe longer. Doc says she has some broken ribs. She's not taking it too well. Beau and I are going to help her, and I'll bet Bull and a couple others will toss in some money when they hear about it. Doc's going to mention it to the preacher's wife, but..." Cash raised his eyebrows in question.

Gabe understood Cash's skepticism. The church women tolerated the saloons, but that's all. He felt certain they'd burn the Dixie and Rose down if they could. "I'll help, and I'm certain Nick and Lena will want to assist. What else?"

"I heard you and Nick were negotiating with Amos to buy the Rose."

"Yes, but it isn't news any of us want shared until the sale is final."

"Understandable. Anyway, Amos has another offer, and apparently, the men who want it sent their gunman twice to speak with him." Cash had seen the man in town, not knowing the reason for his visit until the day before. "This time, he came right out and told Amos not to accept any other offer or he wouldn't be alive long enough to collect the money."

Gabe let out a string of curses. "Is the other offer from Carlyle?"

"And his partner. Amos ignored them and accepted your offer. Nick asked me to let you know Del Utley, the attorney, is drawing up the contract. As soon as it's final, Amos will be leaving town. The sooner the better in my mind."

Gabe nodded, his mind already working on how to protect Amos until he left.

"Is that it?"

Cash pursed his lips, grasping the almost cold cup of coffee between both hands. He glanced up at Gabe, his face grim.

"Tell me."

"The real reason I'm here is Nick asked me to come and get you."

Gabe leaned back in his chair, crossing his arms. "Does he need help with the hotel work? Maybe wielding a shovel?" he joked.

"Lena might marry Carlyle."

Ever since her discussion with Nick and his emphatic conviction she couldn't marry Willie, Lena had struggled. She'd let Nick believe his argument had persuaded her to abandon the possibility of marrying him, but she couldn't shake the grim reality it might be her only way to keep Jack safe without pushing Gabe to honor his proposal.

Gabe had left, angry and feeling deceived, leaving no word on his whereabouts. She didn't know when or if he'd return. If he did, would he still want her? She'd had her chance and lost it, all because of fear he'd reject her once he learned the truth.

It had been three days, the amount of time Willie said he'd give her to make a decision. Nick had already seen him ride in, leaving his horse at a post down the street. He'd be looking for her soon. If she denied him, he'd start a campaign to destroy her, as well as Nick. His threats had been clear and she would be his main target.

Lost in thought as she rested her arms on the bar, her back to the entrance, Lena didn't hear the doors swing open, or the sound of boots coming up behind her. She flinched as a prickling feeling crept up her spine. Glancing toward the mirror behind the bar, she gasped, seeing Willie's reflection, a sneer returning her shocked expression. Fisting her hands at her sides, she took several steps away, rounding on him.

"What are you doing here?"

"I would think that would be obvious. I've come to learn your decision." Willie stepped closer, letting his gaze wander from her silk slippered feet upward until it settled on her lush lips.

Stepping away, she crossed her arms, glancing at Paul on the other side of the bar, ready to intervene. Finding her courage, she glared at him, eyes flickering with indignation.

"I've made no decision." She looked away, unable to stomach the sight of the man she hated with all her heart.

"Of course you have, my dear. You're just not ready to voice it." Willie leaned closer, confident of her answer. "As I said before, I need your decision tonight, Lena. Now, what will it be?"

"I'd advise you to step away from my fiancée. Better yet, why don't you take your sorry ass and ride it out of town." Gabe strolled in, his feral gaze fixing on Willie, his hand resting on the butt of his gun.

Lena whipped around, letting out a relieved breath. "Gabe..." She started to move toward him, then stopped when he shot her a hard look.

"Later. Willie and I have some business to finish." Gabe stepped between Willie and Lena, his face a mask. "Did I not make myself clear?" He could see Carlyle's Adam's apple spasm, beads of sweat forming on his brow. Gabe's hand snaked out without warning, grasping Willie by the collar and yanking him closer. "Get out of town, Carlyle. Never set foot in Splendor again, and never, *ever*, get anywhere close to Lena." He held him close another minute, then pushed him backwards, Willie's back slamming into the edge of a table.

Straightening, he adjusted his shirt, sending a lethal scowl at Lena. "This isn't over." Before he could utter another word, Gabe's fist connected with his jaw, sending Willie crashing to the floor.

"You don't seem to hear so well, Carlyle." Bending to grab Willie's arm, he twisted it behind his back, marching him to the door before shoving him outside, leaving him sprawled on the boardwalk. Gabe's expression didn't change as he turned back to Lena. "Grab a coat. You're coming with me."

Her shaky legs moved toward him, her resolve strengthening with each step. "I'm not going anywhere with you until I know why."

"A whiskey, Paul," Gabe ordered before shifting his gaze to her. "We're going someplace we can talk in private, without fear of interruption. I'm leaving as soon as I drink this." He held up his glass and took a sip. "Be ready by then."

She settled her hands on her hips. "Or what?"

He pushed his hat back from his forehead. "Do you really want to know?"

Her tongue darted out to moisten her lips before she spun away, stomping toward the office. A moment later, she returned, slipping into a heavy wool coat as she approached him.

Tossing back the rest of the whiskey, he stalked toward the door, certain she'd follow. Looking around, he felt a sense of relief at seeing Willie's horse gone.

Stopping between Blackheart and Joker, he waited to help her mount.

"I don't need your help." Lena pushed past him, grabbing the reins as she placed one foot in the stirrup. Bouncing once, then twice, she created the momentum needed for swinging her right leg over the saddle. Adjusting her skirt, she sent Gabe a smug expression.

Pursing his lips to keep a smile from forming, he walked around Blackheart, mounted, and started to ride north.

"Where are we going?"

Ignoring her question, he glanced over his shoulder. "Keep up or you'll lose me in the dark."

They rode for an hour, her stiff posture relaxing as she let herself feel Joker's rhythm. Taking a trail Lena had never noticed before, they wound north, then west, then north again until they came to a creek.

"Not much further." Gabe didn't wait for a response, reining Blackheart along the edge of the water, continuing north.

Lena saw the flickering of lights ahead moments before they rode into a clearing, a beautiful cabin centered on the land.

"Where are we?"

"This is the house Luke built before he met Ginny. He's been letting me use it." Without further explanation, Gabe slid to the ground, walking Blackheart into the barn. "Are you coming?" he shot over his shoulder when he saw her still sitting astride Joker.

Feeling her face heat, she dismounted, following him, coming to a stop alongside his horse.

"We'll take care of the horses before going inside."

"You mean, unsaddle them?" Her incredulous voice almost made Gabe laugh.

"That's what you generally do when you've finished a ride." He put his saddle on one of the stands Luke had built, then removed the bridle. Noticing she hadn't moved, he placed the bridle on a hook. "Don't tell me you've never taken care of a horse."

His question angered and embarrassed her. The truth was, Nick had always paid someone to prepare her horse for a ride, taking care of him when she returned. She had no idea what to do next.

He walked up next to her, letting his arm graze hers, hearing her sharp intake of breath.

"Here. I'll show you."

Standing next to him, feeling warmth radiate off his body, she watched, fascinated by his quick, sure movements. Within minutes, they were placing each horse in a stall.

"Come on. I'll make some coffee."

The cabin seemed bigger on the inside and cozier than she expected. "Luke built this?"

"With help from men at the ranch. He only had weeks to get it done before the first snow fell. Go ahead. Look around." Hearing her walk away, he let out a relieved breath, glad for a few minutes to collect his thoughts.

He'd felt a surge of rage when he spotted Willie so close to Lena, then heard his threatening words, insisting she marry him. It took all his willpower to control his emotions until he could confront the man, registering the look of fear on Lena's face at the same time.

He'd wanted to take her in his arms, tell her they'd work it out, but dealing with Willie came first. Now they had a chance to talk. Gabe needed to hear her explanation to decide if he could put her deception behind him enough to find a future with her and Jack.

"It's lovely." Stepping next to him, she accepted the cup he offered. She held it tight, wrapping both hands around it as she tried to still her shaking.

"Let's sit down." He held out a chair, then sat across from her. "Tell me everything, Lena. And don't leave anything out."

He listened, not interrupting as she explained her history with Willie, her decision to shield Jackson from his father by having him live with Isabella, and his threats if she didn't marry him.

"I have no choice. He'll take Jackson if I don't marry him."

"You *do* have a choice." Gabe reached across the table to cover her hands with his.

"There's no way out of this and Willie knows it."

"The way out of this is for you to marry me and let me adopt Jackson. Carlyle won't be able to touch you or him after that." Gabe's chest tightened at the thought she'd marry Willie to save her child and not for love. He wanted her to accept his offer. He loved her—always would, no matter all the secrets she'd kept from him.

"After all I've done, you'd still marry me?"

"I've known since the first moment I spotted you stepping off the stage in Splendor that you were who I wanted. No matter how hard I've tried to talk myself out of it, I can't help how I feel about you." He let go of her hands. "If you don't feel the same, we can still marry to protect Jack. Maybe in time..."

Her stomach clenched as his voice faded. "How *do* you feel?"

"I love you." His grim chuckle tore at her heart. "There doesn't seem to be any way I can change how I feel."

They sat in silence, Lena deciding she had to share the last of what she'd kept from him. She loved him, didn't want to lose him, but he needed to know what he'd get if they married.

Her chest squeezed painfully. "I love you, too, Gabe, but there is something more you must know. I hoped to never share it with anyone other than Isabella and Nick, but..."

Gabe leaned across the table, lifting her chin with a finger. "Tell me."

She glanced away, her eyes damp with tears. "Jackson and I almost died during his delivery. The doctor thought he could save just one of us and I chose Jackson. No one knows how I made it through, but I did, although it took months to recover. The doctor said I might not live through another childbirth."

It took a moment for her meaning to become clear. If they married, they could never have children. Closing his eyes, he searched deep inside, trying to come to terms with her admission. He loved her, would do anything for her. Could he forsake having a family if they married? The answer came to him in an instant.

Gabe stood and walked around the table, pulling her up and into his arms. Feeling her tremble, he tightened his hold, placing a kiss on her temple as her tears dampened his shirt. He pulled back, not letting her look away.

"I love you, Lena. We have Jack and he's enough for me."

Chapter Twenty-Two

The rest of the night passed in a passionate fog. They made love so many times, she lost count. She'd agreed to marry him, accepting his ultimatum she never keep secrets from him again. The promise had barely left her mouth when he'd scooped her into his arms, carrying her to the bedroom, and stripping her under his heated gaze.

"You're so beautiful, Lena," he whispered as he slipped out of his clothes and settled next to her, stroking her skin while placing fevered kisses along her neck and face, then seizing her mouth in a searing kiss.

Reaching up, she ran her fingers through his hair, drawing him closer.

"You're certain you won't regret not having more children?" Her voice trembled, but she needed to hear him say it again.

"Never," he breathed against her lips as his hands splayed on her back, drawing her close. "You and Jack are all I need. Don't ever doubt it."

"I'd better get you back to town before Nick sends men looking for us." He couldn't contain a grin as he handed her a cup of coffee as she sat in bed, her auburn hair falling around her shoulders as the blanket slipped down, exposing smooth skin. Feeling his body begin to heat, he stepped back, putting distance between them so he wouldn't be tempted to climb back into bed and take her one more time before leaving.

Taking the cup, she leaned back against the headboard. "I hate to say it, but you wore me out, Sheriff. I'm not certain I can stay in the saddle all the way to Splendor." Her eyes twinkled, mouth curving into a smile.

"Then I guess you'll have to ride with me on Blackheart." He raised his eyebrows, knowing having her in front of him would be pure torture. "I have eggs and ham ready. We'll eat, then head back."

They'd just entered the north edge of town when Noah came riding up, pulling to a stop, his face grim.

"What is it?"

"Carlyle. He took some men to Luke and Ginny's yesterday while everyone was at Dax and Rachel's." Noah shot a look at Lena, then lowered his voice. "He took Jack and Isabella."

Gabe couldn't contain the curse that sprang from his lips. "I need to go find them." He started to rein Blackheart around before Noah stopped him.

"Luke and Ginny discovered a note from Willie when they returned. He'll return Isabella in exchange for Lena."

"No!" Lena's anguished voice sliced through Gabe.

Gabe grabbed her reins, stopping her from riding off. "Lena, we'll find them."

"Cash, Beau, and Nick have already ridden to the Devil Dancer mine. Dax, Luke, Bull, and a good number of other Pelletier men have formed a posse. They're already searching."

"I can't sit here and wait. I need to find my son." Lena tried to jerk the reins from Gabe's hand, without success.

"Lena, stop." He slid from Blackheart, handing the reins to Noah, then walked up to Joker, catching Lena around the waist and pulling her to the ground. Wrapping his arms around her, he held tight when she tried to squirm loose. "We will find them, but you must let me do my job. There are two groups of men already out searching. It's just a matter of time before Jack and Isabella are found." He smoothed a hand down her hair, praying he spoke the truth. "They need you to be strong right now. If you ride off, there's a chance Willie will find you."

Gabe could feel her breathing slow and her body relax as he stroked her back.

"Noah, do you know which direction the Pelletiers rode?" Gabe asked, not releasing his hold on her.

"They split into two groups. One rode south, the other west, following Cash and the others. What do you want me to do?"

He pulled away from Lena, cradling her face in his hands. "I need to ride out with Noah. Promise me you'll stay with Suzanne while I'm gone."

She didn't want to promise, but the look in his eyes—worry, sincerity, concern—stopped her. He and most of the other men were trained in fighting, were excellent shots, and some had been trackers during the war. She had no skills for such a search. What she *did* have was an idea of who might know where Willie would take Jack and Isabella.

"I'll stay with Suzanne, although it will be miserable waiting to hear word of what's happening."

Kissing her forehead, he turned to Noah. "You and I will ride out in ten minutes to catch up with Cash and the others."

"Meet you at the livery." Noah took Blackheart and Joker with him as Gabe escorted Lena to Suzanne's.

Once inside, he drew her to him.

"We'll find them, sweetheart. It will be easier knowing you're here in town, safe."

Lena peered out the window until Gabe and Noah passed by on their way out of town. She'd been thankful when he hadn't escorted her into the kitchen, explaining to Suzanne and Fanny her promise to stay. *Although it wasn't an actual promise as much as an agreement,* she thought as she dashed outside and ran across the street to the jail.

Rushing inside, she came to halt at the sight of a man she'd never seen before behind Gabe's desk. He looked her up and down, then tipped his hat.

"Ma'am. What can I do for you?"

"I...um...I was looking for Cash or Beau." She winced at the lie, knowing the two men were long gone on their search.

"They're not here. Can I help you with something?"

She stepped forward, flashing the man a charming smile. "I'm Magdalena Campanel. I don't believe we've met."

"I'm Ebenezer Smith. Most people call me Eb. My brother and our families came into town a few weeks ago. The day of the bank robbery."

"Oh, I remember seeing you. I hope everyone got settled all right." She wrung her hands, searching for a way to get rid of the man for a while.

"Found our land. It's as good as the man who sold it to us said it would be. I guess you can't ask for more than that."

"No, I guess not. Are you guarding the prisoner?" She looked around the corner at the cells, but couldn't see Thomas Pennington.

Eb chuckled. "Not much to guard. He's a quiet dandy. I doubt he'll put up too much of a fuss."

"That's good. Doesn't sound as if there's much to worry about. Well, I suppose I should head over to the boardinghouse and get something to eat." Her eyes lit up as she glanced at him. "I'm guessing you haven't eaten since breakfast. I'd be happy to sit here a while if you want to get some food."

"Well, I thank you for the offer, but I doubt Deputy Coulter would approve of me leaving a lady to watch the prisoner." His eyes crinkled at the corners.

"I'm not so certain. You said yourself he's quiet and I doubt he could escape. Besides, you wouldn't be gone too long, right?" She walked up a little closer to Eb, offering another smile. "I don't mind staying if you're hungry."

Eb rubbed a stubbled jaw between his fingers, considering her offer. His brother, Elijah, had asked him to ride to town late the day before when they realized how low they'd gotten on some crucial supplies. He'd spent the night in town, but hadn't been able to eat breakfast before Cash approached him about keeping watch on the prisoner. Food sounded real good right about now.

"If you're certain, I might just take you up on your offer. I won't be gone long. You stay out here, in the front, and you won't have any problem with the prisoner."

"Don't fret about it, Mr. Smith. While you're gone, I'll write a letter I've put off too long. You take your time."

Nodding, he headed out the door. Lena stepped to the window, watching as he crossed the street to the boardinghouse and vanished inside. Turning toward the cells, she reached into her reticule, pulling out the derringer Nick insisted she always carry. Even though small, it could kill a man if aimed in the right place. And she knew just the spot.

Straightening her spine, she approached Tommy's cell, noting his prone position on his stomach. Dragging the barrel of the gun along the bars as she walked, she waited for him to move.

"Wake up, Tommy." She halted at the cell entrance, pointing the gun in his direction as he began to stir. "Did you hear me? I said, *get up.*"

Rolling onto his back, Tommy lifted his gaze to her, his eyes widening at the sight of the gun.

"What the hell are you doing?" he ground out, his voice groggy and raw.

"It's what you're going to do that's important. You're going to tell me where Willie might go to hide. A shack, old cabin, cave...anywhere he could disappear. And, Tommy, you're going to do it now." She lifted the gun, aiming for his heart.

"I have no idea what you're talking about. If Willie's not in town, he'll be at the mine."

She wiggled the gun back and forth. "Uh-uh. I'm certain you can think of other places he might go. Perhaps a spot only the two of you know about."

When he started to stand, she stepped closer to the bars, her face hardening. "Stay where you are. I don't have much patience right now. And don't think I won't shoot you because right now, there's nothing more I'd like to do."

"Someone would hear you."

"With this?" She cast a quick glance at the derringer. "Well, the good news is this gun is quiet. The bad news is it kills just as fast as a bigger one. Oh, and the deputies are gone, as well as the man Cash asked to watch you. Poor man hadn't had a bite to eat all day."

For the first time, his face showed concern. "You mean it's just the two of us?"

"Very astute of you, Tommy. Believe me, if you don't give me the information I need, you *will* require the services of the doctor."

Tommy rubbed his hands on his thighs. "I need a few minutes to think."

"You have thirty seconds."

Glaring at her, he looked more closely at the gun. "You only have one bullet."

"Believe me, that's all I need." Her nerves began to weaken the longer he refused to give her what she needed. Any moment she expected the door to open and Eb to walk in. "Last chance, Tommy." Her finger began to put pressure on the trigger as her heart pounded in her chest.

"Fine. There is one place he might go. It's an old shack about two miles south of the mine. It's tucked against the base of the mountain. But you'll never find it. The place is buried in bushes and trees."

"I'll find it." She slipped the derringer back into her reticule and turned to leave.

"Wait. Why do you need to find him?"

"He kidnapped my son."

Dashing to the desk, she opened a drawer, pulling out a wanted poster and turning it over. Scribbling a quick apology to Eb about an emergency, she took a look out the front door, deciding her best route would be out the back.

"If you take me, I'll lead you to it." Tommy stood with his hands clasped around the bars.

Lena stared at him, weighing her ability to keep watch on him. A gun with only a single bullet for protection meant he could overpower her with little effort.

"What Willie did was wrong. He should never have taken the boy. Let me help you find him."

Tommy's eyes showed sincerity. She wished she could see into his heart, know if he told the truth. Lena hadn't planned to ride to the shack alone. Instead, she'd go to the mine, find Gabe and the other men, telling them what she'd learned. The odds of making it to the shack with Tommy as her guide were slim.

"It's a generous offer, but I think I'll take my chances alone." The words had barely left her mouth when she closed the door behind her, heading toward the livery.

Staying close to the back of the building, she ran the short distance, knowing Joker would be in a stall. All she had to do was saddle and bridle him, grateful for the lesson Gabe had given her.

It took longer than expected, her fingers trembling as she cinched the saddle in place. After several attempts, she finished, grabbing the bridle and replacing the halter. Pulling Joker behind her, she started for the back gate, then stopped, thinking of her small gun. Throwing the reins over a fence rail, Lena dashed into Noah's blacksmith shop, looking around. In frantic movements, she searched shelves, hooks, and barrels before finding what she wanted—a revolver, wrapped in cloth and tucked behind a box of bullets.

Grabbing both, she slid them into the saddle bags, opened the gate, then rode out, not taking another moment to consider Gabe's reaction. Willie had her son, and by God, she would make sure he paid.

"We don't have any idea where Carlyle is. He took off with a group of the newest men after Pennington left camp. Neither's been back." The tall, scrawny miner held tight to the shovel he'd plunged into the ground, letting his body lean against it. "What do you need him for?"

"He kidnapped a boy in Splendor." Gabe looked around at the men who'd gathered. None of them showed any surprise at his announcement. "Any of you know where he might have taken him?"

Shaking their heads, they turned away, focusing on their work. "Certainly some of you have wives and children back home. What would you do if one of them disappeared?"

The first miner spun around, glaring at Gabe. "Same as you, Sheriff. The truth is, he doesn't speak to any of us. We've all been working with little sleep to pull gold from the mine. Not much time to check out the surroundings." He spat on the ground. "All of us need the work or we wouldn't be here. From what we can tell, the man can't be trusted. Watch your backs."

Gabe stared after him, then swung his gaze to Cash and Beau. He and Noah had caught up with them not far from the mine. No one had heard from the Pelletier riders, so they decided to continue ahead, hoping the miners might know more. If they did, they weren't sharing.

"Where to now?" Cash leaned forward, resting his hands on the saddle horn.

"It depends on..." Gabe's voice faded, his face turning to stone at the rider who approached. Cursing, he reined Blackheart around.

The others followed his gaze, Noah chuckling as Lena rode toward them, her saddle slightly askew. At Gabe's stormy expression, he leaned over. "You may want to hear what she has to say before you rip into her."

Gabe started to respond, then clamped his mouth shut, his lips a thin line as she reined to a stop next to them.

"I have news, Gabe. It's important." Breathing hard, as if she'd been running, Lena shifted her weight to one stirrup in an attempt to center the saddle.

"I'll fix it for you, Lena." Noah slid off Tempest, handing the reins to Cash. Holding up his hands, he grabbed her by the waist and set her down, then went to work adjusting the saddle.

Gabe took longer to regain his calm. The sight of her riding alone, on a saddle barely staying in place, had his heart beating. He guessed they needed to have another talk about keeping herself safe. Dismounting, he closed the distance between them.

"What news?"

"There's an old shack about two miles south of here. That's where Tommy thinks Willie may be keeping Jack and Isabella."

"And you know this how?"

Hands on hips, she looked up at him, her face showing none of the trepidation she felt. "I spoke to him, of course. How else would I know?"

"You're telling me Pennington decided to confide in you while locked in a jail cell?"

Shooting a quick look at Cash, she caught her bottom lip between her teeth. "In essence, yes."

"He *volunteered* the information to you? And here I had such poor thoughts on the man." Cash watched her expression, knowing there was more to the story. "Eb Smith let you talk with him?" Cash asked, surprised that Eb would let her near Pennington.

"Not exactly," she answered, then rushed on. "But you're missing the importance of what I'm saying. We have a place to search, unless you've already found Jack."

Taking her by the shoulders, he turned Lena away from the men, escorting her several feet away. "*We* are not going anywhere. You are going to tell me everything Pennington said, then you're going to stay here until I come back for you." His grip tightened on her shoulders as he spoke, fear at what could've happened to her on the trail pulsing through him.

"Gabe, you're hurting me." She knew distress guided his actions, nothing more. Nonetheless, she expected to see bruising from his tight grip.

Dropping his hands and stepping back, he removed his hat, running unsteady fingers through his damp hair. "How did you get Pennington to talk, Lena?"

Walking to Joker, she grabbed her reticule and returned to Gabe. Slipping her hand inside, she gripped the derringer, pulling it out enough for him to get a glimpse.

"You threatened him?"

"It worked, and I wouldn't have actually pulled the trigger."

Gabe pinched the bridge of his nose. "Cash said Eb Smith was there. Didn't he try to stop you?"

"He hadn't eaten all day. I convinced him I'd be all right watching Tommy while he left to eat." Crossing her arms, she glared at him. "We're wasting time. We need to leave and find Jack." She spun away, grabbed Joker's reins, and put her foot in the stirrup, ready to swing up, then froze as strong hands held her in place.

"You're not going and that's final. We'll come back for you when we find Jack."

"If you leave me, I'll follow. I won't be left behind to worry. It's not going to happen." Crossing her arms, she stood firm, glowering at Gabe.

Swearing under his breath, Gabe looked at the other men, who just shrugged, indicating they weren't going to be any help.

"All right. But you do what I say at all times. If you don't, I swear I'll take you over my knee and make you wish you had." Gabe didn't wait for a response before mounting Blackheart, reining him south.

Chapter Twenty-Three

"Shut up, kid. I've had enough of your whining." Willie's eyes were narrowed into slits, his hands fisted as he glared at Jack.

"He needs to go outside, Willie. You'll end up with a mess if you don't let him." Isabella's calm voice pleaded with him. "He's already waited hours."

"I don't give a..." He stopped himself, rubbing his throbbing eyes with his thumb and forefinger before storming toward the door, throwing it open. "Get out there. But if you try to run, I'll catch you, and Isabella will be the one to pay." His vacant eyes focused on Jack, his son, a boy for which he felt nothing.

Jack ran outside, past the one guard Willie had posted, and disappeared behind a bush. Willie turned a venomous gaze toward Isabella.

"You've turned him into a sniveling weakling."

"He's six years old, not a man. You're being very hard on your own son." Isabella glared at him, hating every inch of the man standing before her.

Willie snorted, glancing back outside. "Hurry up, boy! You're wasting time."

"Do you feel *anything* for him?" Isabella asked, her voice soft, full of uncertainty. She couldn't understand how a father could be so ambivalent about his own blood.

"Why should I? He's been kept from me his entire life."

"I'm aware of the letters, Willie. You knew where to find Jack at any time, yet you showed no interest and offered only threats against him and Lena."

Willie glanced outside just as Jack peered around the bush, then started back, the one guard keeping his eyes trained on him.

"I'm finished." Jack stood in the doorway, his gaze darting between the two adults.

"Then sit down. And stop whining for your mother." Willie closed the door before adding wood to the stove.

"What are your plans for us?" Isabella reached over, putting an arm around Jack's shoulders. She'd been surprised when Willie hadn't tied them, assuming the isolation and his threats would keep them from running.

Taking a seat in a rickety chair, he crossed his arms, spearing them with a smug look. "I've offered to exchange you for Lena. Word has been sent to her about when and where to meet us. If she doesn't appear, she'll never see either of you again."

Isabella felt Jack begin to shake. Looking at him, she could see his lower lip tremble as he began to understand the meaning of Willie's statement. Jumping up from the chair, Jack ran toward his father, pushing him and pounding his chest, tears beginning to stream down his face.

"I hate you. I hate you." Jack's voice, loud and clear, broke as he pounded on Willie's chest, pushing him with such might the chair almost toppled over.

"Enough." Willie grabbed Jack's wrists, wrenching them until he cried out in pain.

"Stop, Willie. You're hurting him." Isabella rushed toward them, slapping at Willie's face, forcing him to let go of Jack before he turned and slammed a fist in her face. Isabella spun away, falling to the floor.

"Aunt Isabella!" Jack cried, wrenching out of Willie's grasp and dropping beside her.

Willie stared down at them, showing only frustration. Stalking outside, he closed the door, leaving them alone. He reached into a pocket, pulling out a cheroot and lighting it, inhaling deeply. The weather had turned cold. As he exhaled, the smoke from the slim cigar and his warm breath hitting the cold air combined to form a wide, white cloud.

He'd sent two men to deliver the message to Lena early that morning. They had yet to return with any news, although he knew she wouldn't put either Jack or Isabella in further danger. Her love of them both would force her to do as he asked. After the exchange, they'd ride to Big Pine, marry, then return to Splendor as one big happy family.

"Did you find any sign of them?" Gabe caught up with Travis, who'd ridden ahead in search of tracks. The two Pelletier groups had merged, then headed for the mine, catching Gabe and the others as they rode off. The sheer number of men allowed them to fan out and cover more ground.

"About a mile from here. Fresh tracks of four riders took a trail up the mountain. I didn't get any closer as I wanted to let you know what I saw." Travis had tracked during the war. When he returned to the family's horse farm, he'd found it destroyed with no sign of his wife or daughter. A neighbor, beaten down and weathered from the war, had told him they'd all perished. Unable to find the heart to begin again, he rode west, making it as far as Splendor before finding work with Luke and Dax. "But there are also tracks of two horses riding out. We may get lucky and catch two people guarding them—assuming we've followed the right group of riders."

Reining their horses toward the others, Travis explained to them what he'd found.

Gabe silently counted the number of men. "We have more than enough men to surround whoever is up there, leaving a small group down here so they can't escape."

"Agreed," Dax said.

"Noah, you pick four men to stay with you, the rest ride with us. Travis, you're in the lead." Gabe knew Noah would understand why he'd been asked to stay behind. His sharpshooter skills might end up being their last chance of stopping Carlyle if he somehow escaped the posse. There would be no chance he'd escape Noah.

Taking it slow, the men traveled up the narrow path, following Travis, who rode about a hundred yards ahead. Once he spotted the shack, he'd ride back and approach on foot with the others.

Gabe thought of Lena. She'd done as he asked and stayed close to him, keeping her silence throughout the ride from the mine—until he'd ordered her to stay with Noah. Her protest had been loud and agitated, her contempt for his decision clear. She wanted to be there for Jackson and Isabella. Once calm, she understood his concern, as well as those of the other men. They didn't want to risk her getting shot or even taken. In the end, Gabe had left the decision up to her. That's when she agreed to stay behind.

Thinking of the argument, his mouth tipped into a grin. Lena had wanted the choice. Once given the reasons to stay behind, safe with Noah, she'd backed off, deciding the concerns were valid. She'd be no help to Jackson if a bullet found her.

"The shack is about two hundred yards ahead. There are two horses, one man standing guard.

Carlyle must be inside, although I didn't get close enough to look." Travis had reined up alongside Gabe and Cash, Dax and a few others joining them.

"We can split the men into groups and surround the shack, but we run the risk of Carlyle using Jack or Isabella as a hostage." Luke spoke without emotion, his years in the war kicking in as if he'd never been away. "Gabe, it might be better to let him think you've come alone, draw him outside so we have a shot at both men."

"That puts you right in his line of fire, Gabe. Let me ride up instead." Cash had little to lose if shot or killed, while Gabe had Lena and Jackson.

"He's more likely to shoot you, but try to use me as an additional hostage. No. I'm the one who needs to go." Gabe checked his revolvers and rifle, then looked at Luke. "Get everyone in position. Signal me when you're ready."

"Riders coming from the west, Noah." Dirk Masters, one of the foreman at the Pelletier ranch, pointed behind him.

"How many?"

"Two."

"Might be the ones Travis thought had ridden off." Noah signaled to the other men, motioning for them to move off the trail. "Lena, you're with me."

Moving well off the trail, he hid her behind a group of bushes several yards behind him.

"Stay there until this is over."

Long minutes passed before the two riders approached, their guard down. Looking straight ahead, they followed the trail, heading toward the shack.

"That's far enough, gents." Noah stood at the edge of the trail, his rifle aimed at the lead rider.

The men pulled up short, fumbling for their weapons.

"I wouldn't try it." Dirk stood behind them. "You have four guns on you."

"What do you want?" the lead rider spat out.

"Are you Carlyle's men?" Noah shifted his weight. There was no way he'd miss from this distance.

"Yeah. What of it?"

"Get off your horses. You'll be staying with us a while."

The man in front glanced around, gauging their chances if they tried to run. They weren't good. Nodding to the second man, both slid from their horses.

"Now drop your guns." Noah moved a few feet closer as Dirk and the others stepped forward.

Within minutes, the men were off the trail and tied up. Noah and Dirk gathered their weapons, noting they weren't indicative of hired gunmen.

"Neither of you appear to be gunslingers. What are you doing working with a man like Carlyle?" Noah looked down at them. From their clothes, they didn't appear to be miners, either.

"That's none of your business."

"It *is* our business when you're part of kidnapping a young boy and woman. The circuit judge isn't too fond of men who terrorize women and children. My guess is you'll hang." Noah set his rifle aside and crossed his arms. "He might be more lenient if you tell us what you know about Carlyle."

The men glanced at each other, their faces full of fear.

"We'll tell you what we know, but it isn't much."

Willie paced inside the cabin as he smoked another cheroot. The two men should have been back by now, perhaps with Lena in tow. Instead of having this settled and being on the trail to Big Pine, he sat in a dilapidated shack, with his brat and Isabella.

"Boss, there's someone coming up the trail," the guard he posted outside shouted through the broken window.

"Our men?"

"No, sir."

Willie leveled a hard look at Jack and Isabella. "Don't say a word. You try to warn whoever this is and I'll shoot him, as well as one of you." He waited until they both nodded, then pulled his gun from its holster and walked outside.

Gabe rode Blackheart forward, stopping as the man on guard raised his gun.

"Get off your horse and keep your hands away from your guns."

He slid to the ground, taking the reins in one hand and walking forward.

"That's close enough." The guard kept his gun trained on Gabe, taking a quick glance at Carlyle.

"So, the sheriff has decided to pay us a visit." Carlyle made a show of looking behind Gabe, knowing he wouldn't find who he sought. "It doesn't appear Miss Campanel is with you. That's a pity." Taking several confident steps forward, he stopped within feet of Gabe, smirking at the stupidity of the man riding in alone. "What did you hope to accomplish coming here without her? Surely you don't believe I'll hand the boy and Isabella over to you."

"*Your son* should mean more to you than just his value as a hostage. And taking a woman? What kind of man does that?" Gabe glared at him, noting Cash and the others making no sound as they came up from behind.

"If you believe you can insult me, Sheriff, you're wrong. I'm long past letting slurs affect me. And to answer your question, I'm the man who is going to marry Magdalena and make her a respectable woman. If she doesn't agree, she won't ever see Jackson again."

Willie must have seen Gabe's eyes flicker when Cash crept along the side of the shack, moving closer. In an instant, Willie backed inside, closing the door at the same time Gabe leaned down to retrieve his gun.

"Don't move, Sheriff." The guard kept his gun on Gabe, although his hands shook as he sensed others moving behind him.

"Drop your gun." Beau's firm voice came from mere feet away. The man turned, seeing several men, their weapons trained on him. Dropping his gun, he held his hands up as Beau moved forward. "Get back there." Beau indicated with the barrel of his gun for the man to join a couple of the Pelletier men behind the shack.

Shots blasted from the broken windows of the cabin, hitting the ground in front of Gabe, missing him by inches. He dove toward some bushes, although they weren't much cover from a flying bullet.

"Come out, Carlyle. We have men all around you. You'll never get past us." Cash had moved to the front corner, opposite where Beau stood, both guns pointed toward the door.

"You forget I have the boy and woman in here. Are you willing to lose them to get me?"

"Are you willing to hang for killing innocent people?" Gabe continued to move until he'd come up alongside Cash. "Let them go and we'll talk. Perhaps the circuit judge will show leniency if you set them free now."

Gabe received a bitter laugh in response. "You and I both know what the judge will say, Sheriff. Here is what is going to happen. I'm taking my boy out of here. I'll leave the woman. You and your men will back away and let me ride off. If you don't, I swear I'll put a bullet in Jackson's head."

From inside, the men could hear the sounds of muffled crying, knowing they came from Jack. Gabe's features hardened as anger flashed through him.

"It may be our best choice, Gabe." Cash's calm voice came from beside him. "Isabella will be safe. Unless Carlyle plans to work his way through dense bushes, there's one trail out of here, and Noah's posted at the bottom of the mountain with Dirk and two other good men. Carlyle won't have any idea they're waiting. He'll never get past them."

Gabe knew Cash's assessment would mean the least killing. Noah could shoot a man between the eyes at a long distance. He'd proved it over and over during the war. The difference would be Lena, who'd be standing near him, watching as he took aim in the direction of Jack.

Gabe nodded. "We'll follow Carlyle as soon as he and Jackson disappear down the trail." Motioning to the other men to back off, he stepped onto the porch. "All right, Carlyle. We'll do it your way."

"No!" Isabella's anguished voice pierced the air. "You can't let him take Jackson."

"Shut up!" Willie's voice preceded a slap.

"I hate you." Jack's cry died quickly, replaced by frightened whimpers as Willie pressed a gun to his head.

"That may be, but you're coming with me." He grabbed a piece of rope, handing it to Isabella. "Tie his hands behind him." Once done, he yanked Jack to his feet, positioning him in front as he walked to the door. "I want a horse brought to the steps and everyone to place their weapons on the ground, then gather over by the tall boulder to the left."

Gabe nodded to his men, who did as Carlyle asked.

Waiting for Gabe to do as he asked, Willie thought through what he'd already done to prepare. As a life-long gambler, he'd made a wager with himself and lost, hoping he could claim Lena and their son. It wouldn't happen. At least not now.

A portion of his wealth had been transferred to several banks, some as far away as Europe. Most importantly, he'd stashed enough across the border in Idaho to live comfortably for the rest of his life. All he had to do was get into the neighboring state, take his money, then disappear into Canada before traveling to Europe, where he'd live in luxury.

"You're betting a lot on Noah's ability to stop him." Dax stood with the others, aware he and Luke had other weapons they hadn't surrendered. "We can try to take him if you want."

"I've got to rely on Noah. He has the best chance of getting Carlyle without shooting Jackson. If he gets past them, we'll follow. He won't get far with Jackson slowing him down."

"If he gets past Noah, he won't be taking Jack with him. I guarantee it." Dax's comment agreed with Gabe's thoughts, although hearing it from someone else gave him no comfort.

"Noah won't miss." His confidence in his friend didn't dispel the growing sense of unease or the knot in his stomach as he thought of Lena. If this failed and Jackson died, he had no doubt he'd lose her forever.

"All right, Carlyle. We've done as you asked."

Willie leaned down near Jack's ear. "Don't think you can get away. Do as I say and no one else will get hurt." He straightened, glancing over his shoulder at Isabella, her hatred almost tangible. "We're coming out."

Guiding Jack, he instructed him to climb into the saddle, using the porch for additional height, as Willie held the reins. His gun never wavered from Jack, even as his gaze darted toward Gabe. Jack's frightened eyes sought and found Nick, his lower lip trembling. Nick nodded in encouragement, trying to convey that everything was going to be all right.

"You do as your father says, Jack, and everything will be fine." It was all Nick could say before Willie sent him an arrogant glare.

Moving his gun from Jack to the men, Willie mounted. Without another word, the two disappeared down the trail.

Chapter Twenty-Four

"What's taking them so long?" Lena paced around the small clearing several yards from the trail, her arms crossed. Glaring at the two men tied and gagged a few feet away, she shook her head, wondering what kind of men could kidnap a young boy and woman.

"They'll be along. You need to be patient." Noah gripped the sharpshooter rifle resting in his hand, marveling at how it still felt like a part of him after all this time.

"It's been hours and still no sign of them. Maybe I should ride—"

"Absolutely not. You'll stay here until Gabe comes back." He saw the flash of anger in her eyes, knowing he'd see the same in Abby's if she were in this position. "It's best this way, Lena. Gabe will return as soon as he has Jack."

"And if Willie gets away?" She stopped pacing long enough to shoot him an exasperated look.

"Then I'll stop him."

Noah's confidence comforted her. She knew most everyone in Splendor thought highly of him and would trust him with their lives. She had no reason to doubt him now.

"A rider is coming from the north." Dirk reined to a stop and jumped off his horse.

"Just one?"

"That's all I saw." His gaze shifted from Noah to Lena, then back to Noah. "It's Carlyle. Jack is in the saddle with him."

Noah cursed, then stood, pointing a finger at Lena. "Stay behind those boulders and don't make a sound, no matter what you see or hear. Do you understand me?"

Nodding furiously, Lena scrambled behind the rock formation, saying a prayer as she waited.

"Get the others in position and stay quiet. My best shot will be if he has no idea we are here, waiting."

"He's all yours, Noah."

Sobs from inside the shack had Nick running, shoving the door open, seeing Travis holding Isabella close, trying to comfort her. Smoothing her hair with his hand, Travis whispered that all would be well and they'd get Jack back. He watched a moment, seeing the concern in Travis' face as he comforted her. He knew they weren't strangers. As a key part of Luke's horse breeding business, Travis bunked at the ranch and often took his meals with them, the same as Isabella had been doing. The tender care with which Travis held her created a lump in Nick's throat.

Kneeling down, he grasped her hands in his. "Isabella, it's Nick."

Her eyes, red-rimmed and glassy, searched his. "Find him, Nick. It will kill Lena if anything happens to Jack." She clutched the front of Travis' shirt as if he were her lifeline.

"We'll get him. That's a promise." Nick stood, looking at Travis. "You stay with her. I'm counting on you to get her safely to Splendor."

"I'll take care of her, Nick. Don't worry."

Giving Travis a quick nod, he dashed outside.

"Saddle up." Gabe had waited as long as he could before giving the order. "Nick, what about Isabella?"

"Travis is with her. He'll get her to town. I'm going with you."

Willie's arms tightened painfully around Jack's chest. "Stop squirming or I'll throw you off the cliff over there."

Jack's eyes widened as he looked in the direction Willie nodded. Sure enough, the ground dropped off, but he couldn't see how deep it went. Clamping his mouth shut, he settled down, fear consuming his young body. He hated Willie. His mother and Isabella had always told him his father would come for him some day. With eager anticipation, he'd looked forward to meeting him, wondering what he'd be like. Now, he despised him.

Jack willed himself to be strong and glanced over his shoulder. "Where are we going?"

Willie thought to ignore the question, then changed his mind. "I have a place over the border in Idaho."

"Will we live there?" Jack's voice wavered. He didn't want to go to Idaho, whatever that was, and leave his mother behind.

"For a while, then we'll move on."

"What about Mother?"

"If you behave, I'll send for her. If not, you'll never see her again."

Jack's anxiety doubled. He'd have to be good if he ever wanted to see his mother again. His young mind couldn't stop there, though. What if he wasn't good enough? It would be his fault she couldn't find him. He'd never see her or Aunt Isabella or Uncle Nick again. He swiped at the tears forming, determined not to let his father see his fear.

"I'll be good."

"Then you and I won't have any problems, will we?"

Jack shook his head. He'd do whatever his father said, anything to see his mother again.

Willie dug his heels into the horse, moving him as fast as possible down the winding trail. He knew the trail south wasn't far ahead. They'd have a hard time finding him once he took the turn.

The sound of a horse whinnying caught his attention. Pulling up, he scanned the area, listening.

"Did you hear a horse?"

"No," Jack lied, hoping it was his mother.

Willie looked around again. After hearing nothing for several minutes, he nudged the horse forward.

Noah's hands clenched the rifle at the sound of their horses. Hidden well off the trail, he knew Carlyle wouldn't see them if the Pelletier man could keep the animals quiet a little longer.

Focusing on the trail, Noah spotted movement. Dirk had been right. Jack sat in front of Carlyle, one of the man's arms wrapped around his waist, holding him in place. As Noah watched, Jack squirmed a little. It wouldn't seem like much to most people, but to Noah, his movements could mean the difference between a clean shot and a miss. He had to take Carlyle in one shot.

"Jack..."

Noah glanced behind him to see Lena a few feet away, her gaze fixed on her son.

"Get back. Now."

Lena glared at him, but took a couple cautious steps backward, watching in terror as Noah lifted his rifle, aiming at Jack.

"No! You'll hit him." Lena started to reach out to grab Noah's arm before a strong hand wrapped around her, pulling her away.

"Let him do his job," Dirk ground out as she struggled to get away. "I swear I'll gag you if you don't stop."

Noah ignored the activity behind him, not taking his face from the stock as he waited. There it was. The shot he needed.

Taking a deep breath, he steadied the rifle, narrowing his gaze, letting everything around him fade away. Squeezing the trigger for the perfect shot, he twitched when an anguished scream came from behind him.

"No!" Lena squirmed, wrenching herself from Dirk's grasp and running forward. What she saw sent terror through her. Willie and Jack lay on the ground, both covered in blood, neither moving. Running toward her son, she dropped down next to him, taking him into her arms as Noah came to a stop next to her.

"You shot him." She glared up at him

"No, I didn't. But I could have the way you panicked."

His words fell on deaf ears. Rocking Jack, her body shook, believing her son gone.

"Mama..."

Hearing the weak, frightened whisper, she pulled back, looking into Jack's eyes.

"Where were you hit?" She lay him down, frantically searching for a bullet wound.

"I hit my head, Mama."

"I know, sweetheart." She continued to search, finding nothing other than a small bump forming on his scalp. Her body trembled in relief as she stroked Jack's hair, then turned to find Noah and Dirk crouching next to Willie.

"He's dead. One shot, Noah. Good work." Dirk slapped him on the back and stood.

"Not where I aimed. It should have been a head shot, not through his neck." Noah shook his head.

"Dead is dead, my friend." Dirk walked over to Lena at the same time Gabe and the others rode up.

Gabe didn't wait to rein Blackheart to a stop before jumping off and running to Lena, his gut churning at what he saw.

She looked up at him, her tear-streaked face recognizing his alarm. "He's fine, Gabe. It's Willie's blood, not Jack's."

Gabe fell to his knees beside them, placing a hand on Lena's shoulder. A grim smile touched his face as he looked down at the boy he had yet to meet.

"So this is Jack." He stared down at the young face, a tiny frown creasing Jack's forehead.

"Jack, this is Sheriff Evans. He helped save you." She reached over and gripped Gabe's hand, squeezing it.

"Hello."

"Nice to meet you, Jack. Now, let's get you cleaned up, son. Then we'll ride back to town." He placed his arms under Jack, carrying him toward Blackheart, then setting him on his feet.

"Here you go." Nick came up next to them, holding out a water pouch, handkerchief, and old shirt. "It's the smallest shirt we could find." He crouched in front of Jack, his chest constricting. Reaching out, he trailed a finger down his cheek a moment before Jack launched himself into his arms and began to sob. "It's all right, son. You're safe and he'll never harm you again."

Lena stood aside as Gabe removed Jack's shirt, wiping the blood and dirt from his face and arms before pouring a good portion over his hair.

"Use this to dry him off." Luke held out another shirt. "You're looking much better, Jack."

Jack peered up at the familiar voice, recognizing Luke right away. "Hello, Mr. Luke."

"Your mother is mighty glad to find you." Luke saw Gabe's confused expression at the exchange. "Guess no one told you Isabella and Jack have been staying at our place."

Gabe shook his head, wondering what else he didn't know.

"Where's Isabella?" Lena searched the other riders, then looked up the trail, seeing nothing.

"She's with Travis. He should be bringing her along any time now," Luke assured her.

"Is she…"

"She's fine, Lena. Probably still shaky, but unharmed." Luke turned to Gabe. "We'll get Carlyle's body and his other men secure on horses. Once Travis and Isabella join us, we can head back to town."

As soon as Gabe finished, Lena wrapped Jack in her arms, closing her eyes at the thought of what might have happened.

"Is he all right?" Noah's deep voice came from behind her.

Loosening her hold on Jack, she glanced over her shoulder, then stood.

"I'm sorry, Noah. I acted foolish and—"

Noah held up a hand to stop her. "You acted like a mother. Jack is safe. That's all that matters."

Resting her hands on his shoulders, she raised up, placing a kiss on his cheek. "Thank you."

He raised his finger to the brim of his hat in a salute before walking away.

"What did you do?" Gabe asked.

Her eyes warmed as her gaze wandered over him. He and his friends had saved Jack and Isabella. She owed all of them more than she could ever repay.

She intertwined her fingers in his. "I'll explain later."

Refusing to intrude, Gabe had given her a week to be with Jack and Isabella. She hadn't shown her face in the Dixie or tried to get in touch with him, and he hadn't asked Nick for an explanation. From what he'd heard, she spent her time at Luke's ranch, staying as far away from town as possible.

As each day passed, the tension he felt increased, believing she may have changed her mind about him. With the threat to her and Jack gone, and the entire town knowing her situation, the need to marry diminished.

He busied himself with his work as sheriff, erecting the new hotel, and the expansion of the boardinghouse. Caro had taken an empty room at Suzanne's, allowing him to move back into his house. They'd had supper together several times, being joined by Noah and Abby most nights. They'd made the announcement of her pregnancy a week before and no one was happier for them than Gabe.

Caro had also made friends with the Pelletier women during her brief time in Splendor, making the decision to stay over the winter. She'd been fortunate. One of the buyers for Noah's last remaining homes changed his mind, opening up a place for Caro as soon as they completed the inside.

Recent snow flurries indicated the approach of winter and the need to finish as much of the outside construction on the buildings as possible before a real storm came through. Looking out the jail window, it appeared that time had come.

As the sun fell behind the western mountains, he slipped into his heavy coat, settling his hat tight on his head, then ventured outside, the wind whipping around him, blanketing the street in snow. Winter had officially arrived.

"Gabe, over here." Nick waved as he walked out of the boardinghouse on his way to the Dixie. "I've told the men to close up as much as they can on the hotel and boardinghouse. With any luck at all, we'll have a few more days to finish outside, then they can work inside as long as possible." Nick took another look at him, deciding what to say. "Come inside. I'll buy you a whiskey."

Gabe followed him, having nowhere else to go. The day before, Cash and Beau had ridden to Big Pine for some well-deserved relaxation. Noah and Abby had already left for their cabin, and Caro had accepted an invitation for supper at Dax and Rachel's, not planning to return until the following morning.

"Two whiskeys, Paul." For a Friday evening, the Dixie was quiet, with few gamblers and almost no cowboys braving what looked to be the makings of a nasty storm.

Nick leaned against the bar, sipping his drink, studying Gabe. He'd been to visit Lena, Isabella, and Jack earlier. They'd all seemed to be adjusting after the ordeal with Willie, Isabella making plans to stay several more months before returning to Philadelphia. He suspected part of the reason had to do with Jack and Lena, while another part might be due to a certain cowboy who worked for Luke and Dax.

"I was out at Luke's today."

Gabe's head snapped up at the comment, but he held his tongue.

"Lena said she hadn't seen you since bringing them back to town. Is there a reason you're ignoring her?"

Gabe blinked in confusion. "What do you mean?"

"She's a little confused, as am I, about why you haven't visited. Have you changed your mind about marrying her?" Nick almost grinned at the astonished look Gabe flashed, his forehead creasing into a frown. He'd tried to reassure Lena the reason for Gabe's absence had nothing to do with her. Now he knew he was correct.

"I thought it best to give her time to deal with what had happened." Staring into his glass, Gabe rubbed his stubbled chin. A slow smile lifted his lips. "I suppose I should ride out there, pay her a visit."

"It's getting late. Why don't you wait until tomorrow when the storm clears and spend the day at the ranch?" Nick looked away, not wanting to give too much away.

"You may be right. I need to spend time with Jack, get to know him. He lost his uncle and now Carlyle. No matter what he did, he was still Jack's father. It may take him a while to warm up to me."

"He's a resilient boy. It may not take as long as you think." When Nick visited them, Jack had spent most of his time talking about the sheriff, saying he wanted to be a lawman when he grew up. Nick wouldn't share the information with Gabe, however. It was best for him to see Jack's admiration in person.

"Guess I'll head home, warm up some beans and biscuits, and get some sleep. I want to get an early start tomorrow." Gabe finished his drink, setting his glass on the bar.

"I haven't had supper. Why don't you meet me at the boardinghouse in an hour and I'll spring for your meal? It's the least I can do after you saved three people I love very much."

It wasn't that Gabe didn't want to share a meal with Nick. Instead, he wanted to prepare for tomorrow. If all went well, it would be a big day. But if it hadn't been for Nick, he wouldn't have made the decision to ride out to Luke's.

"All right. I need to make rounds, then stop by my place."

Gabe didn't expect to find anything amiss during his rounds. The storm made the town seem eerily quiet as he passed each business, poking his head in a few, then moving on. He'd change into a clean shirt at his place, meet Nick for a quick bite, then return home. Now that he knew how much he'd misjudged the situation, he planned to start out right after breakfast tomorrow. Gabe didn't want to waste another minute.

The sky had turned black by the time he stepped onto his small porch. Kicking mud from his boots, he reached for the knob, noticing a light inside. Taking a step backward, he checked the windows. All the curtains were drawn. He didn't recall leaving them closed.

Drawing his gun from its holster, he held it in front of him, slowly turning the knob. As he slammed the door open, a shriek had him swinging his gun toward the kitchen. His breath caught and his body tightened at the sight of Lena standing near the stove with a spoon in her hand, a hand over her mouth—and not a stitch of clothing on under her white apron. Never in his life had he seen anyone so beautiful.

"You scared the daylights out of me." Lena moved her hand from her mouth to her chest, taking a breath. "Do you always enter your house that way?"

Gabe hadn't moved a muscle since seeing her and he sure as hell couldn't form a coherent sentence. Not taking his gaze from her, he holstered his gun, moving toward her in slow, measured steps, trying to drag oxygen into his lungs.

Lena watched as he stalked toward her, a look she'd never seen on his face. Perhaps she'd made a mistake letting herself into his house, throwing away all propriety by making an impulsive decision to welcome him in such a forward way.

Backing up, her hips hit the edge of the counter as he came to stop inches away. Reaching out a hand, Gabe let his knuckles draw a line down her cheek, along the curve of her jaw, then to the silky skin further down. Leaning toward her, he replaced his hand with his lips, hearing a deep sigh escape as Lena wrapped her arms around his neck, letting her head fall back.

"Gabe..."

"Hmmm..."

Her concentration vanished as he continued lavishing her with heated kisses, moving up to settle his lips on hers, nipping at the corners before delving inside. His hands tightened on her back, drawing her close, aligning her body with his. Never had he felt as consumed with desire as he did right now. Moving a hand down, he pulled the ties, letting the apron fall to the floor.

"You have me at a disadvantage, sir." Lena fought for air, heat radiating between them as her skin connected with his fully clothed body.

"I guess we'll have to do something about that then." Capturing her mouth again, he scooped her into his arms, wasting no time as he settled her on the bed. "God, you are so beautiful, Lena." Stripping off his clothes, he lay down beside her, stroking her face, his gaze burning into hers. "Marry me."

A small laugh escaped her lips as she cupped his face with her hands. "I believe you already have my answer, Sheriff." Her eyes crinkled at the corners as her heart pounded in her chest. "And it will always be yes."

Epilogue

Three weeks later...

"How did you ever convince Reverend Paige to come all this way out of town to marry you?" Dax pushed his hat further down on his head to ward off the chill. He figured Gabe and Lena must be blessed. The sun had shown bright, heating the air and earth, melting the early winter snow right on the spot where they took their vows.

A wide grin lifted the corners of Gabe's mouth. "A generous donation to the church." He glanced around at all the friends who had joined them on the hill overlooking the waterfall, a spot that would one day be the location of their home. She'd been excited when he'd mentioned riding up the hill the morning after she'd surprised him in his kitchen. Enjoyment turned to shock when she learned the land belonged to him—to them.

Watching his bride move among the crowd, his heart swelled, still not quite believing his luck in capturing the heart of such a special woman. She'd been through so much and could have been forgiven for never wanting to marry. Instead, she'd chosen to take a chance with him, giving Gabe the love and trust she'd kept locked inside for so long.

"More *punch*?" Dax asked, raising his eyebrows at the subtle reference to the whiskey the men had added to their glasses.

Gabe didn't take his gaze off Lena as he handed Dax his glass. "Thanks." Catching her eyeing him, he winked, getting a blush in return.

"Guess we'll never be able to get away from each other now."

Gabe shifted toward Nick, who'd come up beside him.

"Hope you're not sorry you brought me in as a partner because I don't plan on leaving anytime soon." Gabe's lips tilted up into a grin.

"Good thing. With all the changes around here, I can't imagine running all this by myself." The hotel and boardinghouse were now secured, men working inside on days when storms didn't keep them away. Nick couldn't be more pleased with the progress or the partnership he'd forged with Gabe. "Ah, here comes your bride now."

Gabe snaked an arm around her waist when she stopped next to him, stretching up to place a kiss on his chin.

"You knew precisely what you were doing when you kept me in town." Gabe sent Nick a knowing look, referring to the way he'd assisted with Lena's surprise three weeks before.

"Guilty. I hope it was worth it," Nick answered, a smile lifting his lips.

"Best surprise I've ever had." Gabe shot a look at Lena, seeing her face redden at the memory. "I hope to have that kind of surprise again sometime."

Nick looked between the two, believing there might be more to Gabe's comment, but saying nothing.

With Willie dead, his part of the Devil Dancer mine passed to Jackson, with Lena as the guardian, although there were still legal hurdles to overcome. Over his strenuous denials, Tommy Pennington had been found guilty of physical attacks against Dolly, being sent to the Montana territorial prison. His half of the mine remained in his name, making Tommy partners with Jackson. Gabe and Lena figured they'd address that situation if and when Tommy ever got released.

"What are you all grinning about, besides the obvious?" Cash handed Gabe a full glass, lifting his own in salute.

"Just reminiscing about the last few months," Nick answered before he took a long swallow of his drink. His gaze moved across the crowd, settling on the one woman who'd captured his interest since the moment they'd met. Looking at Gabe and Lena, he made a vow to do more than just be Suzanne's friend—if she allowed it.

"Thought I'd let you know, Gabe, I plan to leave for a couple months. I have unfinished business I need to take care of." Cash hadn't intended on leaving, especially before the heavy snows, but he had no choice. He'd made a commitment long ago to a good friend and had received word it was time to pay up.

"Beau going with you?" Gabe asked, thinking of who he could get to take over Cash's spot as deputy until he returned.

"No. This is personal." Besides the oath he'd made to a friend, he needed time away to reconcile the death of the young bank robber, Bobby. He didn't understand why this killing bothered him so much after all the carnage he'd seen, and participated in, during the war. All he knew was he couldn't continue being awakened most nights with visions of the young man's haunted face emblazoned on his mind. He knew Gabe had sent word to the boy's kin and never heard back. Cash hoped they never showed up in Splendor. He didn't need any more reminders of Bobby's frightened eyes as the life flowed out of him.

"You keep in touch and let us know if you need anything." Gabe leveled his gaze at a man he'd grown to respect and like as a friend. "You'll always have a place here."

Cash tipped his glass toward Gabe and nodded, thankful to finally find a place he fit in and could call home.

"Do you have everything, girl?" Clara McGrath watched as her daughter, Alison, packed the last of her belongings for the trip west. They'd both seen their share of bloodshed during the war, including the death of Alison's father at the Battle of Richmond. Both women had been forced to kill raiders to protect all they had left—a horse farm her grandfather had started forty years before.

"I have what I need, Mama." Allie placed a Colt revolver and ammunition in her trunk, then closed and locked it.

Weeks before, it had taken hours for Allie to calm her mother after word of her brother's death had been delivered. The message had been brief, only saying that Robert McGrath, identified as one of the outlaws, died during a bank robbery attempt in the Montana Territory. The message went on to say his personal belongings were being held by the sheriff of Splendor, with a request to let him know if they'd like to claim them. Allie read it over several times, still not believing the contents.

Although several years her junior, she and Bobby had been close. The grief she felt at his loss ate at her every day, her bitterness increasing, until she and her mother had made the decision behind her journey. She knew the brother she'd grown up with would never be a part of an outlaw gang or involved in a bank robbery. With every fiber in her being, Allie also knew someone had murdered him and walked away.

The reason for her trip wasn't to claim Bobby's belongings or his body. She'd travel the long distance to Montana to find the man responsible for Bobby's death and make him pay. By the time Allie left Splendor, the man who killed Bobby would be dead, the brother she would have given her life for avenged.

Thank you for taking the time to read Dixie Moon. If you enjoyed it, please consider telling your friends or posting a short review. Word of mouth is an author's best friend and much appreciated.

Please join my reader's group to be notified of my New Releases at:
http://www.shirleendavies.com/contact-me.html

I care about quality, so if you find something in error, please contact me via email at
shirleen@shirleendavies.com

About the Author

Shirleen Davies writes romance—historical, contemporary, and romantic suspense. She grew up in Southern California, attended Oregon State University, and has degrees from San Diego State University and the University of Maryland. During the day she provides consulting services to small and mid-sized businesses. But her real passion is writing emotionally charged stories of flawed people who find redemption through love and acceptance. She now lives with her husband in a beautiful town in northern Arizona.

Shirleen loves to hear from her readers.

Write to her at: shirleen@shirleendavies.com
Visit her website: http://www.shirleendavies.com
Sign up to be notified of New Releases:
http://www.shirleendavies.com/contact-me.html
Books by Shirleen:
http://www.shirleendavies.com/books.html
Comment on her blog:
http://www.shirleendavies.com/blog.html
Facebook Fan Page:
https://www.facebook.com/ShirleenDaviesAuthor
Twitter: http://twitter.com/shirleendavies
Google+: http://www.gplusid.com/shirleendavies

LinkedIn:
http://www.linkedin.com/in/shirleendaviesauth
or
Pinterest: http://www.pinterest.com/shirleendavies
Tsu: http://www.tsu.co/shirleendavies

Other Books by Shirleen Davies

Tougher than the Rest – Book One
MacLarens of Fire Mountain Historical Western Romance Series

"A passionate, fast-paced story set in the untamed western frontier by an exciting new voice in historical romance."

Niall MacLaren is the oldest of four brothers, and the undisputed leader of the family. A widower, and single father, his focus is on building the MacLaren ranch into the largest and most successful in northern Arizona. He is serious about two things—his responsibility to the family and his future marriage to the wealthy, well-connected widow who will secure his place in the territory's destiny.

Katherine is determined to live the life she's dreamed about. With a job waiting for her in the growing town of Los Angeles, California, the young teacher from Philadelphia begins a journey across the United States with only a couple of trunks and her spinster companion. Life is perfect for this adventurous, beautiful young woman, until an accident throws her into the arms of the one man who can destroy it all.

Fighting his growing attraction and strong desire for the beautiful stranger, Niall is more determined than ever to push emotions aside to focus on his goals of wealth and political gain. But looking into the clear, blue eyes of the woman who could ruin everything, Niall discovers he will have to harden his heart and be tougher than he's ever been in his life...Tougher than the Rest.

Faster than the Rest – Book Two

MacLarens of Fire Mountain Historical Western Romance Series

"Headstrong, brash, confident, and complex, the MacLarens of Fire Mountain will captivate you with strong characters set in the wild and rugged western frontier."

Handsome, ruthless, young U.S. Marshal Jamie MacLaren had lost everything—his parents, his family connections, and his childhood sweetheart— but now he's back in Fire Mountain and ready for another chance. Just as he successfully reconnects with his family and starts to rebuild his life, he gets the unexpected and unwanted assignment of rescuing the woman who broke his heart.

Beautiful, wealthy Victoria Wicklin chose money and power over love, but is now fighting for her life—or is she? Who has she become in the seven years since she left Fire Mountain to take up her life in San Francisco? Is she really as innocent as she says?

Marshal MacLaren struggles to learn the truth and do his job, but the past and present lead him in different directions as his heart and brain wage battle. Is Victoria a victim or a villain? Is life offering him another chance, or just another heartbreak?

As Jamie and Victoria struggle to uncover past secrets and come to grips with their shared passion, another danger arises. A life-altering danger that is out of their control and threatens to destroy any chance for a shared future.

Harder than the Rest – Book Three
MacLarens of Fire Mountain Historical Western Romance Series

"They are men you want on your side. Hard, confident, and loyal, the MacLarens of Fire Mountain will seize your attention from the first page."

Will MacLaren is a hardened, plain-speaking bounty hunter. His life centers on finding men guilty of horrendous crimes and making sure justice is done. There is no place in his world for the carefree attitude he carried years before when a tragic event destroyed his dreams.

Amanda is the daughter of a successful Colorado rancher. Determined and proud, she works hard to prove she is as capable as any man and worthy to be her father's heir. When a stranger arrives, her independent nature collides with the strong pull toward the handsome ranch hand. But is he what he seems and could his secrets endanger her as well as her family?

The last thing Will needs is to feel passion for another woman. But Amanda elicits feelings he thought were long buried. Can Will's desire for her change him? Or will the vengeance he seeks against the one man he wants to destroy—a dangerous opponent without a conscious—continue to control his life?

Stronger than the Rest – Book Four
MacLarens of Fire Mountain Historical Western Romance Series

"Smart, tough, and capable, the MacLarens protect their own no matter the odds. Set

against America's rugged frontier, the stories of the men from Fire Mountain are complex, fast-paced, and a must read for anyone who enjoys non-stop action and romance."

Drew MacLaren is focused and strong. He has achieved all of his goals except one—to return to the MacLaren ranch and build the best horse breeding program in the west. His successful career as an attorney is about to give way to his ranching roots when a bullet changes everything.

Tess Taylor is the quiet, serious daughter of a Colorado ranch family with dreams of her own. Her shy nature keeps her from developing friendships outside of her close-knit family until Drew enters her life. Their relationship grows. Then a bullet, meant for another, leaves him paralyzed and determined to distance himself from the one woman he's come to love.

Convinced he is no longer the man Tess needs, Drew focuses on regaining the use of his legs and recapturing a life he thought lost. But danger of another kind threatens those he cares about— including Tess—forcing him to rethink his future.

Can Drew overcome the barriers that stand between him, the safety of his friends and family, and a life with the woman he loves? To do it all, he has to be strong. Stronger than the Rest.

Deadlier than the Rest – Book Five
MacLarens of Fire Mountain Historical Western Romance Series

"A passionate, heartwarming story of the iconic MacLarens of Fire Mountain. This captivating historical western romance grabs your attention from the start with an engrossing story encompassing two romances set against the rugged backdrop of the burgeoning western frontier."

Connor MacLaren's search has already stolen eight years of his life. Now he is close to finding what he seeks—Meggie, his missing sister. His quest leads him to the growing city of Salt Lake and an encounter with the most captivating woman he has ever met.

Grace is the third wife of a Mormon farmer, forced into a life far different from what she'd have chosen. Her independent spirit longs for choices governed only by her own heart and mind. To achieve her dreams, she must hide behind secrets and half-truths, even as her heart pulls her towards the ruggedly handsome Connor.

Known as cool and uncompromising, Connor MacLaren lives by a few, firm rules that have served him well and kept him alive. However, danger stalks Connor, even to the front range of the beautiful Wasatch Mountains, threatening those he cares about and impacting his ability to find his sister.

Can Connor protect himself from those who seek his death? Will his eight-year search lead him to his sister while unlocking the secrets he knows are held tight within Grace, the woman who has captured his heart?

Read this heartening story of duty, honor, passion, and love in book five of the MacLarens of Fire Mountain series.

Second Summer – Book One
MacLarens of Fire Mountain Contemporary Romance Series

"In this passionate Contemporary Romance, author Shirleen Davies introduces her readers to the modern day MacLarens starting with Heath MacLaren, the head of the family."

The Chairman of both the MacLaren Cattle Co. and MacLaren Land Development, Heath MacLaren is a success professionally—his personal life is another matter.

Following a divorce after a long, loveless marriage, Heath spends his time with women who are beautiful and passionate, yet unable to provide what he longs for . . .

Heath has never experienced love even though he witnesses it every day between his younger brother, Jace, and wife, Caroline. He wants what they have, yet spends his time with women too young to understand what drives him and too focused on themselves to be true companions.

It's been two years since Annie's husband died, leaving her to build a new life. He was her soul mate and confidante. She has no desire to find a replacement, yet longs for male friendship.

Annie's closest friend in Fire Mountain, Caroline MacLaren, is determined to see Annie come out of her shell after almost two years of mourning. A chance meeting with Heath turns into an offer to be a part of the MacLaren Foundation Board and an opportunity for a life outside her home sanctuary which has also become her prison. The platonic friendship that builds between Annie and Heath points to a future where each may rely on the other without the bonds a romance would entail.

However, without consciously seeking it, each yearns for more . . .

The MacLaren Development Company is booming with Heath at the helm. His meetings at a partner company with the young, beautiful marketing director, who makes no secret of her desire for him, are a temptation. But is she the type of woman he truly wants?

Annie's acceptance of the deep, yet passionless, friendship with Heath sustains her, lulling her to believe it is all she needs. At least until Heath drops a bombshell, forcing Annie to realize that what she took for friendship is actually a deep, lasting love. One she doesn't want to lose.

Each must decide to settle—or fight for it all.

Hard Landing – Book Two
MacLarens of Fire Mountain Contemporary Romance Series

Trey MacLaren is a confident, poised Navy pilot. He's focused, loyal, ethical, and a natural leader. He is also on his way to what he hopes will be a lasting relationship and marriage with fellow pilot, Jesse Evans.

Jesse has always been driven. Her graduation from the Naval Academy and acceptance into the pilot training program are all she thought she wanted—until she discovered love with Trey MacLaren

Trey and Jesse's lives are filled with fast flying, friends, and the demands of their military careers. Lives each has settled into with a passion. At least until the day Trey receives a letter that could change his and Jesse's lives forever.

It's been over two years since Trey has seen the woman in Pensacola. Her unexpected letter stuns him and pushes Jesse into a tailspin from which she might not pull back.

Each must make a choice. Will the choice Trey makes cause him to lose Jesse forever? Will she follow her heart or her head as she fights for a chance to save the love she's found? Will their independent decisions collide, forcing them to give up on a life together?

One More Day – Book Three
MacLarens of Fire Mountain Contemporary Romance Series

Cameron "Cam" Sinclair is smart, driven, and dedicated, with an easygoing temperament that belies his strong will and the personal ambitions he holds close. Besides his family, his job as head of IT at the MacLaren Cattle Company and his position as a Search and Rescue volunteer are all he needs to make him happy. At least that's what he thinks until he meets, and is instantly drawn to, fellow SAR volunteer, Lainey Devlin.

Lainey is compassionate, independent, and ready to break away from her manipulative and controlling fiancé. Just as her decision is made, she's called into a major search and rescue effort, where once again, her path crosses with the intriguing, and much too handsome, Cam Sinclair. But Lainey's plans are set. An opportunity to buy a flourishing preschool in northern Arizona is her chance to make a fresh start, and nothing, not even her fierce attraction to Cam Sinclair, will impede her plans.

As Lainey begins to settle into her new life, an unexpected danger arises —threats from an unknown assailant—someone who doesn't believe she belongs in Fire Mountain. The more Lainey begins to love her new home, the greater the danger becomes. Can she accept the help and protection Cam offers while ignoring her consuming desire for him?

Even if Lainey accepts her attraction to Cam, will he ever be able to come to terms with his own driving ambition and allow himself to consider a different life than the one he's always pictured? A life with the one woman who offers more than he'd ever hoped to find?

All Your Nights – Book Four
MacLarens of Fire Mountain Contemporary Romance Series

"Romance, adventure, cowboys, suspense—everything you want in a contemporary western romance novel."

Kade Taylor likes living on the edge. As an undercover agent for the DEA and a former Special Ops team member, his current assignment seems tame—keep tabs on a bookish Ph.D. candidate the agency believes is connected to a ruthless drug cartel.

Brooke Sinclair is weeks away from obtaining her goal of a doctoral degree. She spends time finalizing her presentation and relaxing with another student who seems to want nothing more than her friendship. That's fine with Brooke. Her last serious relationship ended in a broken engagement.

Her future is set, safe and peaceful, just as she's always planned—until Agent Taylor informs her she's under suspicion for illegal drug activities.

Kade and his DEA team obtain evidence which exonerates Brooke while placing her in danger from those who sought to use her. As Kade races to take down the drug cartel while protecting Brooke, he must also find common ground with the former suspect—a woman he desires with increasing intensity.

At odds with her better judgment, Brooke finds the more time she spends with Kade, the more she's attracted to the complex, multi-faceted agent. But Kade holds secrets he knows Brooke will never understand or accept.

Can Kade keep Brooke safe while coming to terms with his past, or will he stay silent, ruining any future with the woman his heart can't let go?

Always Love You– Book Five
MacLarens of Fire Mountain Contemporary Romance Series

"Romance, adventure, motorcycles, cowboys, suspense—everything you want in a contemporary western romance novel."

Eric Sinclair loves his bachelor status. His work at MacLaren Enterprises leaves him with plenty of time to ride his horse as well as his Harley...and date beautiful women without a thought to commitment.

Amber Anderson is the new person at MacLaren Enterprises. Her passion for marketing landed her what she believes to be the perfect job—until she steps into her first meeting to find the man she left, but still loves, sitting at the management table—his disdain for her clear.

Eric won't allow the past to taint his professional behavior, nor will he repeat his mistakes with Amber, even though love for her pulses through him as strong as ever.

As they strive to mold a working relationship, unexpected danger confronts those close to them, pitting the MacLarens and Sinclairs against an evil who stalks one member but threatens them all.

Eric can't get the memories of their passionate past out of his mind, while Amber wrestles with feelings she thought long buried. Will they be able to put the past behind them to reclaim the love lost years before?

Redemption's Edge – Book One
Redemption Mountain – Historical Western Romance Series

"A heartwarming, passionate story of loss, forgiveness, and redemption set in the untamed frontier during the tumultuous years following the Civil War. Ms. Davies' engaging and complex characters draw you in from the start, creating

an exciting introduction to this new historical western romance series."

"Redemption's Edge is a strong and engaging introduction to her new historical western romance series."

Dax Pelletier is ready for a new life, far away from the one he left behind in Savannah following the South's devastating defeat in the Civil War. The ex-Confederate general wants nothing more to do with commanding men and confronting the tough truths of leadership.

Rachel Davenport possesses skills unlike those of her Boston socialite peers—skills honed as a nurse in field hospitals during the Civil War. Eschewing her northeastern suitors and changed by the carnage she's seen, Rachel decides to accept her uncle's invitation to assist him at his clinic in the dangerous and wild frontier of Montana.

Now a Texas Ranger, a promise to a friend takes Dax and his brother, Luke, to the untamed territory of Montana. He'll fulfill his oath and return to Austin, at least that's what he believes.

The small town of Splendor is what Rachel needs after life in a large city. In a few short months, she's grown to love the people as well as the majestic beauty of the untamed frontier. She's settled into a life unlike any she has ever thought possible.

Thinking his battle days are over, he now faces dangers of a different kind—one by those from his past who seek vengeance, and another from Rachel, the woman who's captured his heart.

Wildfire Creek – Book Two
Redemption Mountain – Historical Western Romance Series

"A passionate story of rebuilding lives, working to find a place in the wild frontier, and building new lives in the years following the American Civil War. A rugged, heartwarming story of choices and love in the continuing saga of Redemption Mountain."

Luke Pelletier is settling into his new life as a rancher and occasional Pinkerton Agent, leaving his past as an ex-Confederate major and Texas Ranger far behind. He wants nothing more than to work the ranch, charm the ladies, and live a life of carefree bachelorhood.

Ginny Sorensen has accepted her responsibility as the sole provider for herself and her younger sister. The desire to continue their journey to Oregon is crushed when the need for food and shelter keeps them in the growing frontier town of Splendor, Montana, forcing Ginny to accept work as a server in the local saloon.

Luke has never met a woman as lovely and unspoiled as Ginny. He longs to know her, yet fears his wild ways and unsettled nature aren't what she deserves. She's a girl you marry, but that is nowhere in Luke's plans.

Complicating their tenuous friendship, a twist in circumstances forces Ginny closer to the man she most wants to avoid—the man who can destroy her dreams, and who's captured her heart.

Believing his bachelor status firm, Luke moves from danger to adventure, never dreaming each step he takes brings him closer to his true destiny and a life much different from what he imagines.

Sunrise Ridge – Book Three
Redemption Mountain – Historical Western Romance Series

"The author has a talent for bringing the historical west to life, realistically and vividly, and doesn't shy away from some of the harder aspects of frontier life, even though it's fiction. Recommended to readers who like sweeping western historical romances that are grounded with memorable, likeable characters and a strong sense of place."

Noah Brandt is a successful blacksmith and businessman in Splendor, Montana, with few ties to his past as an ex-Union Army major and sharpshooter. Quiet and hardworking, his biggest challenge is controlling his strong desire for a woman he believes is beyond his reach.

Abigail Tolbert is tired of being under her father's thumb while at the same time, being pushed away by the one man she desires. Determined to build a new life outside the control of her wealthy father, she finds work and sets out to shape a life on her own terms.

Noah has made too many mistakes with Abby to have any hope of getting her back. Even with the changes in her life, including the distance she's built with her father, he can't keep himself from believing he'll never be good enough to claim her.

Unexpected dangers, including a twist of fate for Abby, change both their lives, making the tentative steps they've taken to build a relationship a distant hope. As Noah battles his past as well as the threats to Abby, she fights for a future with the only man she will ever love.

Dixie Moon – Book Four
Redemption Mountain – Historical Western Romance Series

Gabe Evans is a man of his word with strong convictions and steadfast loyalty. As the sheriff of Splendor,

Montana, the ex-Union Colonel and oldest of four boys from an affluent family, Gabe understands the meaning of responsibility. The last thing he wants is another commitment—especially of the female variety.

Until he meets Lena Campanel...

Lena's past is one she intends to keep buried. Overcoming a childhood of setbacks and obstacles, she and her friend, Nick, have succeeded in creating a life of financial success and devout loyalty to one another.

When an unexpected death leaves Gabe the sole heir of a considerable estate, partnering with Nick and Lena is a lucrative decision...forcing Gabe and Lena to work together. As their desire grows, Lena refuses to let down her guard, vowing to keep her past hidden—even from a perfect man like Gabe.

But secrets never stay buried...

When revealed, Gabe realizes Lena's secrets are deeper than he ever imagined. For a man of his character, deception and lies of omission aren't negotiable. Will he be able to forgive the deceit? Or is the damage too great to ever repair?

Reclaiming Love – Book One, A Novella
Peregrine Bay – Contemporary Romance Series

Adam Monroe has seen his share of setbacks. Now he's back in Peregrine Bay, looking for a new life and second chance.

Julia Kerrigan's life rebounded after the sudden betrayal of the one man she ever loved. As president of a success real estate company, she's built a new life and future, pushing the painful past behind her.

Adam's reason for accepting the job as the town's new Police Chief can be explained in one word—Julia. He wants her back and will do whatever is necessary to achieve his goal, even knowing his biggest hurdle is the woman he still loves.

As they begin to reconnect, a terrible scandal breaks loose with Julia and Adam at the center.

Will the threat to their lives and reputations destroy their fledgling romance? Can Adam identify and eliminate the danger to Julia before he's had a chance to reclaim her love?

Our Kind of Love – Book Two
Peregrine Bay – Contemporary Romance Series

Set in the beautiful lake country of Idaho, Peregrine Bay stories follow the lives of the five Kerrigan sisters and their family.

Read about Selena and Linc in book two. Releasing 2016

http://www.shirleendavies.com/books.html

For permission requests, contact the publisher.
Avalanche Ranch Press, LLC
PO Box 12618
Prescott, AZ 86304

www.ingramcontent.com/pod-product-compliance
Lightning Source LLC
Chambersburg PA
CBHW070345170726
48291CB00001B/190